London. 1940. Why do you go there?
'Because,' Jack said, 'my friend needs my help.
He's the only family I have left now.'
Who?
'My grandfather, Davey Vale.'

Timesmith

By Niel Bushnell

ANDERSEN PRESS • LONDON

2 4 6 8 10 9 7 5 3 1

The right of Niel Bushnell to be identified as the author of this work has been asserted in accordance with the Copyright, Designs and Patents Act, 1988.

British Library Cataloguing in Publication Data available.

ISBN: 978 1 783 44032 0

Printed and bound in Great Britain by
CPI Group (UK) Ltd, Croydon, CR0 4YY

For Sarah and Megan
You make me smile every day.

Timesmith

Bone, stone and sorrow,

Mark the days of yon and morrow.

Thru' fortune, ruin and secrets past,

Sorrow's line will ever last.

First World Proverb, Anon, c. 1700

'It is true that the Concealed Realms are a wonder to behold, but the frozen rivers of Niflheim are a place I would not dare to visit again. I have survived many dangers on these journeys, and beheld the grotesque and insidious, but nothing I have witnessed can compare to the Mists of Niflheim.'

Extract from *On the Nature of the Concealed Realms*
by Magnus Hafgan

1

THE SCREAM

The man buried in the cold earth screamed a motionless scream.

He had long since given up trying to move; his body was rotten and useless. Every message his angry brain threw out went ignored by his wasted, pathetic frame. Yet he *felt* everything.

Worms moved through him, wriggling, feeding, persistently tearing at his human remains. Moisture formed about his darkened flesh, seeping in with needles of ice-cold indifference that cracked his calcified bones. And the sword; even after all this time he felt the mocking metal of the sword impaling his inert heart. In the age since his demise the pain had not diminished. Unimaginable, never-ending pain.

Nothing worked any more. Only his soul, his very essence, prevailed somewhere deep within. He felt the passing of time like the slow, maddening drip, drip, drip of a frozen waterfall. Seconds laughed at him for decades. Decades scorned him for an eternity. He was buried in time.

And yet Rouland endured it all.

One burning thought kept him going. It was a thought about a boy, a boy who had beaten him. Rouland was immortal, unstoppable. He had never been beaten before. The boy's face came into his mind and a new wave of hatred consumed him.

Jack Morrow.

He had bested Rouland. He had plunged a sword through the centre of his heart and suspended his eternal existence. He had buried him in this patch of earth and left him to rot, to die like a mortal man.

But Rouland was not mortal, and his rage sustained him through the lonely, dark years. He waited, and plotted and schemed. He knew his day would come. His followers would find him and restore him and he would have his revenge on Jack Morrow.

Rouland pictured his victory, and he forgot about the pain. He was satisfied. Then as the notion subsided the hurt returned, stronger than ever. Inside the prison of his mind, hate condensed into pools of agony and Rouland's soul screamed...

Captain Alda de Vienne screamed.

Every fibre in her body was being torn apart.

She opened her eyes, blinking away the frozen tears. She turned her head, and her neck cracked loudly. It was broken, like every bone in her body. A flash of pain thundered up her spine. Yes, she still felt pain, in spite of the long years since her death.

She needed to heal. One disjointed arm flayed about, searching for her sword. Her bent fingers touched the cool metal and she gripped it with all her pathetic might. Immediately the healing energy trickled from the blade into her shattered frame, righting her ancient bones.

She lay there for an age, feeding off the sword, her body realigning itself into its proper order. Eventually she sat up and studied her surroundings: the bodies of her sisters lay about her, twisted and inert. They were in the catacombs, deep below London, safe in the dim coolness of their resting chamber.

Her mind was a fog of recent memories. She forced herself to recall what she could: they had journeyed upstream, forwards in time from 1940 to 2008, to do battle with a boy. Why? She could not recall. Her master had wished it, and that was enough.

Her master.

Rouland.

His beautiful image erupted in her mind's eye and she suddenly remembered. Her beloved Rouland had been defeated, his mind was missing from hers, and the loss burned like fire.

Alda de Vienne screamed anew.

* * *

The Sorrowline.

A corridor through time.

A corridor that linked a gravestone to the date of that person's death.

Jack Morrow endured its uneasy currents. The nausea, the wall of remorse, the flood of regret – it was all here, caressing him, willing him onwards. He gave himself over to its hideous beauty, completely and without resistance, feeling himself fall back through the years to the font of sorrow.

It was still new to him, he recalled with a shudder. He had only recently discovered his natural ability to open up a Sorrowline and enter its depths. Already he had been back in time to 1940 – to the heart of London during the nightly Blitz of the Second World War. He had made friends there – friends he now wished to return to.

So he was going back to the past, to London, 1940. He planned to find Davey Vale, his teenage grandfather-to-be. They had already shared a great adventure, and some-where along the way their friendship had grown, in spite of many trials. And he hoped Eloise would be there too. She had been one of Rouland's personal army – the Paladin – an undead knight who had defied her master. Jack had grown to trust and care for her. She had proved her undying loyalty to him during their recent adventures. He wallowed in his own memories and for a moment they blocked out the sorrow around him.

And then the Sorrowline shattered.

Jack screamed.

Blackness. Emptiness. Nothing.

Davey Vale could not scream. There was no air left in his lungs. His fingers gripped Eloise's hand, his only compass in a world of void. They were in the folds of a Grimnire.

They had left the battlefield of 2008 behind them. They had won. Rouland was defeated – Jack had seen to that. The immortal's body had been dragged back in time to 1805 and buried. The Paladin, Rouland's undead knights, had disappeared. And the Grimnire, a mysterious hooded creature, a keeper of Destiny, had taken Davey and Eloise under its mighty cape. Together they fell back through the years, back to 1940 where they belonged.

The dark cape suddenly parted, and Davey and Eloise dropped onto a cobbled street. They were back in war-torn London. Davey smiled, glad to be home. He looked up at the elongated shape of the hooded Grimnire. It was already evaporating into the cracks between worlds. Its body became transparent and vanished. In its place was the sickly sky, darkened by towers of ashen smoke that framed a squadron of German aeroplanes as they retreated to the south. The wail of an air-raid siren rose and fell on the hot wind that pulled at Davey's dark ragged hair.

'Davey!' Eloise cried, her tone full of anguish. He turned to see what she was looking at, and his smile died.

A wall of fire and smoke and soot blew towards them at a ferocious speed. The shattered structure of a once noble building had succumbed to the flames and fell onto the street below. The burning ash thundered towards them like a herd of living fire creatures, propelled by a chaotic wind from Hell.

Davey screamed.

2

COUNCIL OF PEERS

'What happened to us, sister?' Geneviève asked, her deep-set eyes fixed on her captain.

All of the Paladin had recovered enough to stand, and had formed a rough circle around Captain de Vienne. Geneviève was the youngest of the eleven Paladin. She had been no more than sixteen at the time of her death. Not that it really mattered: her life *after* death was measured in centuries. Her old life was a whisper of a memory. Like her sisters, Rouland had resurrected her to be one of his Paladin, his personal knights. Her dark armour was dusty and worn, its metal edges scuffed, the leather straps marked. Captain de Vienne checked the other Paladin: they were in a similar state, some much worse. Even their blood-red cloaks were tattered, torn and burned.

Captain de Vienne had led the Paladin these last one hundred years. Never before could she recall them looking like this.

'We were defeated,' she concluded in a whisper, hardly able to believe her own words. She let them drift in the air until they had taken hold in her sisters' minds. Defeat was unthinkable. They were Paladin.

'How?' asked Geneviève. 'My memory is fractured.'

Captain de Vienne searched her own thoughts and found them in disarray. 'I know not,' she replied. 'My recall is ... elusive.'

'We were with Master Rouland, at St Paul's Cathedral,' Geneviève said hesitantly. 'But it was not now. It was hence. Upstream.'

'Yes,' Captain de Vienne recalled. 'We had travelled upstream, to the future. To 2008.'

'Are we not in 1940 now?' asked another. Her name was Olivia.

'Yes, we are back in our present, our correct time,' Captain de Vienne confirmed. 'This is 1940.' She could not explain how she knew – it was a sense deep within her – but none of her Paladin sisters doubted her.

Geneviève stepped closer to Captain de Vienne and said, 'But what were we doing in 2008? We do not travel in time. We are not Yard Boys.'

'It is unclear to me,' Captain de Vienne said tersely. This hole in her memories infuriated her. Her sisters looked to her for guidance and she could give none. This was a weakness.

'It was a Grimnire,' Olivia said.

Captain de Vienne paused, unable to think clearly. The Grimnire were creatures of Destiny, she mused. They worked to their own discreet plan, whatever that might be. What had a Grimnire been doing here? Why had it taken them to 2008, and then back here, to 1940? Her head throbbed.

'What know you of the Grimnire?' she bellowed, her dark eyes impaling each of the Paladin in turn. One by one they looked away.

'I recall,' Geneviève offered, her voice swallowed up by the room. 'The memory is returning.'

Captain de Vienne paced with a barely hidden rage.

'Our master,' Geneviève continued unperturbed, 'summoned a Grimnire.'

'Why?' Captain de Vienne spat. 'Why would he take such a course? The Grimnire do not lightly trifle in the affairs of men.'

'We sought the Rose,' Olivia said meekly.

The Rose. Suddenly Alda de Vienne's mind opened up to her, and the splintered memories revealed themselves.

The Rose of Annwn. It was the key to her master's plans, a living form of enormous energy that resided in a human host. They had chased the scent of the Rose to 2008. It had been hidden. Hidden where? The memory was elusive and sly.

'There is a boy,' Geneviève said. 'He has the Rose.'

The picture completed itself inside the captain's mind. They had gone to 2008 in search of the Rose. It had been hidden by the boy's mother. She had given it to her son to

9

heal him, so that he might live. 'The boy has the Rose.'

Olivia stepped closer. 'Where is our master? I cannot feel him.'

None of her sisters felt him, Captain de Vienne surmised. But they could *always* feel their master, they knew where he was at all times. But now he was gone from their world and the void inside her dark heart was vast. Captain de Vienne steadied herself as she remembered her master's fate.

'The boy. He was a Yard Boy,' she said as she tried to fortify her composure. 'He and Master Rouland disappeared downstream.'

'He is in the past?' Geneviève asked.

'There is no other explanation,' Captain de Vienne said.

'Then we must follow,' Olivia replied, suddenly filled with conviction.

'How?' Captain de Vienne asked angrily. 'Where should we go? *When?* We know nothing except that we travelled upstream to 2008 where our master fought a boy who wielded the Rose. The boy took Master Rouland back in time. We have been returned to 1940 without him. He is lost to us.'

Olivia gasped. 'Then all is hopeless?'

'No.' Captain de Vienne made a move to reassert her authority. 'We must first find the boy. The boy will lead us to Rouland.' A name grew in the captain's mind. '*Jack Morrow* is the key to our future.'

'And how do you propose we find him?' The voice was new and came from the dark recess of the chamber. It belonged to Dominica. She was pale and dark-haired, like all of the Paladin, but a streak of bold white zigzagged from her temple like a river of molten silver through her hair. Her frame was taller, thinner too, like an athlete's. She approached Captain de Vienne slowly, her contempt for her leader barely hidden. 'How do we find a boy who could be *anywhen* in time?'

Captain de Vienne's eyes narrowed. She had no more answers to give. 'This needs thought.'

'We have no time for thought,' Dominica replied, 'or for pointless discussions in darkened holes. Our master needs us. We must act now.' She turned to face her sisters, deliberately placing her back to Captain de Vienne. 'The Morrow boy was not alone. The Exile was his ally.'

Olivia's face broke into a smile of relief. 'Yes, I recall now. Our fallen sister was with him.'

'Eloise,' Captain de Vienne said at last. Her mind had betrayed her. She was their captain, they looked to her for leadership, yet she was the last to recall what had happened. She was becoming old and weak.

'Yes,' Dominica said. 'Eloise, our forgotten sister. She who defied our Master Rouland and was imprisoned. She is in league with the Morrow boy. She will lead us to him, and he will lead us to our master.'

'But where is she?' Geneviève asked.

Dominica closed her eyes and took a deep breath. 'She is close.' She held out her hands to Geneviève and Olivia. One by one the Paladin joined hands until only Captain de Vienne remained unconnected. Her rage boiled within. She wished to choke Dominica for her insolence. But now was not the time. She took her sisters' hands and closed her eyes.

Together, their minds as one, they saw their forsaken sister. Eloise was nearby, burning. Captain de Vienne ripped her hands free.

'Sisters,' she shouted. 'Ready yourselves for battle.'

As the others gathered their armour, Captain de Vienne summoned Dominica to her side.

'You will not join us,' she said.

Dominica's mouth opened, about to protest. The captain had expected this. She raised her hand and Dominica fell silent.

'I have another mission for you, something of great importance.'

Dominica's temper eased. 'Yes, Captain.'

'Our master is compromised. He may need to be revived. You must bring me Durendal.'

Dominica gasped. 'What you ask, it is impossible. Rouland hid the sword from all of us.'

'You refuse to help our master?' Captain de Vienne said sternly. 'In his hour of need?'

'No,' Dominica replied, some of her fire extinguished.

'But . . . where to begin?'

'The Widow will know.'

Dominica faltered, her eyes flashing like a trapped animal's. 'But she is . . . the Widow is insane—'

'Guard your words!' Captain de Vienne snapped. 'The Widow is to be revered. And she may be our only hope of resurrecting our master. If we cannot find the boy, if he does not lead us back to Rouland, the sword will. And if he is to prevail he will need Durendal. You cannot fail. Go to the Widow and find Durendal. Our discussion is at an end.'

'Yes, Captain,' Dominica said eventually.

'Take two sisters with you. Say nothing more here. Do you understand?'

Dominica nodded.

'Then go,' Captain de Vienne said. The thinnest of cold smiles danced upon her lips as Dominica turned to carry out her orders.

3

FIRE

Davey was burning.

He'd lost sight of Eloise. He'd lost sight of everything. Smoke consumed him and hot splinters bounced off his body. His lungs protested as he forced more noxious air into them. Flames licked his skin and took hold of the edges of his clothes. He had to move or be consumed.

He rolled to his left, patting down the islands of fire that threatened to envelop his arms and legs, and pulled himself up into a half-run, half-crawl away from the thickest part of the inferno.

Columns of smoke danced about him like circling wolves, hemming him in. It seemed that his every turn was blocked by ash and cinder. He no longer trusted his eyes, the heat of the fire acting as his only compass. He kept it to his back and ran away from it. After a moment he was suddenly clear of the tempest, and he saw the London skyline for the first time – his London, 1940's London. It seemed as if it was all ablaze, the flames almost white against the night sky.

'Davey,' a voice cried out pathetically.

He turned to see a shape limping towards him from the fire. As it moved free of the thick smoke he saw with relief that it was the outline of a young woman, perhaps sixteen or seventeen to the eye, in a grubby black dress pulled in by a thick leather belt. His eyes lifted from her buckled boots to the cropped black hair framing a face of porcelain. He instantly recognised the beautiful features of Eloise, and his heart rose. She smiled weakly, and collapsed at his feet. Pale blood pumped from her left shoulder and her arm twisted unnaturally. Davey caught her and stared at the wound, a deep cut that revealed the white of bone. Her eyes rolled languidly as she fought to stay conscious.

He stared in disbelief. Why was she not healing? Eloise had once been a Paladin – an undead knight who could endure almost any assault. He'd seen her survive much worse than this. The energy from her sword was able to restore and heal the most brutal of wounds.

Her sword.

Davey looked down to her empty hand. The sword was gone. Without its energies Eloise would not heal. Davey pushed her aside and scrambled to his feet. He looked back at the wall of fire and knew the sword must lie somewhere within.

He took a deep breath and ran into the smoke.

Almost immediately he was engulfed in a world of hot grey ash. He held his breath for as long as he could, until forced to fill his lungs with the burning smoke. He coughed violently. Pinpricks of fire danced on his face as splinters of burning wood landed on his skin. His eyes would barely open. All his senses told him to run, to get away from this terrible death that taunted him from all sides. But he couldn't. Eloise depended on him.

His vision began to tunnel, the edges fading into blackness. He had to get out now. But then he spotted the faintest of green glows in the choking smoke. He thrust his hand towards it and he touched hot metal. His fingers coiled around it and he pulled the sword towards him, then ran out of the terrible fire, towards fresh air.

Coughing and gasping, he fell next to Eloise. She wasn't moving. He pushed her sword into her hand and prayed that he was not too late. The metal's ethereal glow grew, pulsing like a feeble heartbeat. As the seconds passed, its emanations increased as its stored energy fed Eloise's injured body.

Davey fell onto his back, his own fatigue suddenly catching up with him. He closed his eyes, only for a moment he thought, but when he opened them again he saw the shapes of people around him.

'Get up, idiot!' a voice cried as hands grabbed him roughly about the shoulders.

Standing cautiously he turned to find who had spoken. He had not expected to see the round face of Castilan, the gruff landlord of the Hanging Tavern, glowering at him, and he almost laughed in surprise. Then he remembered Eloise.

'Castilan,' Davey cried. 'Where's Eloise?'

'How the hell should I know?' Castilan coughed as he herded Davey away from the fire.

'She was right next to me, on the ground,' Davey explained.

Castilan shook his head. 'Just you back there.'

They rested in an alleyway that sheltered them from the worst of the inferno.

'No, I wasn't alone,' Davey said breathlessly. 'Eloise was injured, her sword was healing her. She was with me!'

'Lad, you were out cold when I found you,' Castilan said. 'There was no one else nearby. If she was there she's long gone now.'

Davey's mind raced. 'Maybe she didn't see me. Maybe she woke up and didn't know where I was.'

Castilan shrugged.

'Maybe she went to the Hanging Tavern to find me,' Davey said.

The Hanging Tavern was well known to people like Davey and Eloise: people of the First World, a secret world of forbidden knowledge and immense power. The pub looked normal enough, but it was a meeting place between the Second World – the world of the mundane – and the First World. Its walls had seen things that many would consider to be magic.

'Yes,' Davey said, trying to reassure himself. 'Eloise will have gone to the Hanging Tavern.'

'Lad,' Castilan sighed, pointing to the mountain of burning timber that had, until tonight, been a building steeped in legend. '*That* is the Hanging Tavern.'

4

A TORMENT OF GRIMNIRE

Jack Morrow was somewhere else.

There had been a terrible instant of scolding, nerve-wrenching pain, followed by a wave of calming purple fire that soothed him like the waters of a lapping sea over hot summer sand.

The Sorrowline had broken apart, leaving in its wake a field of silver melancholy.

For the first time in an age Jack felt at peace. All the painful memories of his mother's death fell away and his mind was clear.

Deep in his stomach he still felt the giddy turbulence of falling. He stretched out his fingers and sensed the warming currents of energy as they passed over him. He was still travelling, still in some part of the Sorrowline, but this was a place he had never been to before. He was somehow beyond his journey's end, falling further back through time. Or was it forwards in time? He really didn't know. Where was he going? He calmed his mind and reached out to the Sorrowline, asking.

A new thought entered his head, like a reply to his own signal.

Fear not, the thought said. And then, silence. After a pause of serenity the purple fire returned, followed closely by a new wave of pain. He was arriving somewhere.

All at once his senses joined forces and screamed in every octave. There was a noise, like water boiling, which became needles of light piercing his eyes and folded into a taste of metal and blood on his tongue. He took a breath of air, letting its coolness revive him, and opened his eyes.

He was in a vaulted room, its dimensions obscured by a series of massive glass cylinders filled with a red gas. Each one was connected by a network of pipes and cables that snaked over every surface of the chamber.

He lifted his foot to take a step forward but something stopped him. He looked down and banged his head against something cold and hard. A low tone reverberated all around him, like a distant bell tolling. He looked closer and saw for the first time that he was *inside* one of the large glass cylinders.

A surge of claustrophobia overtook him. He tried to breathe, but the red gas tore at his lungs and burned his throat. He hammered his fists against the thick glass. Its grubby surface hardly moved. Jack's eyes began to burn, his heart pounded rapidly, his lungs closed up. He fell to the floor of the cylinder, his hammering getting weaker and weaker with every passing second. His vision blurred behind a wall of tears and his mind shut down. The only thought that prevailed was that he had let his mother down. She had sacrificed her own life for his, and given him a gift of great power, the Rose of Annwn living within him. And now he would die inside this chamber. Had his mother's sacrifice been for nothing?

A new vigour rallied inside him. He would not allow his mother's death to be in vain. With the last semblance of his physical strength he opened his hand and placed it onto the glass. Deep inside his mind the Rose stirred. Instinctively, he channelled it towards his palm, pleading with it to help him. He felt the heat rush into his hand, like a living thing, and suddenly the glass shattered into a thousand lacerating fragments. The noxious gas burst free, and fresh air surged into Jack's brittle lungs. He felt the multiple cuts to his body as the glass fell, but it was a relief after his terrible containment. He coughed violently and opened his eyes again.

In front of him stood three hooded figures almost twice his height. Their dark feathered robes were emblazoned with elaborate overlapping designs, which confused the eye. Ivory chains rattled from their limbs (each had at least four arms extending from their narrow frames), and a complex ticking timepiece hung from every neck. No faces were visible behind the heavy cowls; instead, a swirling column of grey smoke spewed out of the openings, filling the air with a smell like burnt plastic. Each held in its bony hand a long wooden staff capped with a bejewelled scythe. These were Grimnire, and Jack had met one of their kind before.

One of the Grimnire raised its skeletal hand, and gestured for Jack to follow. The three Grimnire turned as one, and drifted past the rows of glass cylinders. Jack staggered after them, his head still reeling. Ahead, a door opened, barely wide enough for the Grimnire to enter, yet endlessly high, its upper part lost in a luminous fog that danced over Jack's head. He crossed through the doorway into a larger chamber. Behind him the impossibly high door closed with a thunderous rumble.

This new chamber was dimly lit; at its edges hung tiny specks of flickering blue-red light. Jack squinted, and realised there was nothing small to these distant illuminations: each was a gigantic furnace which broiled with a purple fire like the one he had seen inside the Sorrowline. The furnaces were connected to a series of glass bells and pipes, which divided and spread like the roots of a gnarled tree, disappearing upwards into the mist. Several Grimnire toiled at each furnace, spading soft ragged forms into the flames. Were they bodies? Jack gasped. Other Grimnire delivered more carcases in immense sacks that they carried on their shoulders. Barely a sound was heard from these infernos, their distance from Jack was so great.

The Grimnire proceeded onwards, through the middle

of the great chamber, and Jack followed. They walked in silence towards a growing speck of white light that had appeared before them out of the mist. The speck became a line, and eventually a doorway. They passed solemnly through the threshold, into a new chamber bathed in a bright light that bleached out all detail.

Jack looked to the Grimnire and saw that they too now shone in harmony with the room. Their dark robes and the crows' feathers that adorned them had turned an ashen white. Even the smoke that belched from inside their hoods had changed: it was now the colour of blood. The Grimnire formed a circle around Jack. Others now joined their number, until he stood at the centre of a vast crowd of Grimnire, their uncountable scythes fading into the distance.

Somewhere far away another giant door opened, and a chill wind blasted from it. The crowd shifted and parted, until a clear path appeared between the door and Jack. Suddenly, with a terrible metallic shudder, the door closed. In its place was a solitary Grimnire making its way towards him. This one wore robes coloured deep red, matching the thick smoke spewing from its hood. As the Red Grimnire passed, the others bowed and when it stopped in front of Jack, the circle closed around them.

'Hello,' Jack said nervously, desperate to break the unending stillness.

The Red Grimnire did not reply; instead, it bowed its

elongated hooded head respectfully. Hesitantly, Jack mirrored its action.

As Jack straightened he heard a dislocated voice. No, *heard* wasn't true; it was as if a flood of images arrived in his mind's eye, and were transposed into a sentence.

You carry the Rose?

Jack's brain tingled, as if a low current of electricity flowed through it. He stumbled back, unable to comprehend the new sensation.

You carry the Rose?

The tingle became a painful spasm. Jack's brain reeled and he fell to the floor.

You carry the Rose of Annwn?

'Yes,' he gasped at last. The spasm subsided to a dull tingle, like the volume on a static radio being dialled back down. The Red Grimnire leaned closer to him.

Where are you going?

'Back to 1940.' This time Jack answered without hesitation. 'I was going back to London in 1940 to meet my friends. I was in a Sorrowline, then I was here.'

Grimnire summoned. You came.

The Red Grimnire glided gracefully around Jack as he pulled himself to his feet.

London. 1940. Why do you go there?

'Because,' Jack said, 'my friend needs my help. He's the only family I have left now.'

Who?

'My grandfather, Davey Vale.'

You carry the book.

The words were not a question. At first Jack was confused, then he remembered the book in his pocket, a slim leather-bound volume called *On the Nature of the Concealed Realms* by Magnus Hafgan. Rouland believed its pages held great secrets that would guide him back to the Concealed Realm of Otherworld. Having been there long ago Rouland was desperate to return, seeking both the book *and* the Rose from Jack. The last page of the little book contained secret messages to Jack from deep in the past. Those messages had guided him to his mother's side and a terrible battle that had taken her life. And, impossibly, the handwriting of those messages was his own. He touched the book in his pocket and said, 'Yes, I have it.'

The Red Grimnire seemed to nod its understanding.

What will you do with the Rose?

'What? What do you mean?'

What will you do with the Rose?

'I don't know!'

There was an audible buzz of disquiet as Jack's answer rippled through the congregation. The air filled with static and the hairs on Jack's neck stood on end.

The Grimnire were conferring.

After a moment the Red Grimnire raised one of its twisted hands, and the assembly fell into silence again. The Red Grimnire approached Jack, standing so close that the smoke billowing from its cowl wafted over his face. As it lowered its head Jack tried to see inside the dark hood, but its interior remained featureless.

Jack Morrow.

The electric sensation rocked through his mind, pulling it into sharper focus.

You are too young to wield the Rose. Too young for the choice.

There was another rumble of static as the congregation reacted to the last statement.

Judgement is made.

With that the Red Grimnire pulled out a golden sceptre from within its robes and pointed it at Jack. The sceptre came alive with long dancing currents of electricity which arced from the base towards its opposite end.

Jack closed his eyes, knowing the end had come.

Wait!

A rattle of excitement rushed though the space. The air was so charged that Jack felt tiny static shocks bounce between his tense fingers. Slowly he opened his eyes. In between him and the Red Grimnire was another of the strange creatures, three of its sinuous arms outstretched in front of it.

The Red Grimnire slowly pulled the golden sceptre to one side, the arcs of electricity subsiding.

A new series of images – a new voice – appeared in Jack's mind.

What of the prophecy of the Last Timesmith? Another Destiny can be achieved.

The Red Grimnire seemed to consider this, then it was as if the two Grimnire communicated directly with each other, debating the finer points of the argument through a dialogue of choral outbursts that reminded Jack of a church organ's keys being struck at random. All the time Jack's eyes darted between the Red Grimnire and this strange protector. Could this be the same Grimnire that he had encountered before, in St Paul's Cathedral? he wondered.

Eventually it seemed an agreement was reached, and the Red Grimnire withdrew the golden sceptre. With a long deliberate nod it spoke again to Jack.

Go, Timesmith. Live out the mercy of the Grimnire. Learn more of the Rose, and beware of Durendal.

The vast crowd parted to reveal another distant door.

Jack nodded to the Red Grimnire then turned to speak to his guardian. 'Thank you,' he said.

As Jack walked towards the door the lone Grimnire whispered a new picture in his mind.

This Destiny is not without its price, Jack Morrow. You will have to choose. When you do, the Grimnire will be there. The Grimnire will have their toll.

The words filled Jack's mind with dread. He shuddered as the door opened and he stepped through into a dazzling white light.

5

SURVIVAL

Her vision was blurred and indistinct. Dark shapes danced in front of her against a wall of flickering light, too painful to look at. Her skin prickled and blistered and she could smell the odour of her flesh burning. She was sure her left arm was broken in at least two places. It hung feebly at her side, bouncing like a heavy rag. Every breath was an ordeal, cracked ribs scraping against her innards with each rasping inhalation. Black smoke scolded her bloodfilled lungs, carrying with it a torrent of burning cinders which fizzed on her lips and throat. Her feet had been burned bare until the skin had become charred and brittle. She could hardly walk.

But Eloise would not give in.

Her right hand ached as it gripped the life-giving sword. Its subtle glow healed . . . but slowly, slowly. She stumbled out of the fire, alone. Where was Davey?

Behind her something exploded, and her world became ash and wood and fire and smoke. She staggered onwards, away from the flames. Survival was her only consideration now.

Somehow she made it to the edge of the Thames. She limped along one of the many wooden jetties, and fell off the end. The water was joyously cold against her burnt skin. She sank to the river bed and lay in the silt. The sword fed from the earth, its hazy green glow brightened with every passing minute. This felt good. She had survived. All she needed now was time. Time to heal.

A sensation sparked in her mind. Someone was coming. Coming to find her. But who? Then, all at once, an image formed. The Paladin, her sisters, were hunting her down. And they knew she was here.

Close by the dirty water broke into a splinter of bubbles as something fell into the river. Another splash erupted to her right, closer than the first. Then a third, behind her. The Paladin were in the water.

Eloise rose carefully, moving the liquid around her as little as possible. She could barely see anything in the churning brown river; the only clues to her assailants' positions were the small changes they made in the currents.

Suddenly someone hit her from the left side. They rolled together along the river bed, throwing up clouds of silt which hung in the water in slowly expanding columns. Eloise swung widely with her sword, hitting something. A hand clawed at her face briefly, then disappeared again into the murk.

Eloise pushed off the bottom and began to swim towards the middle of the river. This was the deepest point, a better place to lose her pursuers. She had barely set off when the blade of a sword glinted out of the darkness and hammered into her right shoulder. The pain was intense. She almost dropped her own sword. A face appeared in front of her, a face she knew only too well: Captain Alda de Vienne.

Hatred filled Eloise. She tried to put aside her feelings, tried to ignore the kaleidoscope of memories that erupted in her mind's eye, but the rage had already consumed her. She could never forget what had happened, long ago.

She lifted her sword but Captain de Vienne was far too fast for her, and grabbed her about the wrist. The captain's sword, a mechanical blade fitted to replace a severed hand, was still deep in Eloise's shoulder. Suddenly the blade turned to the side and the filthy water flooded into her lungs as she let out an anguished scream. Her strength was ebbing away, her injuries too great. She was only moments away from blacking out.

Eloise looked up; a vast dark shape was coming towards her out of the gloom. A deep throbbing pulsed through the water as the shape flew towards her. Captain de Vienne seemed to sense it too. She stopped twisting the sword and spun round just as the metal hull of the battleship smashed into Captain de Vienne's face, breaking her skull. The impact dragged them along the length of the ship, colliding again and again with its rusty hull. For a moment Captain de Vienne lolled about in the water, her hands still holding

Eloise, then, as her white blood began to mix with the river, she fell backwards. Eloise gripped the captain's arm and pulled at the blade embedded in her shoulder. The sword shifted slightly, then with an almost unbearable shock wave of pain, it came free.

The battleship's great propeller thundered down on Eloise, churning the water. She pulled herself under, out of the ship's path and swam deeper. Her shoulder screamed out in pain, but there was no time for rest, no time to heal. The other Paladin would smell the blood and be upon her in seconds. She swam for the north bank, rising up to the surface. The thin line of an anchor appeared in front of her. She dragged herself up it and burst free of the water, into the night air, leaping the great distance to land on the wooden surface of a fishing boat. She heard several powerful splashes as the dark shapes of the Paladin rocketed through the air and landed nimbly on the deck beside her.

'You have my sword,' Captain de Vienne said. 'I will have it back.' The words stumbled and slurred from her bloody mouth, her fractured jaw hanging low on one side of her mangled face. Eloise managed a triumphant smile. The sword in her hand had once belonged to Captain de Vienne, but she had lost it, and the hand that held it, when two boys had freed Eloise from her eternal imprisonment. Briefly she wondered what had happened to Jack and Davey.

'You wish it back: you must take it from me,' Eloise replied through gritted teeth.

Captain de Vienne glanced down to where her right hand had once been. 'We do not want you dead,' she grimaced. 'Tell us where the Morrow boy is and you may live.'

Eloise laughed icily. 'Your memory is short. You think I would trust you? After what you did to Cayden?' She felt a wave of emotion overrun her as his name fell from her lips. She moved in the same instant, up the mast pole, clawing at the timber, stabbing into it with the sword, gaining purchase and height with each swing of her arms until she met its summit.

The door to the boat's cabin flung open and a stout fisherman ran out. 'What's all this?' the fisherman demanded. 'This's my ship!'

One of the Paladin – Véronique – grabbed him by his jowly throat and flung him into the air. The man's scream faded rapidly as he disappeared into the darkness, followed by a distant splash.

Captain de Vienne turned her attention back on Eloise, high above her. She raised her mechanical arm and, with a heavy click, the blade doubled in length.

'You cannot take *this* sword from me, sister!' she cried, and swung her arm at the mast. The weapon sunk into the wood, cutting it to its centre. Captain de Vienne pulled the blade out and swung again. With a hideous creak the mast began to topple. It fell towards another vessel moored alongside. As the mighty wood smashed overboard Eloise seized her opportunity and leaped to the next craft.

With an inhuman speed the Paladin gave chase along the mast's length, descending on the other boat in seconds. It was the briefest of head starts, but it was enough for Eloise. The sword in her hand fed her, healing her wounds, filling her with a ferocious will to survive.

Véronique was first to strike, her sword raised high above her. She fell on Eloise as she raced to the bow of the boat. Eloise blocked the attack, her living sword throwing off sparks as it gouged through the nail-infested deck, igniting ropes and timber.

A second Paladin – Corinne – joined the skirmish, blocking Eloise's path. As they fought they ascended the ship's rigging and, again, Eloise jumped to the next boat. Corinne was first to follow, but Eloise was ready. As the Paladin fell towards her she turned, rolled, and impaled her sister with her sword. Corinne fell over Eloise's head and rolled along the burning deck, clutching her stomach. Eloise took Corinne's weapon from her shaking hand and rose to her feet. She stood over the fallen Paladin, a sword in each hand, a dark graceful shape against the burning sky.

Quickly she turned and ran up the deck and leaped onto the dockside, pushing aside two sailors carrying buckets to douse the fires. Behind her Véronique screamed as she swung from the boat's burning rigging, doggedly closing the gap between them until their blades met in a blur of anger. Eloise made full use of both weapons, swinging them in a frenzied onslaught that overwhelmed and disabled her attacker. Véronique fell to her knees, her chin on her chest, as Eloise leaped free of the rest of the approaching Paladin and sprinted along the dockside, weaving into the crowd drawn by the noise.

Eloise heard Captain de Vienne cry out as she gave pursuit. She turned a corner and stole a glance behind her: Geneviève, Anouk and Margaud were close to their captain.

Four Paladin were more than a match for her.

6

THE FIGURE IN THE DOOR

When the fire finally abated the Hanging Tavern was nothing more than a twisted pile of cinder and half a dozen blackened struts which pointed heavenwards at disordered angles. Nothing of value had survived the bombardment.

'That's my home,' Castilan said, his voice catching. 'That's my whole life right there.'

Davey barely heard him, his mind elsewhere. He stepped forwards in a daze through a swirling field of ash.

'Hey!' Castilan shouted. 'It's not safe, lad. Get back here!'

Davey carried on. Fire still raged about him as other buildings in the narrow street succumbed to this terrible death. Plumes of noxious black smoke belched upwards, pushed on by super-heated air, choking him with the rancid particles. A man ablaze staggered out of a burning structure and fell nearby. Davey rushed to his side but the man was already dead. His every impulse was to turn and run away, to free himself from this terrible place, but something kept him moving forwards, searching, searching.

'Eloise!' Davey shouted out repeatedly, coughing each time he pulled in a lungful of the hot air, but no one replied. He felt the soles of his feet burning and he knew his search was futile. And yet still he carried on.

Another building cried out, like a dying beast, then collapsed into the street. Davey ran for cover, narrowly avoiding the onslaught of brick and wood. The dust and smoke suddenly cleared, and for a moment a blast of cold, fresh air resurrected him. He wiped his stinging eyes with the arm of his shirt and squinted ahead.

A brick wall survived, partially collapsed on both sides, but enough remained to frame a red door, still upright, like a cut-out stage prop in a tawdry East-End parlour show.

He was stumbling towards the sight, over mounds of rubble mixed with the bodies of the young, closer to this absurd vision, when the handle turned and the red door opened. Davey could hardly believe what he saw. A figure emerged from the doorway, silhouetted by the fires burning beyond.

'Eloise?' Davey cried again. His fingers clawed at the mountain of debris, pulling at broken chairs, smashed bottles, torn curtains, towards the figure in the door.

There was a violent pop, as if the sky had fallen in on itself. At that moment the ash clouds parted, and Davey saw the figure clearly for the first time: not Eloise, but a boy, his white shirt smeared with dirt and blood. He appeared out of place, uncomfortable in his own skin, with a weariness about his eyes. Davey saw the boy's untamed mop of cherry-brown hair blowing in the breeze and recognised his future grandson at once.

'Jack?' Davey gasped, stunned and confused.

The boy in the doorway glanced up at the sound of his voice and saw Davey. Tears formed in his eyes as he ran to his friend. They met at the brow of the rubble hill, grabbing each other in disbelief.

'Davey,' Jack said, 'is it really you?'

'Who else?' Davey laughed.

Jack looked about him in a daze. 'I'm back! I'm back in London! It's 1940, isn't it?'

Davey gestured to the devastation around them. 'Well, it ain't 2008!'

A wide grin broke over Jack's face, and Davey laughed too.

'It's good to be back,' Jack said. His eyes took in Davey's tattered appearance. 'What happened to you? And where's Eloise?'

'That bloody Grimnire dropped us right in the middle of a bleedin' air raid, didn't it!'

'Don't talk to me about the Grimnire,' Jack mumbled. He saw Davey's inquisitive expression and said, 'I'll tell you later. Tell me what happened to you first.'

'Not much to tell,' Davey replied with a shrug. 'That Grimnire fella dropped us here, right in the middle of a fire. Me and Eloise, we got separated—' His voice disappeared.

Far away a sound began to grow.

'Run!' Davey pulled at Jack's shirt and the two boys stumbled over the rubble, along the street, away from the wailing noise.

'In here,' Davey cried, and pulled Jack down a flight of steps, to a basement entrance. He pushed at the shattered door and ran inside, just as the entire building shook violently as a bomb fell to earth close by. A wall of smoke and debris rushed past outside. The small windows exploded, showering them with fragments of wood and glass. What remained of the old door gave way and fell onto Jack and Davey, pinning them to the floor. Davey crawled further under the feeble protection, pulling Jack in with him.

They lay there for long minutes, listening to the chorus of fire and destruction, until the thick air forced them back into the street.

A firestorm had taken hold, and any hope of searching for Eloise was consumed by it. Reluctantly, and with a heavy heart, Davey turned away from the flames, away from what had once been the Hanging Tavern.

'She's in there,' Davey said heavily. 'Eloise.' He slumped onto a pile of rubble that had recently been someone's bedroom.

'But we have to do something,' Jack spluttered.

'What?' Davey replied angrily. 'I've tried! Can you walk through fire? Can you?'

Jack sat next to him and put his hand on his shoulder. Davey shrugged it off, hiding his tear-stained face. He shook himself upright, his back to Jack. 'No point moping about here. Everyone goes in the end, right?'

'But she's Paladin, she can survive.'

'Survive *that*?' Davey pointed at the advancing wall of fire, its heat and intensity growing stronger with every passing second. The flames licked at the edges of the surrounding buildings, taking hold of the rooftops, dropping like twisted phoenixes onto the scorched ground below, spreading, feeding. He kicked at the rubble in frustration. 'Come on, before we burn 'n'all.'

They sought sanctuary in the doorway of a sweet shop, far enough from the fires to be of some safety. The two impossible friends turned their backs momentarily on the carnage of the Blitz and stared instead at the jars of sweets.

'She'll get out of the fire, I'm sure of it,' Jack said.

Davey sighed heavily. 'I hope so.'

Jack nodded. Eloise had been dead already, a long time ago. Her former master, Rouland, had resurrected her as part of his elite inner circle, his Paladin. She was OnceDead now, unable to die, as long as her sword sustained her. The fires might consume her, might disfigure and torture her, but in spite of how much she might cry out for release, she would not die.

'So, what you been up to then?' Davey said with forced casualness.

Jack faced the jars of sweets, his eyes far away. He seemed different somehow. Older? No, that wasn't it. He was changed, more absorbed, with authority in his stare. 'After you left 2008 I went home.' He turned and looked at Davey, his features marked with sadness. 'Did I tell you my dad's in prison?'

Davey shook his head, listening intently.

'Our flat, it wasn't much, but with Dad in prison and me' – he half smiled – 'me here, they took the flat away. I've got nowhere else to go now.'

'You did the right thing,' Davey said, trying to sound paternal. 'I'll look after you here. After all, I'm your grandad, right?'

'Right.' Jack offered up a rigid smile. 'I tried coming straight back here, to find you. But I've been somewhere else first, Davey.'

'What d'you mean?'

Jack shook his head, squeezing his eyes shut. 'I, I don't know. I was in the Sorrowline, heading back here, to 1940, when . . .'

'When what?'

'I was somewhere else, with the Grimnire.'

Davey exclaimed, 'The Grimnire!'

Jack nodded pathetically. 'I don't know what happened. There were hundreds of Grimnire, thousands probably. It was a massive place. And there was a Grimnire dressed in red. I think I was on trial. But they let me go.'

'Is that all?' Davey asked, sensing more.

'They warned me,' Jack said, 'about something, or someone, called Durendal.'

'Durendal?' Davey mused. 'Never heard of it.'

'Me neither. I bet Eloise would know what it was.'

Davey felt his stomach turn over at the mention of her name. He closed his eyes and tried to calm his mind. 'Where are you?' he said quietly. He felt as if he could sense her like a darting, flickering image just out of focus. Jack's hand touched his shoulder and Davey opened his eyes. 'What?'

'Are you . . . are you sensing something?' Jack's face was stern, like stone.

Davey shrugged casually. 'Nah, not really.'

Jack's hand fell away and the space between them seemed to grow. 'You are, aren't you!'

'I'm not an Operator, Jack!' Davey replied angrily. In the future, in 2008, Jack had met Davey as an old man. Old David had become an Operator – someone who could control energy with their mind – and he had been consumed by bitterness and hate. He had joined forces with Rouland, and his actions had led to Jack's mother's death. Davey knew all this as well as Jack – he'd seen his

41

future self with his own eyes and the knowledge of his destiny weighed heavily on both boys.

Secretly, Davey had felt the first stirrings of his mental ability. He'd tried to ignore it, but it was there.

'Tell me the truth!' Jack demanded. His cheeks flushed with rage, his hands coiled into fists.

'I'm sensing things, all right? I can't help it! But I ain't *him*, Jack. I don't have to become him.' His voice fell to a terrified whisper. 'Do I?'

He saw Jack's anger subside, replaced with an uncomfortable formality. 'No, you don't. You shouldn't hide it, though, Davey. You have a gift, you should learn to use it properly.'

The last word seemed to ride on a wave of unresolved anger. The closeness that they had enjoyed only moments ago had gone, torn away, leaving a vast hole that Davey felt might consume him.

He watched Jack wrestling with his doubts. Then Jack seemed to come to a decision. 'Use it. See if you can find Eloise.'

'You sure?'

Jack nodded firmly.

Davey closed his eyes and tried to find the elusive images again. At first there was nothing, then he saw a dark figure moving quickly against flames. He gasped.

Jack's voice broke in. 'What can you see?'

'Something. I don't know,' Davey replied honestly.

He looked to the west, to the centre of the city. 'She's over there, somewhere towards Piccadilly Circus.'

'You sure?'

Davey stared at Jack. 'No, of course I'm not sure! It's just a feeling, a hunch, that's all.'

'It's all we have,' Jack said with a thin smile.

Davey laughed involuntarily and they began to move westwards, through the debris.

7

THE BATTLE OF TRAFALGAR

They were like an unstoppable wind, surging along the foggy night-time streets, sometimes rushing through the middle of traffic, sometimes plummeting along the narrow paths, sometimes even rising up the very walls of the buildings, clawing, grabbing, ascending. Around them Londoners screamed and withdrew into shop doorways, cars swerved and braked, all in a ballet of slow motion compared to Eloise and the Paladin.

Eloise led the way, choosing the path that suited her best, her goal always in mind. Behind her Captain de Vienne, Geneviève, Anouk and Margaud followed like a pack of wild hunting dogs.

Ahead the road turned, and the awnings of an elegant hotel became an easy stepping stone for Eloise. Her fingers clung to the grooves in the stonework, lifting and pulling her upwards to the metal rails of a first-floor balcony. She leaped free, suspended for an instant over a double-decker bus – its top-floor passengers' faces frozen in a tapestry of shocked confusion – until her hands found

44

the top of a street lamp. Instantly she jumped from it, back towards the hotel's façade. Behind her the Paladin kept pace.

The hotel's extinguished neon sign groaned under Eloise's weight as she landed on it, sending a group of pigeons into the bleak air around her. The muscles in her torso tensed and twisted. She was airborne again, heading up to the second floor. Her fingers ached as she gripped the narrow ledges and grooves in the stone. One tiny miscalculation and she would fall to the street below. One mistake is all the Paladin would need to destroy her for ever.

Along the wall she clawed like a loping spider, her muscles laughing at gravity. Behind her she heard a grunt and the sound of metal scraping into stone. One of the Paladin had misjudged and fallen.

Ahead, another balcony appeared out of the grey mist. Eloise reached for it, landing softly, hardly slowing down as she tried the glass door. It was unlocked.

She was a blur of black as she entered the hotel room and closed the door behind her. Outside she saw two dark shapes pass by. It would only take them seconds to realise where she was.

She ran past the room's sleeping couple – both oblivious to the desperate chase happening around them – towards the door that would take her deep into the hotel's maze of corridors. She did not like this confinement, it was dangerous. She wanted to be outside again. Silently, swiftly, she made her way to the top floor, found the staircase that led to the rooftop and left the stuffy corridors behind.

The moist night air cooled Eloise's face. She looked out over the London skyline: dark, in hiding from the German pilots. In front of her lay her goal: the wide expanse of Trafalgar Square, shrouded in a misty fog. For a moment the distant thunder of bombs ceased and Eloise felt she had London to herself.

In the centre of the rooftop she found a pole with telephone cables shooting out of it in all directions, like an artificial web.

Her eyes followed one of the lines out into the street where it met a junction box on the wall of another building. She quickly judged its length. It would be enough. Eloise pulled sharply and the cable came free from the box. She reeled in its length until it sat in a pile at her feet.

Time was running out. They were coming for her. She pulled the sword she had taken from Corinne from her belt, tied the end of the cable to its hilt and stepped onto the edge of the roof. She would have to time this perfectly.

Her target was almost lost in the damp gloom. She focused and saw Nelson's Column standing proudly in the centre of Trafalgar Square. Eloise aimed the sword and threw it at the top of the column. It whistled through the air, dragging the cable behind it until, with hardly a sound, the sword pierced the old stonework. She had judged well. The cable hung taut between the column and the rooftop.

Behind her she heard motion. The door to the rooftop shattered, and the Paladin burst through. Quickly she spun her sword round and latched the hilt over the cable. She grabbed it with both hands and ran off the edge of the rooftop. Her heart seemed to stop, and all sound blurred away. She felt like a bird, gliding through the moist air, nothing holding her back. The pain fell away and she was, for the briefest of moments, happy.

The sword slid along the length of the cable, down towards Nelson's Column. Behind her on the rooftop she saw the dark shapes of three Paladin. She knew what would happen next. There was a faint glint of a sword being swung, then Eloise felt the tension disappear from the cable and she began to fall. She spun the sword back round and grabbed the cable, wrapping it round her wrist several times. At the same time she swung her weight out to her left, forcing herself into an arced decent. The cable jerked to the left, and Eloise swung around and behind the column. The cable pulled itself tighter around the stonework, dragging Eloise around it once, twice, three times. As she disappeared behind the column again she let go and fell to the pavement, rolling to a halt. The sound and pain returned.

Somewhere high above Captain de Vienne cursed, her

distant howl absorbed into the mist. Eloise picked herself up and ran towards one of the two large pools of water that lay either side of the column. She was almost upon it when—

'Eloise!'

The voice was oddly familiar. She focused beyond the pool, into the misty night, and saw two boys running towards her: Davey and Jack.

'You're alive!' Davey said with a grin. 'We've been looking all over for you!'

Eloise warmed at the sight of her two friends. Then she remembered the chase. 'The Paladin, they are here.'

'Don't worry!' Davey smiled as he produced a coin from his pocket and tossed it into the wide pool. The water shimmered and glistened, then an opening appeared beneath it. 'I've always got a way out.'

'This is a junction?' Jack said, amazed. 'Trafalgar Square is a junction?'

'One of the main entrances into the First World,' Davey explained quickly. 'Too busy for my liking. Too many forms to fill out, but we ain't got time for a quieter way in.'

Above them the sky lit up with anti-aircraft fire as the distant drone of German bombers began again in earnest. The flash of a memory erupted in Eloise's mind, of the first time she had used a junction chamber. She was just a girl, and she had been terrified. Her mother had explained it to her, how it was a secret way from the London of the

Second World to the hidden depths beneath it, to the First World. She had been afraid of water and cried until she had found herself safely on the other side. The sensation of falling was gone almost at once, and yet the memory remained even now, after all these long decades.

A distant explosion filled the damp fog with a sickly light, shattering Eloise's memory. Cut out against the temporary flash of colour was a trio of sinister figures, dark and malevolent.

'Quick,' Eloise said to Jack and Davey. 'Into the junction, before it closes. I will hold them back.'

'No,' Davey cried. 'You've gotta come with us.'

'They seek Jack. They will follow me, so I cannot go with you.'

Jack rushed up to Eloise. 'We stay together.'

Eloise saw her sisters approaching rapidly and knew what she must do. 'Forgive me.' She picked Jack up by his shirt and threw him into the pool. As he disappeared into it the surface glowed, shifted, and the junction closed.

'What have you done?' Davey gasped.

'Saved him. You have another coin?'

Davey fumbled in his pockets until he found a small silver coin. He held it up for Eloise to see the First World crest embossed into it.

'Good,' she said. 'Follow me, and stay out of the way.'

'Aren't we going in?'

49

'No. The coin is not for us.'

Without another moment's hesitation Eloise ran towards the Paladin, her sword in front of her. Anouk was the first upon her and their swords clashed, green sparks illuminating the giant lion statues that guarded the column.

Eloise jumped onto one of the statues, and Anouk followed. As she leaped into the air Eloise's sword made contact, ripping through Anouk's ancient armour and tearing at the flesh below. Anouk fell to the ground, moaning softly. The other two Paladin, Margaud and Captain de Vienne, approached cautiously.

Eloise sprang off the lion, and somersaulted towards the far pool. Margaud swung her sword high over her head, crying out as she flung herself at Eloise. The battle was fierce, their swords a blur. Eloise retreated backwards into the pool, parrying every blow. Margaud waded into the water purposefully, as if she sensed her opponent weakening. Captain de Vienne watched and waited, unaware of Davey hiding behind the lion statue.

Then, one of Margaud's jabs found a way through. The sword pierced Eloise's side, the tip protruding from her back. For a moment the pair were frozen, like a new statue, then Eloise fell on one knee, unable to draw her breath. Margaud pulled her sword free and raised it over Eloise's head.

'Wait!' said Captain de Vienne. 'She will answer to me.'

Eloise, her head down, saw Davey scramble closer, unobserved, like a mouse amongst giants. His fearful gaze found Eloise. She blinked slowly, her eyes looking to the water, then up to Margaud. Davey nodded quickly.

As Captain de Vienne crossed the low wall and stepped into the pool of water Davey crept forward silently. He tossed the coin into the air towards the pool.

Captain de Vienne stood over Eloise. She raised her mechanical hand high in the air and, with a click, the blade slid out. Only Eloise saw the tiny coin as it fell towards them. She shifted her weight onto her back leg. Her muscles tensed.

'You will tell me where the Morrow boy is, Eloise. Pain always reveals secrets. I think I will start with your eye,' Captain de Vienne said. Her sword arm began to spin noisily as it inched closer to Eloise's face.

Close by there was the smallest of splashes. At the same moment Eloise leaped out of the pool. Even before she had landed the water had begun to glisten and give way. Captain de Vienne gasped as her feet began to fall. She clawed about her for something to hold onto, but she found only Margaud. The pair fell into the junction and disappeared completely. Eloise landed awkwardly on the pool wall, her eyes blurring with the pain from her side. The water fizzed again and the junction closed.

The square was instantly veiled in silence. All was

still, the thick mist like an emerald-grey shroud muffling even the air raid siren.

Eloise gasped to catch her breath; one of her lungs was full of blood. She prayed her sword would heal her quickly. A hand reached out and touched hers. She opened her eyes and saw Davey.

'Are they gone?' he asked quickly.

'For now.'

'They won't find Jack down there, will they?'

'Ealdwyc is a big place. The junctions are far apart. They can sense *me*, not him. They will soon return here – to me. I will lead them away.'

'Can you walk?'

Eloise pulled herself upright. The pain was terrible, but she would bear it. Davey put his arm around her, supporting her fragile broken body as they retreated into the bleak night.

8

ALONE IN EALDWYC

'No!' Jack cried as the Trafalgar Square junction fell away, its tepid colours mixing together into an inky blue-black. Air rushed about him as the brief sensation of falling receded. Out of the nothingness new shapes and colours formed themselves into order as Jack came to rest with all the force of a feather on a metallic high chair. He looked about him, stunned: he was in a large room with many other chairs, all the same as the one he found himself in, all of them empty. In one corner of the room a small electric lamp hummed into life, breaking the muddy-brown hue of the space with a circle of yellow.

'Name?' The voice was old and gruff. It seemed to be coming from behind the light.

'What?' Jack replied. 'Who's there?' He tried to raise his hand and shade his eyes from the glare, but something was stopping him from moving.

The voice sighed. 'Name! What is your name?'

'Jack.'

'First or last?'

'First or last what?' Jack asked, confused.

'Name! Is that your first or last name?'

'First. My name is Jack Morrow.'

The sound of a pen scribbling over paper rattled round the vast chamber.

'Jacque? With a Q?'

'No, Jack, with a K. It's spelled J, A, C, K.'

The old voice tutted. There was the noise of paper crumpled into a ball and being thrown onto the stone floor.

The hidden speaker cleared his throat. 'J, A, C, K. Marrow. M, A, R—'

'No, no,' Jack interrupted. 'It's Morrow. M, O, R, R, O, W.'

The voice muttered and complained as another piece of paper was thrown to the floor.

'Morrow. Two o's, two r's? Are you sure?'

'Yes. Can I go now?' Jack asked.

'Reason for visit?' the old voice said.

'I . . . I don't know—'

'State the reason for your visit to Ealdwyc,' the voice shouted angrily.

Jack thought quickly and said, 'I'm visiting friends here.'

'How long are you staying?'

'Oh . . . just a few days. Maybe a week,' Jack replied optimistically.

'Any contagious diseases?'

'No.'

'Are you carrying any forbidden substances?'

Jack shuddered, remembering the small book he carried in his trouser pocket. It was a highly prized antique, a rare volume stolen from 1813 by him and Davey.

'Tobacco? Alcohol? Cheese?' The voice broke Jack's thoughts apart.

'No,' he replied tensely.

There was a heavy thud as an inky stamp struck paper.

'Welcome to Ealdwyc. Enjoy your visit.'

Whatever force had been holding Jack in the chair was suddenly released. He quickly checked the book was still safely in his pocket, and as his fingers touched its leather surface relief flooded his body. He stood up slowly.

The gruff voice spoke again: 'Move on, move on. Quickly, now.'

Jack stepped away from the chair, down several shallow steps, towards the light.

'Not this way.'

'What?' Jack asked.

'Way out is over there.' If the owner of the voice was pointing Jack could not see it. He looked about the chamber until he noticed a door on the opposite side. He walked towards it, pulled the handle and stepped through the threshold.

Jack was not prepared for what lay beyond that unassuming door. He found himself on a narrow walkway, a path that had been perfectly carved out of the side of a steep rocky outcrop. In front of him was a vast chasm, a great opening which wound ever downwards, seemingly without end. The abyss was perhaps a mile in diameter, and all around its surface paths and inlets had been hewn into the rock. He looked directly across the wide opening. Spires and cathedral-like pinnacles clung onto the edge, jutting out into nothingness, like arrows of stone. The architecture was oddly familiar, a reflection of the Second World city he'd just left, but on a much grander scale, defying gravity.

Jack leaned over the carved wall that ran along the edge of the great rift. Warm currents drifted upwards, blowing Jack's scruffy hair about in the breeze. The heat felt good on his dirty skin. Smells drifted on the wind: spices frying, fish in garlic, burning coal, manure. Life.

Everywhere he looked he saw movement. People were going about the interconnecting corkscrew pathways that lined the walls of the chasm. He saw fires, and lights, some flickered by gas, others giving off the distinctive cool persistence of electricity. Dozens of flags hung from the buildings on long poles over the pit. All had different designs on them, crests of some sort.

Suddenly a giant bird, black like a raven, swooped upward from the depths. It glided round in a vast arc, the rising air taking it higher and higher. On its back sat a man in a saddle, guiding it with an outstretched hand. Another bird followed it, then another. The three riders chased each other into the darkness high above, their cries disappearing on the wind.

Jack stood and watched for almost fifteen minutes, never tiring of the ever-changing view, of the great metal sculptures that sat on pillars of marble, of the boat-like ships that floated away from either side of the chasm with their beautiful golden sails unfurled to catch the thermals, of the many waterfalls that tumbled into the rift only to rise up again as rainbow-laden mist clouds. He had been to the First World before, had seen some of its spaces, but none of it came close to the wonders of this view.

'Are you new here?'

Jack broke off his gaze to see a young girl standing by his side. She appeared to be of a similar age to Jack, perhaps twelve. Her hair was long and wild, auburn streaked with lighter shades of sandy brown, and stood out like a mane around her shoulders. She wore a dark dress, edged in white lace, the sort of thing Jack had only ever seen in history lessons. The fabric appeared expensive, but the edges were worn and splattered with dirt. Her grubby face was proud and mysterious, like someone of great importance who had fallen all the way back to earth. Her deep green eyes pierced Jack, never blinking.

'You must be new here. The locals don't stare and gawp the way you do. Where are you from?'

Jack looked from the girl to the impossible view. 'London. My name's Jack.'

She smiled broadly, 'Hallo, Jack. Hilda Jude. Pleased to make your acquaintance'

Jack suppressed a giggle. He'd never met anyone called Hilda who wasn't grey and toothless. This strange girl was immediately fascinating.

'What's so funny?' the girl enquired, her hands on her hips. 'Are you laughing at me?'

'No, sorry. It's just, well, where I come from Hilda is an old name.'

Hilda frowned. 'I'm older than I look.'

'And you live here?'

'Sometimes. I live in lots of places.' Her eyes wandered to the spectacular sight. The rock wall was streaked with quartz crystal, which caught and reflected the many points of light. Patterns played over its surface, always moving.

'What about you, Jack?' Hilda continued. 'What brings you to Ealdwyc?'

Jack shrugged. 'I don't think I had a choice.'

He thought of Eloise and Davey. He had wanted to stay and fight with his friends. They had saved his life, but at what cost? He wondered with a shudder if they were still alive.

'Your friends?' Hilda asked casually, hardly sounding interested.

Jack's spine tingled. He turned to face Hilda. Her eyes were closed and a broad smile filled her round face.

'You read minds?' Jack said angrily.

'Who doesn't?' Hilda shrugged, like it was the most normal thing in the world. 'Don't worry, Jack. I'm still practising. It's almost as vague as reading tea leaves. My Aunt Jesse does that. She thinks it's clever.'

Jack fumed.

Hilda smiled playfully, edging closer to him. 'For example, I can tell that you're concerned for your friends' welfare, but I could no more tell you their names than list what you had for breakfast. Any dim and sordid secrets you have up there are safe.' She tapped on his forehead, her fingernail sharp on his skin. Jack pulled away. This stupid girl was a nuisance, he thought. His face felt hot with blood. He looked about him; they were alone. A terrible thought conjured itself into being. He could easily lift the girl up. The edge of the wall was low enough. It would only take an instant. He could watch as her scream faded into the bottom of the chasm.

His cheeks flushed and he realised his hands were clenched into tight fists. He forced them to open as he inhaled deeply. The horrific image dissipated, leaving a terrible nausea in the back of his throat. The over-whelming anger diminished. He felt ashamed and confused. Why had he thought such a thing? Then he sensed the power resting inside him stir and he understood: the Rose of Annwn was restless. Jack swallowed, trembling with a rush of fear. His mother had given him the Rose, using its energies to save his life. He could sense its potential, desperate to stretch, to grow, tempting his mind to use it. Jack forced himself to resist it, pushing its influence aside.

Hilda had taken a step away. She stood casually, hardly looking at him, but Jack saw that she was tense. Had she read his mind again? Did she know? Could she tell what had happened to him? *The Rose happened to me*, he shouted inside his mind. He felt it in every part of his body, like a burning beacon. It sat like a dark spider in the web of his mind, clawing to be set free. The Rose made him greater than any man. He could do anything. He could wish the girl away, for ever. The rush of power was intoxicating, almost overwhelming, rising up again.

Jack shook his head and the disturbing thoughts subsided.

He needed to focus. He recalled the Grimnire's warning and he knew what he must do next: find out what Durendal was.

'I have to go,' he said quietly, and began to walk away along the curved path.

'Jack, wait.'

He didn't stop. He daren't.

'Don't go,' she shouted after him. 'I can help you find Durendal.'

Jack halted abruptly and turned to face Hilda. 'What did you just say?'

'Durendal,' she said meekly, looking anxious. 'I know how you can find it.'

'How did you—'

'You were practically shouting it.' Some of her confident manner began to return, and Jack's anger grew again. He didn't need her to tell him what to do. He had already defeated Rouland in battle. He had blocked his thoughts from him. But that had been soon after he had been given the Rose. His mind had been clear, controlled. Now that clarity had dissolved into a fog of indecision.

Jack stepped closer to Hilda, breathing deeply to slow his rage. 'What do you know about Durendal?'

9

RESOLUTIONS

The first rays of the morning sun kissed the top of the old building. Eloise sat motionless, letting the warmth of the dawn sink into her blistered face. Every moment lessened the pain. The wound to her side had knitted together well enough, but it would be many hours before she would be fully restored. The battle in Trafalgar Square had taken a great toll. Now all she wanted was time, peace and solitude.

'How long do you think we should stay here?' Davey sat nearby, noisily eating a loaf of bread.

Eloise sighed and opened one eye. 'Davey, please.'

'Yeah, yeah, I know, you need a break. But I hate staying still,' Davey said, his mouth full of half-chewed bread. 'It's not gonna take the Paladin long to get back to London, is it? And when they do they're gonna find us and . . .'

Eloise held up her hand. 'We are safe enough here for a few more minutes.'

Davey began to pull chunks of bread from the loaf. He threw them onto the roof where a handful of eager pigeons fought over them. Eloise closed her eyes again, calming her mind.

'What do you suppose Jack's doing?'

Eloise sighed deeply, wishing she was alone. 'Keeping hidden, I hope.'

'You don't think the Paladin will find him, do you?'

'No,' Eloise said firmly, putting aside her desire for peace and quiet. 'They will already have left Ealdwyc. By now they will be back in London. It is me they sense. It is me they hunt. They did not see Jack enter the junction chamber to Ealdwyc. They do not know he is there.'

Davey nodded hesitantly. 'He's a tough nut anyway. He'll look after himself.'

She saw the concern on Davey's blackened face. She was glad of his company after all.

'How did he find you?' Eloise asked.

'The Grimnire. They dumped him here, like they did you 'n' me.'

Eloise stared at Davey. 'What do they want with him?'

Davey shrugged, wiping his coat down. 'They warned him, I think. Didn't make much sense.'

'What was the warning?'

'He didn't know. Me neither. They warned him about something called Durendal.'

The word shook Eloise. It was a long-forgotten name that she had buried deep within her. To hear it again now, after all these years, was deeply disturbing. Her mouth opened but she could not bring herself to repeat that name.

'It ... it is a great weapon.' Eloise's voice trembled.

'Durendal? A weapon?'

'Do not speak its name again to me.'

Davey tutted. 'What sort of weapon?'

'It is a sword,' Eloise said slowly. 'Rouland's sword. But it is more than a weapon, it is the sum of the hateful deeds it has done. Even Rouland feared it.'

'But Rouland's gone now.'

'You do not understand, Davey. The Paladin swords sustain us. When we are injured they can heal us.'

'I know that!' Davey said indignantly.

Eloise continued, 'When they are used in battle they drain the life from their victims. But Rouland wanted more. He forged a new sword, a terrible mix of metal and secret knowledge. His sword ...' Eloise faltered. That name again.

'Durendal,' Davey offered.

'It did more than feed off its victims, it consumed them completely. It is said that he found a way to capture their souls in that weapon, to contain them for all eternity. Over time its energy grew, and Rouland fed off it until he feared he might lose himself to it. He kept it hidden, only daring to use it when it was necessary.'

'So if it's hidden then we don't need to worry.'

Eloise struggled to her feet. 'But the sword fed off

Rouland too. He and the sword are connected. It can find and restore him. The Paladin know this. They will be searching for it. And if the Grimnire warned Jack about it then they must think the Paladin might succeed. Our next move is clear to me now.'

'Is it?' Davey said.

'Yes,' she replied, bracing herself against her own fear. 'We must find it first.'

'You know where it is?'

Eloise sat in quiet contemplation for several long minutes. She felt as if there were answers buried deep within her, far out of reach. When she had been imprisoned by Rouland a century ago he had fragmented her memories, torn them apart so that his secrets would be safe. Over time small recollections came back to her, disjointed and useless. But some things she could never forget. Terrible dark deeds haunted her still, of her life before everything changed. Before Cayden.

She realised Davey was staring at her. 'I do not know the sword's location, only rumours,' she said at last. 'It is hidden between realms.'

Davey laughed. 'Well, no one's gonna find it there!'

Eloise nodded thoughtfully. Then she remembered something, a wise face from her ancient past. Might she still be alive? Hope flickered inside her.

'Take me to the nearest junction to Ealdwyc.'

Davey sighed. 'It's a big place.'

'To the Old Quarter: Folunain.'

'Why?' Davey asked, throwing the end of the loaf off the roof. 'What's in Folunain?'

'Someone who can help, if she is still alive. Someone who might yet know where the sword is hidden.'

10

COMPTON'S PRISM

The wide passage descended steeply away from the Great Pit of Ealdwyc. As Jack followed its winding path it reminded him of a Mediterranean street leading down towards some hidden shore. In front of him was Hilda, her steady footsteps leading him on. Above their heads were lanterns, which glowed and dimmed as they passed by. The ebbing and flowing of the orange lights made it seem as if the street was breathing, widening as they approached then shrinking again behind them.

'Where are you taking me?' Jack asked when the pathway narrowed and zigzagged in a new direction.

Hilda smiled knowingly. 'Not too far now.'

They came to a wider opening where two pathways met. In the centre of the space was an olive tree surrounded by chairs.

'How do things grow here?' Jack asked. 'Without the sun, I mean.'

'Ask a gardener,' Hilda replied. She followed the path to the left, leaving Jack staring at the olive tree. He paused for a moment then turned to join Hilda. She was almost out of sight. Jack ran down the pathway to catch up with her.

'Where are we going?' he asked more forcefully.

'You don't know?' Hilda replied nonchalantly as she opened a rickety doorway and stepped inside.

Jack's face flushed with pent-up anger as he rushed through the door to keep up with her. She seemed to be doing her best to annoy him. 'Well, if I knew I wouldn't be asking you, would I?'

Hilda led Jack down two flights of stairs and into a dusky room clad in oak panels. The air smelled of polished brass. 'This is a morphic prism, of course.' She spoke as if addressing a small child.

'Which is?'

Before Hilda could reply another voice bellowed at them from the darkness. 'Oi! Watcha think yer doing in 'ere?'

Jack noticed a man sitting behind a small desk, illuminated by the feeblest of candles. He slammed his hands down, sending dust particles dancing around the flame, and stood up noisily, grunting and huffing. Then the man reached up and pulled at a large lever fitted to the stone wall and the dark space was flooded with a cool blue light.

Jack could see him properly now: the stranger's hair, what there was of it, sprouted in sparse clumps from his shiny head. As he moved, the fine mane drifted like grey seaweed in a gentle tide. His poxed, stubbled face scowled at them.

'Not fer kids. Be on yer way,' the man said, his little eyes squinting at Hilda and Jack.

'We'd like to use the prism,' Hilda said, all smiles and charm.

'Well, you cannit. Shove off.'

'We won't be long, sir,' Hilda soothed. Jack supposed the man had never been called 'sir' before. He seemed to flush and fumble at this newly acquired title.

'Well, that is . . . you cannit, sorry.' He blushed.

'My father,' Hilda continued, 'is very rich and powerful. You know Lord Jude of Gogmagog?'

The man thought for a moment and said, 'Nope. Never 'eard of him! Now, really, go on, git!'

'I have money. All we want is to use your machine for a few moments.' Hilda pulled out a small purse as she spoke and began to count out gold coins into the man's thick hand.

The man smiled. 'It's prolly my supper time, anyways.' He pushed the coins into his trouser pocket and tapped the side of his wide nose with his finger. 'Don't wanna know yer names, and don't be askin' fer mine. Right?'

Jack nodded, trying not to look at the printed card that sat on the man's desk. It read: *Vannevar Lawrence Compton, Morphic Field Engineer.*

'Come on, quick, quick!' said Compton.

He beckoned them towards a complex apparatus that would not have looked out of place inside an astronomical observatory. The device was huge, made up of a series of interconnecting tubes which stretched up to the high ceiling. At its pinnacle was a faceted crystal which turned slowly, throwing dynamic reflections onto the walls. Beneath the grand mechanism was a reclining seat.

'Who's goin' in?' Compton asked.

'He is,' Hilda said, pointing to Jack.

Compton patted the leather chair. 'Sit,' he said firmly.

'What for?' Jack asked.

Hilda pulled him up close and whispered, 'You want to know what Durendal is, don't you?'

'Yes, but—'

'Then this is how. The prism will help you.'

'How?' Jack said angrily.

'The morphic prism,' Compton said with an air of professional pride, 'is a clever bit o' kit, an' no mistake. See, you don't *need* to know something, not exactly anyway. As long as someone, *anyone*, alive or dead knows it then you should be able to find the answer. It's not perfect, an' it's not fer everyone, but when it works it bloody works!'

'It taps into the collective resonance of all First Worlders,' Hilda added. 'Think of it as a library of every-one's thoughts.'

'Now, quickly,' Compton shouted, 'before I go changin' me mind.'

Jack reluctantly climbed into the seat and lay back.

'Keep still, while I gets you sorted.' Compton quickly rolled Jack's jacket sleeve up.

'Ow!' Jack looked at his arm – a needle had been injected into his vein and blood began to drip through a tube, into a dirty bottle.

'Keep still! Need ter tune the prism to you.'

Jack put his head back on the leather and tried to relax.

Compton took a small sample of Jack's blood from the bottle with a dropper and placed it onto a piece of coarse paper. As the blood soaked into the paper it revealed a series of coloured shapes.

'Ah,' Compton said as he studied the changing paper. 'Nought point two five two variance frequency. Quite high. Yer ever need glasses?'

'No,' Jack replied.

'Suffer from blackouts?'

'No.'

Compton returned to the paper. Its surface was now a maze of shapes that changed colour from moment to moment.

'Temperance up high 'n'all, but should be fine,' Compton noted as he fastened a pair of leather straps over Jack's chest, pinning him into the chair.

'This way, little miss,' Compton said as he pulled Hilda behind a metal shield the size of a door. Jack heard the sound of switches being thrown, and a deep rumble rose from somewhere under the chair. The great machine was coming to life.

'Is this safe?' Jack asked.

A pair of eyes appeared at a tiny letterbox opening in the thick metal plate. 'Absolutely fine,' Compton said. There was a sudden white flash as electricity pushed through the prism. Light cascaded outwards in sharp beams, bouncing off angled mirrors which refocused them together into a blinding pinprick, like a laser. The beam hit Jack in the centre of his forehead, and the room melted away.

Jack fell through the chair, or at least that was how it seemed. His body boiled away. Nothing remained. Then, from nowhere, a voice erupted.

'You OK, young 'un?' The voice was high-pitched and distorted.

'Who's there?'

'I said no names. You'll be feelin' a bit out of sorts; that's normal.' The voice narrowed and dropped until it was recognisably Compton's. 'It'll pass after a mo.'

'I'm OK,' Jack said, his teeth gritted firmly together. His world still reeled around him, but the sensation lessened with every passing second. The walls of the room returned, as did the chair, and the terrible nausea in the pit of his stomach calmed.

'What... what happens now?'

'Just relax, let yer question form in yer mind's eye,' Compton instructed.

'The answers will come,' Hilda said hopefully.

Jack tried to clear his mind of other distracting thoughts. *What is it I need to know?* he wondered.

'Durendal.' The booming voice was monotone and deep with vibrations that rattled through the chair.

'What? Who's that?'

'It's all right, young 'un. Just the horns,' Compton said. He pointed to a row of conical openings hanging from the wall. 'They amplif... amplificate... they make it sound louder. Yeah?'

'They make what sound louder?' Jack asked, confused.

'Yer thoughts!' Compton tutted.

Jack closed his eyes again and tried to relax. He formed a new question in his mind. *What is Durendal?* he asked.

The amplifier horns filled with static that hissed and popped. Then the voice returned: *'Durendal is the living sword... Rouland's sword.'*

Jack shuddered. Even now he seemed to be haunted by Rouland. He tried to form a new question: *Where will I find it?*

The machine throbbed as the prism shifted above him,

and the massive speakers sounded again: *The book will show the way.*

The hair on the back of Jack's neck prickled. He knew instantly what this meant.

'Yes!' A voice cried out through the rolling hiss. 'Where is the book?' There was a naked urgency to the question. There was fear there too, laced with impatience and anger, and he realised that this voice wasn't coming from the machine – it was inside his mind. 'Where is the book? Tell me now!'

The question suffocated him. Jack opened his eyes. 'Let me out of this chair!'

'What? Already? But you're not deep enough yet,' Compton said gruffly.

'Let me out, now!' Jack cried, desperate to be free of the sickly angst.

'Keep yer shirt on.' Compton pulled at the straps that held Jack in place, until he fell free of the chair, gasping for breath. Eventually the sensation passed. Jack pulled himself upright. In front of him was Hilda. She stared at him, her wide eyes full of fear.

'What happened to you?' she asked.

'Don't you know? You seem to know everything else!'

Compton stared at the complex device. 'That'll 'ave to do, fer now. You've knocked the ocular alignment off. I don't think yer right fer the machine. Yer best leave.'

Jack looked again at Hilda and fresh doubts swept through his mind.

Just then he heard a loud thud and the door to the Morphic Chamber swung open. Four men entered wearing what looked like a military uniform: dark blue frock coats with polished silver buttons and a winged lion emblem across the chest.

'Protectors,' Compton cursed under his breath and skulked out of sight behind his desk.

One of the men removed his custodian helmet and approached Jack. 'Mr Morrow,' he said in a clipped voice, 'you will come with us.'

11

THE CHRONOGRAPHER OF FOLUNAIN

The streets of Folunain were old and narrow, more like primitive miners' tunnels than the rest of Ealdwyc's grandeur. The walls were roughly hewn and painted white. No statues or carvings decorated this place. It was functional – the tentative first part of what would eventually become the splendour of the great city.

Eloise and Davey walked quietly along the warren of anonymous streets. To the untrained eye this passageway looked just like all the rest, but Eloise knew her way well enough. She felt uneasy, burdened by her guilt and fear as she returned to this place. It was as if each new step dragged up more of her past. Ever since her escape from imprisonment she had hidden her turmoil from her new companions, pushed her regrets deep down, shielding herself from their friendship. But now the past was rushing up to greet her and she could see no way to avoid its embrace.

They turned a corner into a new street. Part of the ceiling had caved in, depositing a pyramid of rock which partially blocked the tunnel.

Davey sighed. 'Is it much further? We've been walking for hours.'

'And you have moaned for most of that time.' Eloise smiled. Her strength was returning to her, her wounds almost healed. The deeper she went into Folunain the more she felt the medicinal radiance of the earth spreading into her through the sword. Soon only the scars in her mind would remain.

She climbed nimbly over the rocks, ignoring the sharp pain that still pierced her side. As Davey followed her he said, 'It wouldn't hurt to find somewhere to rest, maybe have a quick drink.'

'You were impatient to leave London! Now you would have us rest? Would you like the Paladin to join us? The further we go the harder it is for them to track me. We will rest soon enough.'

Davey groaned.

Ahead, the regular straight walls of the street gave way to a wider curved thoroughfare with many doorways and crossing tunnels. Where the street widened market stalls and food sellers filled the space with overlapping smells and conversations.

Eloise had made sure they had passed no one on their long walk through Folunain, often pausing, listening, until it was safe to continue unseen. Now stealth seemed impossible. She carefully concealed her sword, releasing her grip on it for the first time. Its sustaining energy disappeared and her head became light. She almost cried out.

Davey saw her discomfort. 'You all right, sweetheart?'

'Do not call me that,' Eloise said through gritted teeth, immediately regretting her harshness.

Davey smiled, seemingly unoffended. 'You're doin' all right, I reckon.' He held out his arm to her. She allowed herself to return his smile as she leaned against him. It felt good to be cared for, it had been so long since anyone had. Yet the urge to push him away, to depend on no one, remained. Trembling, she realised she did not have the strength to stand alone, not without the sword in her hand, and she gave in to Davey's kindness. They walked towards the marketplace like a young couple on an early morning stroll, mingling with the traders, breathing in the smells of fresh bread and cooked meats, discreetly gliding past the shoppers until they came upon a rough doorway set back in the whitewashed stone. Eloise looked about, checking they were not observed, and tried the door's handle. A little brass bell rattled over her head, and she and Davey stepped inside.

The workshop was full of grand-looking clocks, all ticking away quietly. A wide table displayed more timepieces, some as large as a dinner plate, others smaller than a fingernail. All bore the same high quality in their gleaming metallic surfaces.

Eloise's fingers found her sword beneath her cape and she pulled herself away from Davey. Her head was still unsteady, but she had to focus – she could not allow herself to rely on others. Not again.

Sitting in a rocking chair was an old woman, her body wrapped in a shawl. Long silver hair hung freely at her shoulders, framing her wrinkled – yet still strikingly beautiful – face. Her slack jaw and closed eyes gave the appearance of someone enjoying a blissful sleep, but then her slender nose twitched and she sniffed at the dusty air.

Davey ignored her, casually picking up one of the larger timepieces from the table, turning it over and studying the craftsmanship.

'Over sixty years old, built by my grandfather, Valhine Carhoop, clockmaker to Ealdorman de Lacy,' the woman said without opening her eyes. 'A lovely chronoscope, biometrically attuned to three realms.'

'We are not buying,' Eloise said, her heart racing.

The old woman opened her eyes wide in surprise. She stared at the visitors with a mix of shock and disbelief.

'Elly? Is that you?' she asked in a whisper.

Eloise smiled, fighting the urge to rush to the woman. 'Hello, Fran.'

The old woman stood slowly, her face contorted in a flood of emotion.

'My beautiful Elly! As I live and breathe. But I thought you were dead.'

'I have been dead for a very long time.' The memory of her confinement passed through her like a shock wave.

'Oh, don't split hairs! You know perfectly well what I mean. I haven't seen you in, what?' – the old woman rubbed her chin – 'about a hundred years?'

'I was...' Eloise fought the emotions. Her face remained like a mask. 'I was imprisoned.'

The old woman nodded thoughtfully. 'I heard stories, but no one knew what to believe. Everything fell apart after you disappeared. We all went to ground. I never thought to see you again. You really are here? You haven't changed. Amazing.'

'What of the others?'

'Long dead, that's the short story anyway. The details aren't for telling here.'

'Long dead?' Davey butted in. 'You seem to be doin' all right. How old are you? What's keepin' you ticking?'

'This is Davey,' Eloise said apologetically. 'Davey, meet Francesco Carhoop, the best Chronographer in the First World.'

'Charmed, I'm sure.' Francesco smiled. 'You know it's rude to ask a lady's age?'

'Yeah!' Davey said grinning impishly.

'I'm...' Francesco thought for a moment. 'Well, I must be over one hundred and ten by now.'

Eloise smiled warmly. 'You are older still. I do not believe you have forgotten.'

'You're right not to believe. I choose not to remember. It really doesn't matter after the first century. What about you, young man?'

'What about me?' Davey replied defensively.

'How old are you?'

Davey shrugged, 'Old enough. Think I'm probably fifteen by now. Give or take.'

'You don't know?' Francesco frowned.

'I look fifteen, don't I?' Davey's voice had lost its confidence.

'Then let us agree that we are both the age we should be.' Francesco chuckled as she walked to the window and pulled a dusty blind down over it.

'Fran,' Eloise said, eager to discuss more pressing matters, 'we need your help.'

Francesco pushed two heavy bolts into place on the door. She dragged a thick velvet curtain across the doorway, throwing the dim workshop into near darkness. After a moment all of the clock faces glowed gently, the incandescent light reflecting off metal and ivory.

'It's never a social call, is it? Never tea and crumpets. It's always favours, and life and death, and the end of the world.'

'I am sorry,' Eloise said grimly. 'Next time I will bring crumpets.'

Francesco laughed. 'How could I ever refuse you?' The old woman dropped back into the rocking chair. 'I looked for you, you know? I tried to find you,' she said regretfully. 'After everything that happened, after Cayden was . . .'

Eloise nodded silently, wishing Francesco hadn't said his name.

'So,' Francesco continued with a sigh, 'what is it you want from me this time?'

'Information,' Eloise replied. 'What have you heard of Rouland?'

Francesco lowered her voice to a whisper. 'Streets are full of rumours. You know he killed the Ealdormen?'

'No.'

'The whole council: dead. That's what I've heard anyway. Who knows the truth? But the Noble Houses are up in arms, all squabbling amongst themselves, leaderless. There's panic on the streets, people rushing here and there, full of portents of doom. And Rouland has disappeared, to who knows where.'

Eloise's eyes narrowed. 'Rouland has been defeated. His body lies frozen, hidden.'

An optimistic smile broke over Francesco's thin lips.

'But there are those who plan for his return,' Eloise continued. 'They seek his sword.'

'Durendal.' Francesco cursed under her breath.

'Yes. Then you do know of it?'

'A little. Too much, perhaps.'

Eloise half smiled. 'We have all paid a price for our past lives.'

Davey looked between them, his deep brow creased. 'How come I get the feeling you two ain't telling me everything?'

'Some things you need not know,' Eloise retorted. She felt it again, that gnawing fear that her emotions might take hold, that she might break down under the weight of her past. She realised the other two were staring at her.

Francesco held up a conciliatory hand. 'I have nothing to hide any more, Elly.' She looked at Davey and said, 'Once, long ago, I worked for Rouland. I was very young and my family were in his service.'

Davey frowned. 'What sort of service?'

Francesco gestured around the shop. 'My father built timepieces for him. I was less fortunate.' The old woman chuckled to herself. 'I was a maid, one of his household staff. That's how I met Elly.'

Davey shrugged. 'Don't sound too bad.'

'It was never good.'

'How's a maid gonna help us find a hidden sword?' Davey said as he casually fiddled with the timepiece. Francesco took it out of Davey's hands. She polished it with a cloth and carefully returned it to its rightful place.

'A maid learns things, overhears secrets, is told things in great confidence.'

Davey scoffed. 'Rouland wouldn't tell a maid nothing!'

'Not Rouland, no. But there was one in his care, someone he was fond of, known as the Widow—'

'Who's she then?' Davey interrupted.

Eloise's frustration welled up. 'When Rouland imprisoned me he tore my memories apart. There is much from that time I do not recall.' She could remember the violence, the killing in his name, the sinister deeds completed without question. All of it was there every time she closed her eyes, waiting for her in the darkness. But the details were gone.

'I didn't know her true identity,' Francesco added, 'and I knew better than to ask too many questions. She was a disfigured old woman whose mind was . . . well, she would talk to me. She told me things only she knew.'

'About the sword?' Eloise asked urgently.

Francesco nodded. 'She spoke of Durendal, yes. She knew where Rouland hid it, when he was not using it.'

'Where?'

'A Concealed Realm of mist and ice called Niflheim.'

'So we go there 'n' find it,' Davey said, 'before anyone else does.'

Francesco stared at the boy. 'Are you not listening? It's hidden in a Concealed Realm. No one can find it.'

'Bet I could,' Davey said arrogantly.

'You know what concealed means?' Francesco replied angrily.

Eloise shot a cold stare at Davey and he backed away. She turned to her old friend: 'Can you help me, Fran?'

Francesco paced round the workshop, touching her creations with her long fingers. The constant ticking of the innumerable clockwork mechanisms seemed to grow, feeding off the tension. Then all at once the clocks chimed the hour of nine. The shelves rattled as the combined sound rose like a chorus of mechanical whale song. As the sound ebbed away Francesco's eyes grew wider.

'Only Hafgan and Rouland have charted the Concealed Realms. Others have tried and failed to discover them. But there is still one who might help you. He has come closer than most. His name is Jonah Hardacre.'

Davey's face recoiled in sudden recollection. 'Hardacre? Captain Hardacre, of the *Orion*?'

'You know him?'

'Know him? I know everyone!' Davey laughed. 'I think I still owe him money, come to think of it. Ain't he dead?'

Francesco smiled dryly. 'Hardacre tried to follow Hafgan's path into the Concealed Realms. Tried and failed, many times. His failures, his dabbling in forgotten knowledge, have turned his mind inwards. They say he's quite mad but, after Rouland, Hardacre is perhaps the foremost living expert on the Concealed Realms. If anyone knows how to get to Niflheim and find Durendal then it would be him.'

'Where can we find him?' Eloise asked.

'Ah,' Francesco sighed, 'that is the hard part. He resides in the Tower of Halbane. It is a prison for the criminally insane.'

'A madhouse?' Davey said.

'Yes.'

'Then you must take us there at once,' Eloise replied.

'And do what?' Francesco asked, her white eyebrows rising up to wrinkle the thin skin of her forehead.

'We must set him free so that he can take us to Niflheim.'

12

THE LAST EALDORMAN

'What do you want?' Jack asked nervously.

The three men circled around him and Hilda, closing in slowly.

'You will come with us,' repeated the one nearest the door, irritation rising in his voice. Their uniforms were neat and polished, like guards from a parade, but Jack couldn't tell if they were police or soldiers. What had Compton called them? *Protectors?*

'Come on, sunshine,' another of the men said. 'Do as the sergeant says.' He pushed Jack's shoulder, herding him towards the door. Jack reeled round, anger swelling up inside him again. Then he saw Hilda in between him and the man, her eyes somehow calming him.

'Sergeant,' Hilda addressed the man nearest the door. 'Tell us your orders and we will happily come with you.'

The sergeant puffed out his chest. Hilda seemed to have taken him by surprise. He scratched his chin, pulled at the edge of his neatly trimmed moustache and said:

'I don't have to tell you my orders, miss. Now, you'll do as you're told and—'

'Whose House do you serve?' Hilda demanded.

The sergeant coughed uncomfortably. 'House of Sinclair. Now, I must insist, miss. Don't make this difficult.'

Hilda nodded and turned to Jack. 'We'll go with them.'

'Why?' Jack asked pensively.

'It'll be quite all right,' she replied, already walking out of the door with the sergeant. Reluctantly, Jack followed her. The other two men fell in behind him as they left the morphic prism chamber.

In the street outside, more Protectors flanked a strange-looking vehicle. It had a squat curved body made of plates of polished metal. A cabin protruded from the front with a bubble of riveted glass windows that reminded Jack of an old-fashioned diver's helmet. Six appendages stuck out from the sides of the vehicle, their joints folded up like the legs of a sleeping spider. At the rear was some sort of engine, Jack mused, a glowing glass-like sphere with a rotating arm that swung about it.

A large hatch opened in the side of the craft to reveal its interior. Hesitantly, Jack followed Hilda and the sergeant inside. Leather upholstered seats lined the cylindrical interior, each one contoured to hug tightly to the body. As Jack sat down he felt secure and restrained all at once.

'Is this a good idea?' he asked Hilda, remembering that he barely knew her.

'They're not going to hurt us,' she said flatly, looking away.

Jack scowled. 'You didn't answer my question.' He regretted following her; his stomach turned. Intuitively his hand reached up and found his mother's pendant that hung around his neck. He pulled it out from under his shirt, turning it absentmindedly between his fingers. He recalled removing it from her dead body as a final reminder of her. Just touching it seemed to calm him, as if he was closer to her again. He realised Hilda was watching him and he pushed the pendant back inside his shirt.

As the last Protector took a seat the hatch closed with a loud clunk. There was a noise, like something spinning rapidly, and the vehicle lurched to the side. Jack gripped the arms of the seat and peered through the glass portholes in the cabin at the front: the world outside was falling away.

'We're flying?' he asked quickly.

Hilda tutted. 'Jack, don't be a baby. Of course we're flying.'

Jack caught the sergeant smirking as he removed his helmet.

'Where are you taking me!' Jack demanded.

At that moment the vehicle fell into darkness. Jack looked to the portholes: they were in some sort of tunnel, moving faster and faster. The vehicle rattled and shook, the feeble lamps flickering with every vibration.

The sergeant smiled again, more warmly this time. 'Nearly there now, young man,' he said as he replaced his helmet.

A bell rattled from the cabin and a blinding flash of light burst through the small openings. As the light faded the carriage began to slow and, Jack sensed, to descend. With a final shift from left to right the craft came to rest. Jack heard gas escaping outside, then two Protectors stood and opened the hatch.

Jack climbed out into a pretty courtyard with a small fountain lapping peacefully at its centre. He could hardly believe his eyes. The light here was dazzlingly bright, pouring from lamps high up in the ceiling, which filled the space with heat.

They walked through the courtyard, past exotic plant life, towards shallow steps that led up to an impressive entrance.

'Where are we?' Jack said quietly.

Hilda shrugged. 'I can only presume this must be one of the Sinclair family's houses.'

They stepped through the doorway into a circular hall, its smooth walls covered with grand oil paintings of stern-looking individuals. The paintings' dark eyes seemed to focus on Jack, making him feel small and insignificant. Each painting sat above a recessed alcove.

Most were bare but two held a skull and fragments of bone. He looked away to see an open door leading to a large sitting room.

'Come in, please.' The gravelly voice belonged to a man sitting with his back to them. Nearby was a small fire that spat and crackled over a fresh log. As Jack approached he began to see the detail in the man's sunken face: thin, wrinkled and blotched with age, with a crown of straw-like hair around the sides of his head. Then the beginnings of the scar came into view. It began at his chin, raw and deep, and stretched up to the side of his mouth. The skin had been torn away here to reveal the teeth and upper jaw. Dark stitches held the flesh in place in a rushed criss-cross pattern that disappeared beneath a patch covering his left eye.

'Unsightly, I know.' The man's voice crackled like the fire.

Jack realised he was staring at the torn face.

'Don't be afraid, I mean you no harm.' The man tried to smile, but the effort was obvious. 'My name is Jodrell Sinclair. I am the elected Ealdorman for the Noble House of Sinclair and I am the last of the Ealdormen.' Weakly, he gestured for them to sit in two chairs near his.

Jack saw the man's thin hands – like a skeleton draped in wet paper.

'The last?' Hilda asked as she sat down.

Jodrell stared wistfully into the fire. 'The Ealdormen are all dead. The council chamber runs red with their blood.'

Hilda leaned in closer. 'How?'

'Rouland,' Jodrell said slowly. 'He summoned us all to the chamber, and like obedient dogs we came. He locked the doors and killed us. He thought me dead, disfigured and bleeding beneath the bodies of my friends.' Sinclair raised his bony hand, the fingers clicking as he opened and closed them. 'His sword fed on us. Part of me will never heal.' His hand dropped onto the chair and he retreated into the fire again. 'But I had strength enough to escape unseen. I am a dead man walking.'

After a moment he seemed to recover some of his strength and his one remaining eye fell on Jack. 'So, you are Jack Morrow,' Jodrell said eventually, his long silences punctuated by the pops of the burning wood.

Jack shuddered as his muscles filled with the urge to escape.

'You are wondering how I know your name, yes? You gave it freely to Customs on your entry into Ealdwyc.'

Jack recalled his arrival through the Trafalgar Square junction. He had told his name to the first person he had met. How had he been so stupid?

'You must be more careful in future,' Jodrell said, as if voicing Jack's inner thoughts. 'My sources are many and far-reaching. It is lucky for you that the Customs officer is loyal to my house. Your current situation could have been much worse. The city is bristling with rumour and chatter. Is it true you have contained him? You have bested Rouland?'

Jack shifted uncomfortably in his seat. He felt Hilda's eyes upon him as well.

'Oh, come now,' the old man said, 'I know a great many things about you. You can have no secrets from me.'

'What do you want?'

'If the rumours are true, that Rouland has been vanquished, then there is a power vacuum which must be filled. The alternative is anarchy. Rouland wiped out the Ealdormen, the ruling elite. Now, with Rouland gone, the First World stands at a tipping point. If we do not have a firm hand at the tiller then all may be lost.'

'So you want to take over?'

The Ealdorman grimaced as he took a long breath. 'No, no. I no longer have the strength to lead. But I do not want to see the First World fall into decay. I refuse to see the Noble Houses crumble, their histories lost in petty bickering. I simply want a smooth transition from one leader to the next as quickly as possible. Of course, in return for my allegiance, my protection, I would have some sway with that new leader. The power behind the throne, if you see what I mean.'

Jack nodded hesitantly. 'I think I do.'

Jodrell grimaced. 'No, I don't think you do. Word is

spreading of Rouland's demise. Even now the Noble Houses plot to fill the void. They will each nominate their own champion, none will agree and we will have war. Only one person can possibly unite the Houses behind him. Only one person stands between order and chaos. It must be the one who has defeated Rouland. It must be you, Jack Morrow.'

Jack suddenly went cold, his skin tingled. The magnitude of Jodrell's proposal fell upon him in waves, each one heavier than the last.

'But I'm no leader. I'm not old enough,' Jack muttered, his thoughts colliding with each other. There was a dark part of his mind that rejoiced at the thought of this. To be in control of such a fantastic place. To be a king amongst men. The notion took hold, growing insidiously. The things he could do with such power! And yet... and yet, he was not a king, he did not want to lead. The responsibility terrified him. An image of Eloise and Davey appeared in his mind, and the thoughts of power retreated into the shadows.

'Your age is of little consequence,' Jodrell boomed. 'What you do not know I will teach you. Your role will be that of a unifying figurehead; I can help with the more tedious duties of office.'

Hilda's eyes burrowed into Jack, and he remembered their mission. *The sword.*

'No, I'm sorry,' Jack said at last. His voice trembled with doubt. 'I'm not your leader. I have other things to do.'

'Other things?' Jodrell said indignantly. 'We are talking about the survival of an entire society, the preservation of a history and way of life that is ancient and precious. What "other things" can possibly be of more importance?'

'Rouland,' Jack said, the name like a bad taste on his tongue. 'Rouland could return.'

Jodrell sat back in his chair, thinking. 'If Rouland is returning then we must be prepared. It makes our work all the more urgent. We must complete the transition to a new leader before it is too late.'

Hilda stood up quickly, her cheeks red. 'Jack is not going to be your puppet leader, Mr Sinclair.' She turned quickly to Jack. 'Come on, we're leaving.'

The Ealdorman rose uncomfortably from his chair. 'Be silent, girl! This is not your decision to make.'

Jack touched his mother's pendant again and stood up. 'She doesn't have to decide. I've already made up my mind. Goodbye.' He walked quickly to the large door.

'I am afraid this was not a request, Mr Morrow. There is far too much at stake,' Jodrell bellowed, his voice clipped and firm.

Jack and Hilda pushed through the door, into a hall full of Protectors barring their way. Jack felt Hilda grab his arm, and suddenly everything went white. For the briefest of instants a nauseous vertigo overtook him. The sensation dissipated rapidly and the white faded away. When his eyes cleared he saw that they were alone in the hall. The Protectors, and the Ealdorman, were gone.

'Are you OK?' Hilda asked.

'I – I don't know. What just happened?'

The deep murmur of Jodrell's voice resonated from behind the door.

'Come on!' Hilda urged.

Jack rushed after her, out through the doorway that led to the courtyard. It was mercifully empty. The Protectors and the vehicle they had arrived in were nowhere to be seen. He could hardly believe their luck.

The courtyard ended at a low wall. Jack jumped onto it and peered beyond: the smooth courtyard gave way to a jumble of rocks and boulders that dropped away steeply into the darkness.

'We can't get down there,' Jack said, 'not without a rope.'

Hilda pointed to his left. 'Look, there are some steps cut into the rock.'

Jack followed Hilda's pointed hand and saw a winding path, old and disused, hugging the steep slope.

'It's better than staying here, I suppose. But what happened back there?'

Hilda didn't reply. She was already making her way towards the irregular steps. Jack rushed to follow her down the uneven path, zigzagging into the dark embrace of the slope.

13

THE CLEVER COUSIN AND THE MADMAN

'I don't know, Fran. You're asking a lot of me,' the chief warden said with a hint of nervousness. 'You know how much bother I'd get in if anything happened in there. They say he's a wild one. He put that poor harbourmaster in hospital!'

Davey and Eloise watched as Francesco led the nervous chief warden deeper into the narrow corridors of the Tower of Halbane. Ahead was a single locked door; behind it hid a madman.

'How's your mother?' Francesco asked as she nodded at the locked door. The chief warden, a slight man in his early thirties, rubbed his insubstantial chin hesitantly. 'Mum? She's fine. Why?' He placed the old key in the lock.

'She was asking me how you were. You don't eat enough, apparently.'

The chief warden blushed. 'It's got nothing to do with her. I'm my own man now. She's always using the family to check up on me.' The key turned in his hand and the locking mechanism tumbled deep inside the door.

'It's a big family, Pablo,' Francesco smiled, 'and the cousins' network has its roots everywhere.'

The chief warden frowned. 'Don't I know it.' He pulled the key from the lock and stepped away from the door.

'Do yourself a favour, Pablo: go see your mother this weekend. And give Aunty Belle my best.' Francesco turned her back on her perplexed cousin and pushed the thick door open. She stepped over the threshold, nodding for Davey and Eloise to follow her. The chief warden hovered around the doorway nervously.

'It's all right,' Davey said cheerfully. 'The captain's an old mate,' and he closed the door behind him.

The room was cool and dark. A brittle breeze blew in through a barred opening in the wall where a tall man stood looking out at the limited view. A mane of raggedy silver hair framed his wind-worn leathery face. In spite of his confinement he stood erect, his hands resting behind his back, like a great nobleman surveying his estate. Captain Jonah Hardacre barely acknowledged the arrival of the three strangers into his diminished kingdom. Only when Davey coughed did he finally turn to face them. His cold blue eyes pierced each of them in turn.

'A Paladin, a Chronographer, and' – he looked at Davey – 'a runt?'

Davey's jaw tensed. 'You don't remember me, Captain?'

'Should I?'

'He's a friend,' Eloise offered.

'A friend?' Hardacre laughed. 'That is a generous gift indeed, little man! One, I am sorry to say, I cannot return. For I am of limited means, as you see, and friendship requires certain' – he paused, considering his words – 'certain liberties. Something I no longer possess.'

Davey's smile retreated. 'You must remember me! Davey Vale! I was on the *Orion* with you, for a few weeks, until . . . well, I'm sure you remember.'

'I would remember a runt,' Hardacre whispered. Davey fumbled in his pockets for a cigarette, his ego momentarily bruised.

Francesco addressed the prisoner softly. 'Jonah, do you remember me? I am Francesco Carhoop.'

The man boiled with scorn. 'Of course I remember you. Do you think me witless?'

'Perhaps,' Francesco replied. 'It's said that you tried to chart the Concealed Realms and it drove you insane.'

Hardacre's face broke into a wide smile and a booming hollow laugh rattled the cramped space. 'You may be right. I *have* been to those places and seen things that would boil most men's minds. But I know who I am, and I am not mad. I followed in Hafgan's path, I know the way to the Concealed Realms. But some people fear knowledge. They fear what I might discover out there.'

'You cannot deny attacking the harbourmaster. You leave a trail of debt and quarrels in your wake,' Francesco said patiently. 'You are not held here as part of some great conspiracy. You are here because you are full of anger.'

Hardacre looked away, his jaw clenched. 'The harbourmaster was an officious prig. I dislike paperwork.'

'So do not act like you are the wounded party!' Francesco's tone was suddenly heavy with authority. 'You are unruly and impatient. What I need to know is, have you really been to the Concealed Realms, and can you go there again?'

'I may be many things, woman, but I do not lie about my travels!' Hardacre leaned against the cold rock, a thin shaft of light cutting over his chiselled, weary face. His lean body was bruised, yet a rage burned still in those cold eyes. 'You know this! Why else would you be here? Tell me, what do you want?'

'Your help,' Eloise said. 'We wish to journey to the Concealed Realms, to Niflheim. We need a realm ship and a captain who can take us there.'

'Niflheim? You flatter me. Even I have never been there. The man you seek is Rouland. He claims to have travelled there, many times. You, Paladin, will know this.'

'I am not in allegiance with Rouland,' Eloise said. 'But you are right, I was once Paladin. I threw off that title many years ago and paid the price for my betrayal. Besides, Rouland has been defeated.'

Hardacre's eyes widened. 'This is news to me. If I was not detained I would raise a glass to his demise. But if

Rouland is truly gone then the path to Niflheim is lost for ever.'

'What if you had the notes of one who had been there before to guide you?' Eloise asked.

'Rouland left a guide?'

'No. His secrets lie still with him.'

'Then the way is lost. No other has travelled there and returned. None except Hafgan himself.'

Davey smiled. 'See, I might be just a runt, and I'm not a big one for books, if truth be told, but I've seen Hafgan's book, and I know exactly where it is now.'

Hardacre's eyes locked onto Davey. 'Do not tease me, boy! Do you think I have not searched for it myself?'

'Then start treating me with some respect!' In spite of Davey's lesser size and age he stood his ground, puffing out his chest in defiance to Hardacre.

'Respect must be earned,' Hardacre said, the edge gone from his voice. 'You have changed much since your days on the *Orion*, Davey. It is a change for the better.'

Davey nodded. 'I'm still brilliant: I stole that little book, and I can take you to it.'

The older man gasped, then smiled. '*On the Nature of the Concealed Realms* by Magnus Hafgan,' he whispered. 'You know where to find this book?'

'He speaks the truth,' Eloise said. 'I have seen its secrets.'

'Where?' Hardacre insisted, crossing the floor to Eloise.

'Where is this book?'

'Here, in Ealdwyc.'

Hardacre turned back to Davey, his face full of doubt. 'How did you find it?'

Eloise frowned. 'That is a story for later. Our time here is limited. Join us and we will take you to the book. In return you will take us to the Concealed Realms.'

Hardacre stroked his bearded chin, watching the trio. 'You can free me? How?'

'My cousin is very stupid,' Francesco said with a wry smile. 'Look outside.'

Hardacre pulled himself up on the bars that covered his tiny window. Outside was the great expanse of Ealdwyc, at its centre the Great Pit. Dots sat in the air, mighty birds riding the hot currents that rose from its fiery core.

'The birds,' Hardacre said. 'They do not move.'

He looked again to be sure: the creatures were far away, but there was no mistaking their inertia. Like figures in some fantastic painting they hung against the rock, their wings caught in an instant of time. Hardacre turned to face Francesco. She held in her hands one of her timepieces.

'You did this?' Hardacre asked, laughing in amazement.

Francesco smiled proudly. 'We're inside a Fracture, a bubble of time. But it will not last long. So, Captain: will you take us to Niflheim, in return for your freedom?'

Hardacre laughed. 'If your claim about Hafgan's book is genuine.'

'It is,' Eloise said coolly.

'Then we have a deal.'

Eloise unsheathed her sword, hidden until now inside her garb, and struck at the locked door. It yielded at the first blow, swinging gently open. Eloise stepped through it, followed by Francesco, Davey and Hardacre.

Pablo the chief warden stood in the corridor, frozen. From his perspective he had just stepped out of the cell. Now, as Francesco's chronoscope caught up with him so did time.

'Finished already?' Pablo asked as he saw Francesco running past. Then he saw Hardacre. 'Hey! Wait!'

Francesco grabbed her cousin by his collar. 'I'm sorry, Pablo. I'll make it look like you struggled.'

'Struggled?' Pablo replied nervously.

Francesco's arm swung up quickly, catching him nimbly on the side of his head. Pablo gasped as his legs crumpled underneath him. Eloise caught his unconscious body and lowered him gently to the floor.

'I'll never hear the end of this,' Francesco noted wryly.

Davey chuckled to himself as they left the tower. By the time the chief warden understood what his clever cousin had done, she, Davey, Eloise and the madman would be lost to the vast warrens of the city.

14

VIOLATION

The cool darkness wrapped around Jack, drying the film of sweat on his forehead. The lights of the Ealdorman's grand dwelling were just visible high above, twinkling like an artificial constellation. It had taken them an hour to get this far, an hour of aching climbing over worn, broken stones. The lights of a ship had broken the darkness some moments ago, drifting in to land in the courtyard. Since then they had rested, watching for signs of movement from above, sure that the Protectors would be coming after them, but they had seen no one.

In spite of his relief at their escape something about it bothered Jack. What had really happened back there? Why had the Ealdorman and his Protectors disappeared? How had they escaped so easily? He felt as if the answer was hiding from him, eluding his probing. What was he missing?

He noticed Hilda staring at him. Then, suddenly, he heard a distant noise from far above. Searchlights appeared at the rim of the Ealdorman's estate and the faint echo of voices drifted on the breeze. The Protectors were finally coming after them.

'Time to go,' Hilda said quickly.

Jack rose wearily, forcing his tired legs to work. The steps continued down in front of them, further and further into the depths.

'Where do you think this leads?' he asked.

'It's an old path,' Hilda mused. 'Do you see the pipes running alongside the steps?'

Jack looked closely. He hadn't noticed the pipes snaking in and out of the rocks, following the edge of the steps down the steep slope.

'They're water pipes,' Hilda continued. 'There might be a lake down here, or a pumping station.'

'Will it lead us back to Ealdwyc?' Jack asked hopefully.

Hilda thought for a moment. 'I don't know. I think we're a long way from Ealdwyc.'

Jack said nothing. He looked up the steps to the distant building. As he watched he saw a set of lights move in formation, drifting out beyond the edge of the steps and dropping quickly towards them.

'Oh no!'

'What is it?' Hilda asked.

They watched together as the spider-like silhouette of a craft floated down from the courtyard, its searchlights trained on the rocks.

'We must go!' Hilda rasped as she broke into a clumsy

run, dropping down the steps two at a time. The low murmur of distant engines grew louder above them. Jack raced after her, narrowing the space between them until he was at her heels.

The steps became shallower and longer until they came to a wide plateau that hugged the edge of a vast lake. Jack felt a throbbing in his ears, a rhythmic pulse of sound that grew stronger and stronger. He glanced back; the searchlights traced over the steps towards them.

He grabbed Hilda's hand and sprinted along the path, following its curving length. Jack heard the vehicle's engines roar as clouds of dust pushed past them. Ahead, the path dipped into a low opening in the rock wall. Jack flew into its shadows and the beam of the searchlight swung over the entrance. The vehicle hovered close by, pushing dust and pebbles into the mouth of the cave. The searchlights crossed the entrance again, scanning left and right, then the vehicle rose up slowly, its lights moving away from their hiding place. The roaring jets became quieter, the throbbing pulse of the engines waned and Jack began to breathe again.

'They've gone,' he said at last, amazed and relieved.

Hilda brushed at the grit and dirt on her dress. 'Good riddance!'

'Which way now?' Jack wondered aloud. 'We can't go back that way, not with that thing out there.'

'What was it the morphic prism said to you?' Hilda asked. 'Something about a book? Didn't it say the book would show you the way?'

She was right, Jack remembered. His fingers touched the stolen book deep in his trouser pocket. He pulled it out and stared at the leather cover.

Hilda was suddenly at his side. 'What's that? Is that the book?'

'No!' Jack replied defensively, hiding it from her.

'May I see it?' she asked, her fingers reaching for it.

Jack spluttered, 'It's private.'

'Please,' Hilda urged with a tight smile. 'Let me see.'

'I said no!' Jack stepped further away, turning his back to Hilda. He opened the book, tilting it to the feeble light. 'It's useless anyway! We can't see a thing in here.'

Hilda kneeled down, sifting the soil and rocks through her fingers, guided by the soft glow that emanated from the ground in dim patches of blue. She picked up two small rocks and wiped them on her dress until the dirt fell away to reveal two jewel-like crystals. Gently she rubbed the stones together until a faint glow appeared inside each of them. A sound resonated out from the rocks that reminded Jack of the hum of the old fridge that had squatted in his kitchen for more years than was probably good for it, the defiant pulse of an electric survivor. He smiled as he remembered its dented surface, covered in long-ignored drawings.

'Let there be light,' Hilda said with a satisfied smile and handed one of the glowing balls to Jack. The blue light intensified in his hand, illuminating the rock around him. His palm tingled. 'What are these?'

'Their proper name is Crystallumen, but everyone calls them lumen stones.'

As their eyes grew accustomed to this new light the cave revealed itself to be a deep rectangular tunnel. Gouged toolmarks on the walls gave away its man-made origins, and pipes wormed along its path. Here and there steam escaped from joins in the pipes, warming the already-hot air.

Jack turned his attention to the book again. He flipped to the back page, visible now in the soft light. He knew what he would find: a page of letters in a neat grid. He had discovered information in this codex before, and he hoped it might show him the way again. He had realised recently that the page was written in his own handwriting, an addition to Hafgan's indecipherable notes, and had contained coded messages from his future self. His eyes studied the text anew as, in the gentle light of the lumen stones, he saw that some of the letters were glowing. At first it was hardly perceptible, but as he squinted at the paper the faint glow became more apparent. Towards the top of the page was the letter D, its dark ink turning more and more golden. Next he found a U, then an R. He quickly found more of the radiant letters until they spelled DURENDAL. Satisfied, he continued on: the next letter in the sequence was N.

Jack's senses prickled. He turned to see Hilda prying over his shoulder.

'Maybe I could help you?' she offered apologetically.

Jack turned away again, hugging the book into his chest so that only he could see it. He followed the code down the page until two new words formed. He closed the book and returned it to his trouser pocket.

'Do you know a place called Newton Harbour?' he asked.

'Newton Harbour? Of course I do,' Hilda said purposefully. 'Why?'

Jack hesitated, then said, 'I'm going there to find Durendal.'

'What makes you think you'll find it there?'

'I just do, OK?'

'Well, I think it's only polite to tell me, don't you?' Hilda said indignantly. 'After all, if we're travelling together to Newton Harbour then—'

'I didn't ask you to join me!' Jack interrupted. 'Come to think of it, why *are* you with me?'

'You interest me,' Hilda said without hesitation, a smile on her round face.

Jack stopped. He felt a surge of anger and confusion. He suddenly grabbed Hilda by the arm and his eyes pierced hers. Something deep inside was nagging away at him, something to do with Hilda.

'Jack, you're hurting me!' she cried.

He heard the tremble in her voice, saw the instant fear in her eyes, yet he would not let go – the Rose would not let go. Emotions welled up inside him: distrust, anger, fear. All at once he was consumed by their intoxicating strength.

'Jack, please. You're hurting my mind.' Painful tears rolled down Hilda's cheeks.

'What are you hiding from me?' Jack demanded, letting the Rose expand inside him, letting it free, letting it consume him, letting it into Hilda's mind.

He saw what he was doing: he was killing her, and he knew it. Yet he couldn't let go. He was pushing into her brain, into her secrets. It wasn't difficult, all he had to do was let the Rose take control. Her mind was giving way and he pushed further in.

Her tears filled with blood and became red lines on her grubby skin. Dark drops fell from her nostrils and became thick tributaries that joined at her lips and ran down her chin.

'Jack, stop it! You're killing me!'

He could smell the blood, he could taste the fear, he could hear her racing heart – like a thunderstorm trapped in her chest – and he couldn't stop. Next he would rip open her mind and read its contents like a book. Like Rouland could.

Like Rouland. The thought terrified him.

Suddenly he saw an image in his mind of Rouland's cruel face, smiling. He stood amongst strangers, threatening them, toying with them. Did Hilda know these people? Was this her family?

Far away he heard Hilda scream.

Suddenly, as if coming out of a trance, Jack released her. She fell to the ground, sobbing uncontrollably. Jack recoiled away from her. A horrid realisation overwhelmed him: he had become a monster. He fell to the ground, the sound of his own sobs chorusing with Hilda's.

'I'm . . . sorry.' His apology was worthless. He moved closer to her and she flinched in fear.

'Don't touch me!' she screamed.

He retreated and sat with his back against the cave wall, watching her out of the corner of his eye, waiting until her sobbing subsided.

'I can't control it,' he said at last. 'It's too strong.'

'Don't bother with excuses,' Hilda scolded, and she turned away in disgust. Her shoulders moved in rhythm with her quiet tears.

'I have this thing in my head,' Jack said slowly, his words falling like one soft confession after another. 'It's a sort of power, called the Rose of Annwn. It was a gift from my mother. I thought it would make everything OK, but . . . it's not working out like that. I think it wants to take over, and I'm not strong enough to stop it.'

Hilda's tiny voice grew, full of the heavy breath of tears. 'You have to be stronger. You can't let it take over. You have to be its master, not the other way round, or you might as well kill yourself now.'

Hilda's resolution warmed Jack, calmed him. It was like being scolded by his mother: he was afraid, but there was safety at the core of her anger, like love. He missed his mother more than ever. She had carried the Rose before him and he wondered how she had coped. She had always seemed calm, in control of her emotions. If she was here she could help him. But she was dead. She had given him the Rose and left him alone. His hand touched the pendant under his shirt – the last piece of his mother. Even his friends had left him. His family was gone.

Family.

Suddenly he recalled what he had seen inside Hilda's frightened mind.

'Hilda. Your family. Your parents. Are they dead?' Immediately he regretted asking her.

The girl's shoulders tensed. After a moment she straightened her back and wiped her face dry. She looked at Jack defiantly. 'Jack, you need help.'

'I – I do?' Jack was confused. Her statement took him completely off guard.

'Yes, you obviously do. Can't you see that?'

Jack fumbled for an answer. 'Well, I . . .' Then the image of him overpowering Hilda appeared in his mind, and he blushed with shame. 'I can't control it. You'd be safer away from me.'

'Probably. But I think you are safer *with* me. I can help you, if you let me.'

'How?'

She kneeled on the ground next to him and her voice became a whisper. 'Close your eyes and relax. I'm going to step into your mind. Don't fight it, I won't hurt you.'

Jack did as Hilda asked and, after a moment of calm silence, he felt the cool presence of someone else in his thoughts. He had come to recognise this strange sensation and, with the Rose, he could easily block it. He resisted the urge to push her out. Instead, he opened the way and let her in.

Time seemed to stretch out. The light from the lumen stones slowly ebbed away until Jack and Hilda sat in darkness, their minds becoming one. It was the strangest feeling. The pathways of his mind seemed stronger now, and the Rose felt less of a threat, more of a tool that could be harnessed and used in the proper way.

He felt a wave of calm pass over him. Suddenly his terrible potential didn't seem so bad. He was in control again.

'Hilda,' he whispered, 'thank you.'

Her voice replied out of the darkness. 'In time you can learn to soothe your own mind, but for now I can help you.'

Jack wallowed in the tranquillity, hoping it might never end, but all too soon he felt Hilda slipping away from him.

'The trick,' she said, her voice sounding weak, 'is to keep that notion of peace in your mind, even when you are alone. Do you understand?'

'Yes, I think so.'

'I must rest.' There was the familiar sound of two stones being rubbed together and the cave filled with the lumen stones' meagre light again. Hilda looked older than before, the inquisitive twinkle in her eyes diminished.

Jack's thoughts drifted to Davey and Eloise. He hoped they'd escaped from the Paladin. He wished they were both here, next to him in the dark. Davey was destined to be Jack's grandfather and the notion weighed heavily on his mind, filling him with doubts too big to see around. When Jack thought of Davey it was with a mixture of friendship, guilt and fear. He had so many questions left unanswered. Even for Jack the future was dark and uncertain.

'You think a lot about your grandfather, don't you?' Hilda said softly.

Jack blushed, trying to think of something else. Should he tell her he was a Yard Boy, that he was from the future?

'You're from upstream, aren't you, Jack.'

He tensed, then exhaled. It seemed pointless to hide it from her when he could hardly keep his thoughts to himself. 'I'm from the future, yes.'

'A Yard Boy.' Hilda nodded thoughtfully. 'I see. And you've met your grandfather here, in 1940. How old is he?'

Jack laughed to himself. The idea was still absurd to him. 'Davey's thirteen or fourteen, I think.'

'And he knows?'

'That's he's my grandad? Yes.'

Hilda pondered this. She seemed happier now the focus of the conversation was not on her. Then, just as Jack was bracing himself for more questions, she stood up and began to step along the dark tunnel.

'Is that it? You're going?' Jack spluttered.

'You'd prefer to sit here and chat about your family for the rest of the afternoon? I'm sure it's all very interesting, but I think we should move on before Jodrell's Protectors catch up with us, don't you?' She stood waiting for him.

Jack sighed heavily, realising he still couldn't weigh this strange girl up. Quietly, almost obediently, he fell in line behind her.

15

STRANGERS ON A TRAIN

'I know a quicker way to Newton Harbour,' Davey offered to anyone who would listen. 'We don't have to come all the way down here.'

Eloise smiled patiently. 'Do you think it is wise for an escaped madman and a former Paladin to walk the streets of Ealdwyc? You know this, Davey.'

'Yeah, but I know some good routes 'n'all, shorter routes...'

'This is safer,' Francesco said firmly, ending the discussion.

Eloise stood and joined him as he rested against the railing that ran along the pathway. 'If we are to travel to the Concealed Realms we must first get to Captain Hardacre's realm ship.' Her voice was soft, caring, and yet Davey felt his frustrations boil up.

'I ain't a kid, Eloise! I know what we're doing! I'm just sayin' that you might listen to me sometimes. I know my way 'round!'

Eloise touched the back of his hand. It still shocked

him how cold she was, and he pulled away. He saw an instant of hurt on her face and he wanted to say something to make it better. But he couldn't think of the right words, and his frustrations only grew.

Eloise stepped away from him.

Davey cursed himself as he gazed over the walkway that extended out into the heart of the pit. High above was the body of the city, its lights twinkling in the hot rising air. Below was the yawning chasm that led deeper into the earth.

'Those vents,' Francesco said, pointing to a maze of pipes that lined the edge of the pit, 'siphon hot air upwards, to every corner of the city.'

Davey stared at her. Did she think he cared? he wondered.

Francesco continued, 'When the air gets up to the top it's fed through organic sponges. They control the temperature and humidity, keeping Ealdwyc pleasantly cool.'

Davey half smiled, teasing her. 'I'm not much of an engineer type. I'm more of an ideas man, a leader. You know?'

Francesco looked from the pipes to him and frowned. 'Oh, I know all right,' she tutted. 'Too many are like you. They walk past these wonders every day and haven't got a clue how it all works. Worse still, you don't *want* to know.'

'Don't need to!' Davey replied. 'Someone else's job.'

Francesco sighed. 'It wouldn't take much for all this to

go, you know? If people like you don't take an interest it'll all fall apart and be forgotten.'

'What's got into you? How come everything's my fault all of a sudden?'

Before Francesco could reply Eloise approached them. 'We must go,' she said tersely. 'I can sense the Paladin are closing in.'

'Suppose that's my fault too?' Davey asked with a wave of his arm.

Eloise stared at him dispassionately, then looked at Francesco. 'They will be here soon.'

'They're tracking you?' Francesco replied.

'Yes.'

Francesco checked her watch and smiled. 'Time to move then. Our ride will be along any minute.'

Hardacre stood away from the others, apparently lost in his thoughts. He shook himself into life and said gruffly: 'The dead woman's right. We can't stay any longer.'

'Dead woman's got a name!' Davey said angrily.

Hardacre laughed at him. 'I'm sure she has, my young man, I'm sure she has.' The captain turned to face Eloise, his eyes narrowing contemptuously. 'But the dead belong buried in the earth, not walking upon it.'

Francesco grunted loudly. 'Play nicely, Jonah. We're all on the same side.'

'The dead do not take sides.' Hardacre's smile ruptured into a scowl. 'As long as you lead me to Hafgan's book I will keep my end of the bargain.' His icy eyes broke their long stare. He pushed past Eloise and descended a creaking ladder to a lower level.

'Remind me,' Davey said to Eloise, 'why did we spring him? He's a barrel of laughs, ain't he?'

Eloise seemed to hesitate for a moment, her face tightened into a frown, then she followed the captain down the ladder. Davey watched her until she disappeared from view. He felt a strange dread in his bones that caught his breath. He'd learned to listen to his instincts over the years and they'd kept him alive on more than one occasion. Now his fingers tingled too as he stared into the darkness ahead.

'You coming, lad? We can't waste any more time,' Francesco said to Davey as she climbed onto the ladder.

He looked behind him, imagining the Paladin somewhere nearby. For a moment he didn't know which way filled him with more dread: the Paladin behind him or the unknown darkness ahead. His limbs jittered, willing him to abandon the others, to find his own way out, alone. He was good at being alone. He knew how to survive. Then he thought of Eloise and Jack. He knew they wouldn't abandon *him*. He pushed his fear deeper into his gut, denying it air, until it became insignificant. He took a step towards the ladder. He placed his hands on the rail and lowered himself down to join the others.

'Less dallying, Davey! You hang around any longer

you'll ruin everything,' Francesco noted. 'I thought I was supposed to be the slow one.'

Davey shrugged, flashing a broad smile like a white cloak to hide his fear. 'Who you callin' slow?'

He pushed past the old woman and tucked himself in close behind Eloise. They descended further, down a roughly cut tunnel that dropped in deep steps until it became level again and ended at a wide opening where the floor fell away into darkness.

'What now?' he said, standing close to the edge of the precipice. 'We can't cross that, can we?'

'We don't need to,' Francesco replied breathlessly as she came up behind him. 'This is the mainline railway.'

Davey peered into the dark void and saw the faint traces of a railway line suspended in mid-air.

Francesco checked her watch again and chuckled quietly. 'Just made it.'

From far away a low rumble grew. Something large was approaching, slowing as the thunderous racket increased. Steam filled the opening, quickly condensing into hot droplets of water that coated the rock. As the smoke thinned the vast metal carriage of a train halted in front of them, letting out one final tired scream of its brakes. The carriages sat above and below the railway line, two levels impaled by the track. Each was a polished metallic blue, decorated as intricately as the stonework of the city. From above a pipe dropped into the top of the train and locked into place with a deep clunk.

'Watering point. Quickly, we don't have long,' Francesco urged. 'Follow me.'

Without hesitation she leaped over the edge and dropped onto the roof of the train.

Davey laughed in surprise. 'She's a fit old bird, all right.'

'She is not to be underestimated.' Eloise smiled knowingly.

Francesco looked up at the others, waving for them to join her. At that moment the water pipe disconnected itself and retreated upwards. The train groaned again and the pulse of its mighty engines coursed through the length of its carriages, ejecting hot steam outwards. As the train began to move away Davey jumped down next to Francesco. Hardacre and Eloise followed behind, scrambling to find purchase on the shiny carriage as it picked up speed. Below them Davey saw the wide void of the Great Pit, its hot fumes rushing past them, heating the metallic surface.

'This is the plan?' Davey asked Eloise over the din. 'Jump onto a moving train?'

'It is a good plan,' Eloise replied. 'We can move quickly away from the Paladin.'

'And the train's going to Newton Harbour,' Francesco added as she crawled back carefully towards the end of the carriage. 'Quicker than your route, Davey.'

The others followed her as she lowered herself into the gap between the two carriages. They squeezed together, holding on as the train accelerated to its full speed. The uncomfortable heat eased as, in an instant, they were plunged into the cool darkness of a tunnel. The air was sucked away from them and the pressure dropped. There was a painful burst of light and they were free of the tunnel. Fresh air invaded Davey's lungs and, as his mind began to clear, he realised he had let go of the railing. He looked up and saw Jonah Hardacre holding him firmly about the chest. The older man simply nodded and, when Davey had recovered his grip, he removed his arm.

'Be ready,' Hardacre shouted over the scream of the engines, 'Another tunnel ahead.'

Davey nodded as he took a deep breath. This tunnel was longer than the first, but he endured it well enough. When they came out they were in a vast fissure, a yawning opening in the rock that expanded for several miles to either side of the track. The rock ceiling seemed oppressively low here, as if it might tilt down and crush those below it at any moment.

Dwellings dotted the opening, like barnacles to the hull of a ship. Clusters of homes were cut out of the rock forming giant steps, each one higher than the next. Roads and pathways meandered between the houses in steep zigzag lines, disappearing into the higher parts of the cavern. Vast lanterns, longer than the train, hung from the ceiling like glowing creatures of the deep. The land below was bathed in warm ochre hues, like a perpetual midsummer evening. Here and there were formations, long twisted structures that joined the ground to the ceiling, like hot blown glass. Even here people had chiselled and cut, making rooms in the rock. As the buildings became taller and more impressive, the train began to slow.

'We're coming into a station,' Francesco shouted. 'Back up top!'

She did not wait for the others to question her decision and by the time the train had hissed to a stop in the station they were all cocooned on the roof.

The doors to the train clattered open and a swarm of passengers emptied out onto the platform. Davey watched the shifting sea of people from his hiding place above them. He saw reunited friends greet each other, workers hurrying here and there, a porter lifting the heavy bags of an old lady. Then, something glinted in the shadowy recesses of the platform.

Eloise saw it too. 'The Paladin! But how?'

'They came from the train!' Francesco replied.

'They were closer than I realised. They must have boarded it when we climbed aboard,' Eloise whispered urgently. 'I must go. They will find me!'

Davey instinctively grabbed Eloise's hand. He remembered Jack's reaction when he'd told him he could sense things. He recalled the dread in Jack's face, the fear that

Davey might one day become twisted by it. But he saw no choice now. If the Paladin found them hidden here they would surely die. Even so it terrified him to try, like he was letting some dark beast out of its cage. He calmed his thoughts. In his mind he chanted, *Turn away! Nothing here!* willing, wishing, hoping the Paladin would not sense Eloise's hiding place.

Turn away! Nothing here!
Turn away! Nothing here!
Turn away! Nothing here!

The rest of the world fell into a blur of forgotten grey as Davey stared at the Paladin, amplifying his thoughts, projecting them outwards.

Turn away! Turn away! Turn away!

The Paladin hesitated, as if distracted, then approached the train.

'What are you doing?' Eloise whispered.

Davey realised he was squeezing her hand. He looked back to the Paladin.

Nothing here! Nothing here! Turn away!

The Paladin walked up to the train, studying it with an air of frustration. She paced along the platform before stopping almost directly under their hiding place. Davey held his breath.

Turn away! Nothing here!

Another Paladin appeared from inside the train. 'What is it?'

'She was here,' the first Paladin said to her comrade. 'She was here, I am sure. Now...now she is gone.'

'I will check the lower carriages,' the other Paladin replied. 'If she is here we will find her.'

The Paladin nodded, then both stepped back inside the train.

Somewhere at the end of the platform a whistle blew. Another replied and the massive train crawled out of the station. Davey closed his eyes and allowed himself to breathe again.

'How?' Eloise said. 'You blocked them. How did you do that?'

'I dunno,' he said at last. It was true enough. He had acted without thinking. Suddenly a familiar image appeared in his mind like a shard of ice through his thoughts. It was a picture of a powerful figure, full of malice and hate. It was his future self – Old David – on that terrible night in 2008. He had become an Operator, someone who could control others with his mind. He had grown bitter and twisted, corrupted and controlled by Rouland. His rage would lead to the death of his own daughter: Jack's mother.

This glimpse into the future had gnawed at his thoughts ever since he had first learned of it; he prayed that it could not be so, that the future would unfold in a new direction. But he could not deny it to himself any more. He felt something stirring inside him, some natural ability pushing itself to the surface, willing him to test it. Today it had saved their lives. Tomorrow? He didn't know. He caught Eloise's eye and knew she must be thinking the same thing as him. He looked away, suddenly ashamed.

She took his hand again. 'Davey, you do not have to be that old man.'

He smiled briefly, but even that defence seemed ineffective. He pulled his hand away from hers.

Hardacre scowled. 'This isn't safe. Those Paladin are onboard and are going to find us.'

'I fear it is already too late,' Eloise said, her eyes fixed on the far end of the train. Something was moving along the roof towards them. The train gave out a low roar and a cloud of hot steam belched upwards, obscuring the view along the carriages.

There was a cluster of sparks as a sword struck the train's rooftop in broad strokes. Finally a dark figure emerged from the steam and leaped into the air. The Paladin's extended limbs clawed towards them. Eloise's sword swung at the attacker, piercing the Paladin's leg, yet still her assailant clung on, raising and swinging her weapon in retaliation. Eloise fell to the left, the sword missing her by just a few centimetres. She parried, this time her blade broke the Paladin's arm, the hand almost severed, and her sword clattering away into the dark. There was a moment of shock that flashed over the

Paladin's pale face as Eloise thrust her weapon deep into her heart, feeding. Eloise raised her booted foot, pressed it into the Paladin's stomach and pushed her off the sword. The Paladin fell backwards into the dark.

'Sister.' The voice startled Eloise. It was Paladin, and it was coming from *behind* her. Davey and the others turned in unison to see the other Paladin advancing towards them.

The Paladin bared her teeth in a broad grin, her body tensed for battle. 'You will come with me, sister.'

16

THE BRIDGE

'How do you know we're going in the right direction?' Jack huffed. 'For all you know we could be walking *away* from Newton Harbour, not towards it.'

Hilda's smile betrayed her irritation. 'Trust me. We're going the right way.'

'You seem to know a lot about this place.'

'I already told you,' Hilda replied curtly. 'I used to live here.'

'With your family?'

Hilda froze for a moment, then her smile returned. 'My Great-aunt Eva.'

'But what about your mum and—'

'Are you hungry?' Hilda asked, talking over Jack. 'I am. We should find somewhere to eat. It'll be getting dark soon. The lights have already begun to dim, look.' She pointed to the egg-shaped lanterns that drifted lazily overhead, tugging on their tethers as they shifted in the breeze.

They had left the crudely hewn caves far behind, descending deeper. After an hour the tunnels became wider and higher until several paths joined together at the bottom of a narrow gorge in the rock. Dwellings rose up above them, hugging the cliffside. Each one was reached by steps and paths made from wooden platforms raised up on the bodies of felled tree trunks. Lights twinkled in the windows of the wooden homes, and strings of lanterns bathed the rickety bridges in a cool evening glow. Below, in the narrow cut between the walls of the fracture, Jack and Hilda walked, staring at the world of activity above their heads. To Jack's eyes it was like a disorganised harbour of temporary jetties and shacks, with the shoreline long gone. The dim path was littered with rubbish from above. Rotten food and discarded junk was piled up into stinking mounds that sustained a colony of oversized crab-like creatures, which scuttled into the shadows as Jack and Hilda approached them.

'We could go up there,' Hilda offered half-heartedly. 'We could get some food, maybe a bed for the night.'

Jack's empty stomach rumbled painfully. He looked up at the twinkling lights. 'Do you know where we are?'

'Obviously. It's a little trading post, called Guthrum, I think.'

'Will there be Protectors there?' Jack asked hesitantly.

Hilda shook her head. 'It's a small settlement. I don't suppose they'll bother with this place. It's not far from Newton Harbour, but it's off the beaten track. I imagine we should be safe there.'

Jack stared up at the houses again. 'We'd best keep going.'

'We won't stay long,' Hilda replied, already scaling a frail-looking ladder. 'Come on.'

'No.'

'What?' Hilda stopped halfway up the ladder.

'I'm not going up, not yet,' Jack said firmly.

'Why ever not?'

'Because you're not telling me something.'

Hilda scowled. 'I haven't told you lots of things. I haven't known you long enough.'

'That's not what I mean,' Jack replied angrily, 'and you know it.'

Hilda sighed and returned to the cave floor, her feet stamping angrily onto each step. 'Right-ho,' she said, facing Jack. 'Out with it.'

Jack hesitated at first, then he quickly said: 'You're hiding something to do with your family.'

'Am not!'

'Hilda! I know you are. I've been inside your mind!'

Hilda's eyes widened with fear, her mouth half open. Then her face changed. Immediately she looked younger, like a lost child. She slumped against the wall of the gorge and slid down to the ground until her knees came up to her chin. 'They're dead,' she said flatly. 'My mother, my father, my brother; they're dead. Happy now?'

'But...' Jack's voice trailed away. He was certain there was more to it than that, something more complex. 'Was...was it recently?'

'It was years ago,' Hilda shouted, her voice trembling. 'But I don't see that it's any of your business.'

Jack opened his mouth to speak, but he felt stupid and his questions escaped him. He could look inside her mind, he realised. Even as he considered it he felt the Rose responding, pleading to be let loose on the girl's frail brain. Jack closed his eyes and took a deep breath.

I'm in control, he said to himself over and over again until he felt the sinister urges ebb away. After a moment he opened his eyes. Hilda had stood up and was dusting down her dress, her back to Jack.

'You're right. I'm sorry,' Jack offered apologetically. 'We should probably go.'

'Finally!' Hilda said without looking at him. She returned to the ladder and began her ascent again.

Jack stared about him at the crab-covered debris and shuddered. He waited for Hilda to step onto the first platform, then he began gingerly to climb up the steps after her.

The paths of Guthrum seemed deserted. Lights still flickered in the tiny windows but the rush of activity Jack had observed from below had now ceased.

They moved cautiously along a sturdy wooden bridge that hung between the houses. Its rigid planks swayed slightly underfoot, like the deck of a ship in a calm sea.

'Where is everyone?' Jack wondered, the hairs on his neck already standing proud.

Hilda looked equally cautious. 'Something's not right.'

'Let's get out of here.'

Jack quickened his pace, and Hilda broke into a jog next to him.

Somewhere far away a bell rang three times, low and hollow. At the same moment Jack saw movement ahead of them. He reached out and grabbed Hilda's arm. 'There's someone on the bridge.'

Slowly a rounded shape emerged from the shadows. Its body was tall and broad and sat atop thick limbs that looked like dried bark. Rows of overlapping plating receded down its powerful back – each one like a layer of gnarled driftwood. Jack thought it might be a tree, or a wood sculpture, until he saw it stiffly walking towards them across the bridge. The creature raised its massive head. Its face was elongated, with a snout and mouth like a wolf's, but much larger, covered in moss, ivy and twigs. Six sinister green eyes glowed malevolently from beneath a brow of leaves, each one twitching and turning to take in the view. Abruptly the eyes stopped their rotation and locked onto Jack and Hilda. For a moment the creature was still, then it dipped its long head, revealing a stag-like crown of twisted horns, and began to howl. The noise, like the falling of a tree, made Jack shudder.

'What's that?' he whispered as he pulled Hilda closer.

'A Gremmen,' she replied quietly with a gasp. 'They lived here long before this was built – before we came here. They're feral now. It will try to eat us!'

The Gremmen howled again as it thumped the planks of the bridge with its hoofed feet and broke into a loping run, charging with its mighty arms like a gorilla across the bridge.

'What should we do?' Jack asked Hilda, panic in his voice. 'We don't have any weapons.' He felt unprepared, almost naked, as the Gremmen approached them.

'We go back,' Hilda replied nervously. 'We have no choice.'

Jack and Hilda began to retreat, but the Gremmen was already closing the gap between them, advancing with the swiftness of a hungry animal.

'Jack,' Hilda screamed, 'you must use the Rose.'

Jack stole a glimpse over his shoulder. The Gremmen was at his heels. He didn't want to let the Rose free again, not until he'd had time to control it properly. But there was no time, no choice. He closed his eyes and prepared to unleash the wild power within him.

He turned to face the Gremmen, his hand outstretched in front of him. He let the Rose's power uncoil like a loosened spring. His palm lit up as energy flew from his fingers in an uncontrolled burst.

The Gremmen cried out, stunned. It fell to one side, losing its footing as it skidded to a halt. The creature pulled itself up onto its hands, its eyes blinking slowly. Green sap fell from the side of its head, soaking into the wooden beams.

Jack saw the injured creature prone in front of him. The Rose exulted, feeling the Gremmen's confusion. Part of Jack knew the skirmish was over, that the animal would soon retreat back into the darkness to lick its wounds. But the Rose was intoxicating. He felt like a god, consumed by power. He laughed to himself as he allowed the energy within him to find his fingers again. He stepped towards the Gremmen and touched the knotted surface of its head. His fingertips tingled. He could take this creature's life in an instant, he realised. His eyes narrowed as a crooked smile crawled from his mouth. Jack's arm tensed and—

'Don't,' Hilda said faintly.

It was as if her voice had broken a spell over him and Jack withdrew from the injured creature. Behind him he heard Hilda crying. Nervously he turned to look at her. Tears streaked her face, and her hands trembled defensively in front of her as she edged away from him. 'The Rose,' she whispered, 'it's horrible. It wanted you to kill. You almost did it!'

Jack shivered involuntarily. A wave of guilt flooded over him as he saw what might have been. He yearned for the peaceful calm he had felt with Hilda soothing his mind. Now his thoughts were in chaos, a ruin of self-loathing:

Not strong enough, not on my own.

Alone.

Cold.

The Rose, it's too much.

Too strong.

I'm not strong enough. Not without Hilda...

Alone.

Then he saw Hilda step closer to him and take his hand. 'You *are* strong enough, Jack,' she replied out loud. 'You have to be.'

The dark thoughts lessened at the sound of her voice. He needed this strange girl, he realised. Without her he felt as if the Rose would consume him completely. He would be lost to its will.

Hilda tugged his hand. 'We should go.'

Jack nodded and, as he turned to set off, he saw more shapes coming towards them over the bridge. His heart quickened as he turned to see others blocking their retreat.

'More Gremmen?' Jack wondered aloud.

'Men!' Hilda replied.

Jack squinted his eyes at the gloom. Hilda was right: the figures were men, marching over the bridge towards them. His momentary relief was quickly quashed as he saw that each wore the unmistakable uniform of a Protector. One unholstered his gun and aimed it at Jack. Instinctively he raised his hand.

'Please, Jack,' a voice bellowed out from behind. 'Can't you see we're trying to help you?'

Jack stared in disbelief as Ealdorman Jodrell Sinclair stepped painfully forward, the light glinting off his exposed teeth.

17

BLOODLINE

'Lay down your sword,' the Paladin growled, 'and your friends may yet survive.' Her hand lunged forward and grabbed Davey about the throat, holding him like a feeble rag doll.

Eloise looked to Francesco and Captain Hardacre – standing between her and the Paladin – and nodded for them to hold their positions.

The Paladin's name was Aurore, Eloise recalled with a shudder. She was ferocious, wild and unruly. When Eloise had been one of the Paladin she had reprimanded Aurore on many occasions for her wilfulness.

'What are your terms?' Eloise asked, knowing Aurore could not be trusted to keep her word.

Aurore smiled coolly. 'Your surrender, sister. Lay down your sword and swear you will come with me. Do that and I will spare these people.'

'And if I do not?'

Aurore's cat-like smile widened. 'Then I will kill them all.'

Davey's face reddened as Aurore's fingers tightened about his throat. Eloise calculated her options. She had to free Davey, now.

'We both know,' Eloise replied with a thin smile, 'that you have no intention of letting these people live. You have always lacked discipline, Aurore, never understood the benefit of tact or compromise.'

'Compromise?' the Paladin scoffed. 'You dare to lecture me? You? The Exile. The one who defied our master. You don't deserve to exist.'

'That, Aurore, is true of us both.' Eloise leaped over her companions and was upon the Paladin, dragging Davey out of her opponent's grasp. For an instant there was a flash of red, and Davey gasped as he fell to the roof of the train. But then Aurore was lunging forwards again and Eloise focused completely on the Paladin. The rooftop became a blur of swords as she pushed Aurore away from her fallen companion. Sparks flew as their blades tore into the roof, slashing through the metal. The carriage reverberated with the cries of frightened passengers and the train began to slow. Eloise swung blow after blow, each one nimbly blocked by Aurore. Suddenly the Paladin pounced on Eloise, somehow breaking through her defences. Aurore's boot stamped firmly onto Eloise's hand, her sword at her throat.

'Do you know how long I have wanted to taste your blood?' Aurore cackled. 'All those times you humiliated me! Thinking you were so special, always Rouland's favourite!'

She lifted her sword, ready to kill Eloise. There was a hail of rapid staccato pops, painfully loud. White blood erupted from five circular holes in Aurore's chest. She looked down in disbelief, then back at Eloise.

'How...how...?' The words stumbled from her lips as she keeled over to one side. Francesco appeared through a cloud of gun smoke, a small weapon in her shaking hand. The design of the gun was as neat and intricate as the timepieces that had adorned her workshop.

'Never underestimate an old woman.' Francesco smiled. She let go of the gun and it disappeared into her sleeve with a delicate click.

Eloise whipped the sword from Aurore's hand and swung it under the Paladin's throat. 'You are still undisciplined, Aurore. Will you never learn?' She raised her foot and kicked Aurore's side, sending her tumbling from the top of the slowing train, down into the chasm below. Eloise allowed herself a small moment of relieved satisfaction. Then she saw Davey and she immediately ran to his side. His face was a deathly pale colour, his eyes flickering in and out of focus. His clothes were wet with blood, cold and sticky. She had not been fast enough, she realised with regret. Her friend had been badly cut by Aurore's sword.

'He is close to death,' Hardacre said, leaning over him. 'We must be swift if he is to survive.'

'Magog station is right ahead. We have to get him off there,' Francesco said breathlessly.

The train juddered as it came to a final stop. Without hesitation Eloise leaped down onto the platform, discarding Aurore's sword and sheathing her own. Around her shocked passengers fled from the carriage. Eloise ignored them; there was no time for secrecy any longer. 'Pass him to me,' she shouted to Francesco and Hardacre.

Davey's limp body was lowered over the side of the train, into Eloise's waiting arms. She held him to her, letting his head rest against her neck. She could still feel his warmth but it was so feeble.

Hardacre jumped down next to her and helped Francesco down. The confused passengers looked on, startled by the appearance of a Paladin. Some retreated in surprise, while others – the younger ones – were drawn forward, full of curiosity. The noise grew until it seemed as if the entire platform was shouting, jostling to see what had caused the commotion. Whistles blew in the distance: Protectors called to the disturbance.

'This is not good,' Hardacre grunted.

Eloise took out her sword and swung it high, shouting, 'Keep back!'

This only served to excite the crowd further, and the masses swelled towards them. Suddenly the air popped with the vibration of a fired shot. The platform fell into silence, save for a crying child in the distance. The crowd retreated from Francesco, her arm outstretched with her gun smoking from her hand. A path opened up in front of Eloise and she ran from the platform, Davey in her arms. Hardacre and Francesco followed her as they disappeared into the sinister alleyways of Magog.

'He's bleeding everywhere,' said Francesco, her chest wheezing from their escape. 'Davey's dying. He needs a doctor.'

'Too dangerous. If we go to a doctor we will be caught,' Eloise replied.

'Then he will die,' Francesco responded angrily. 'Is that what you want?'

Eloise stared at Davey's immobile body. She hesitated, uncertain what she should do.

'Here,' Hardacre said, pointing to a dark pathway.

Eloise followed the captain. A trail of blood dripped from Davey's body, down her arm, and splashed onto the stone floor with frightening regularity.

They stopped at a vast opening filled with a great metal structure. Eloise recognised its rusted form: it had once been a magnificent piece of machinery, responsible for purifying and pumping water around the cave system. But its days of decay were many, and anything of use had been stripped away until only a fragile skeleton remained.

'Put the boy down,' Hardacre ordered.

Eloise hesitated. 'Here?'

'Do it, woman!'

Eloise lowered Davey onto the floor. His breathing was shallow.

'Give me your sword,' Hardacre said as he pulled off his grubby prison shirt to reveal a mass of tattoo-like markings on his torso. The swirling lines spread over his arms and neck as well, but became denser as the patterns converged at the centre of his chest. He ran his palm along the edge of Eloise's sword and dark green blood began to drip from the new cut. The marks on Hardacre's body seemed to pulse and he placed his bleeding hand onto Davey's wound.

'What are you doing?' Eloise asked.

Hardacre did not respond. Sweat beaded on his face as his skin became pale. The tattoos throbbed rhythmically, pulsing towards his wounded hand – towards Davey. The faintest of green marks began to appear on Davey's neck, bursting up under his skin. The lines grew more complex, spreading, growing. The finest of tendrils curled up behind his ear and down to his collarbone, merging with patterns budding on his chest.

'Gremmen sap,' Francesco whispered to Eloise. 'It can heal the sick.'

Eloise recoiled in shock. 'Gremmen sap? It is addictive.'

Francesco nodded grimly. 'Your friend will have to take it for the rest of his life, or...'

'Or he will be driven mad,' Hardacre said feebly as he slumped down next to Davey. Eloise stared in wonder as a warm green glow filled Davey's cheeks. His breathing became stronger and, after a moment, his eyes flickered open. At first the pupils shone an emerald green, then they faded back to their natural dark brown. He looked lazily from Hardacre to Eloise.

'He'll live,' Hardacre said distantly. 'Let him rest.'

'What happened?' Davey asked, rubbing his neck. The new tattoo had faded into his skin until it was barely visible. 'What'd you do to me?'

'Saved your life,' Hardacre replied with a shrug. 'This book better be worth all this trouble.' His cold eyes narrowed as he stared at Eloise.

'I will keep my side of the bargain,' Eloise replied.

'And I mine. We're close to Newton Harbour now.'

Davey raised himself up on one elbow. He took shallow, painful breaths as he flexed his fingers, watching his hand move in front of him. He stood up timidly, testing the muscles in his legs.

Eloise watched him, relieved at his recovery. 'In future,' she smiled, 'leave the dying to me.'

'No fun in that, is there?' Davey replied.

'How'd you feel?' Hardacre said, studying him.

Davey hesitated. 'Different, I suppose.'

'I gave you some of my blood.'

'You did what?'

'It was the only way to save you in time. I've been taking Gremmen sap for many years. It's in my blood. You have sap in *your* blood now.'

Hardacre picked up his shirt off the floor and pulled it over his tattoos. 'Two systems in conflict: blood and sap. It'll change you. You're gonna live a long life, that's for sure, much longer than most men.'

'First Worlders always live longer,' Davey scoffed. 'Look at Carhoop there, she should be long dead!'

'You've lost none of your charm!' Francesco scowled. 'I think I preferred you when you were dying.'

'First Worlders do live longer than Second Worlders,' Hardacre said, ignoring Francesco, 'but you have Gremmen sap in you now, Davey. You'll grow more slowly.'

'Don't sound so bad,' Davey sniffed.

'It's a stress on a human body, especially one as young as yours. There's a rage that comes along, every few years in the spring, like a growing pain. It can tear your mind apart. It's called the *Furor Vernum*, the Rage of Spring. I've suffered it twice so far and it took all my will not to give in to despair. It can drive you mad.'

Davey nodded thoughtfully as he touched the new marks on his neck. 'It beats being dead, right?'

Hardacre frowned, refusing to meet Davey's stare. 'It will be some time before it afflicts you. But you'll have to be strong. In time, I can teach you how to cope. And you'll have to drink Gremmen sap to keep you sane.'

144

'Where the bloody hell am I supposed to get Gremmen sap from?'

'A Gremmen,' Hardacre replied flatly. He picked up Eloise's sword and handed it back to her. 'If we leave now we can be in Newton Harbour in less than an hour.'

'Wait!' Davey exclaimed. 'What about—'

'No more questions! Not now,' Hardacre interrupted. 'Time to move on. We can talk onboard the *Orion*. Get up, lad.'

Davey begrudgingly obeyed. He didn't have the strength to spar with Hardacre.

'Are you well enough to go on?' Eloise asked softly.

Davey took her arm. He seemed fragile, aged and weak. 'Tough as nails, me!' he managed with a forced chuckle.

Eloise returned his smile, but inwardly she shuddered. Old David had those marks on his neck, she recalled. What might the Rage of Spring do to Davey's mind? It was as if the future was hurtling towards them, fixed and unavoidable.

18

THE FORGOTTEN SHIP

The lift cranked to an abrupt halt, its wire walls creaking and complaining. Davey pulled the wide door to one side and noticed that the lift had stopped a few centimetres short of the floor level.

'Watch your step, ladies and gentlemen.' He waved them out with a wide spread of his arm. The lift had taken them far below the busier dockyards, to some of the smaller berths. There were fewer people here and the place echoed with the noises of repairs to ships far above. Oil and water dripped down in fragile lines that fell into the darkness between the gangways, taking with it any sense of optimism or cheer. This was a largely forgotten level, a place where realm ships came to die.

'There she is,' Hardacre grinned, pointing along the walkway. 'The *Orion*!'

The ship was old, its worn rusty skin a patchwork of oxidised browns, umbers and yellows. Hints of its original paintwork endured – lonely patches of deep red that would have been impressive when it was new. But time had eaten away at it until the metal had been burned clean in places. Newer, unsympathetic repairs sat uncomfortably next to original plating, creating a patchwork that told the story of the *Orion*'s many adventures as well as any book might.

It was small for a realm ship, Davey noted, with only three decks to its height. It had the same curved bulbous front as most other realm ships but its flight deck sat proudly above in a bubble of metal struts and glass. Three equally spaced fins protruded out of its surface and sloped towards the rear, giving the ship a grace that outshone the functionality of its riveted body. The *Orion*'s engine rings slowly ploughed over each other in long hypnotic arcs. A series of foil sails, which overlapped like gills along the ship's sides, danced in the gentle breeze from the engine rings and sent a kaleidoscope of light and colour refracting onto the platform around the ship. Jets of gas spilled from vents on its side in rhythmic intervals – exhaust fumes from its idling engines – but it was as if the ship were alive, breathing in and out in long languorous breaths. Even seen at this distance, the ship moored by guide ropes, Davey thought it was beautiful. He looked at Hardacre and understood that he shared the same emotion.

'Is someone on board?' Eloise asked, nodding to the slowly turning engines.

Hardacre shook his head. 'It's automatic. They have to keep turning to keep the ship afloat.'

'They can keep going for ages,' Davey added enthusiastically. 'As long as there's gas in the tank the engines'll keep on turning...' His voice trailed away as he noticed something that sent a shiver down his spine. 'The entrance ramp's down!'

'Why on earth would it be down?' Hardacre mused. 'Unless...'

'Unless someone *is* aboard,' Francesco said.

'Something is wrong,' Eloise said through gritted teeth. 'This is a trap.'

Francesco took Eloise's hand. 'What do you sense, Elly?'

'My sisters,' she replied, drawing her sword slowly from its scabbard. 'They are here.'

'The Paladin?' Hardacre said brusquely.

Eloise nodded. 'They sense me. We are discovered.'

They heard footsteps on the metal entrance ramp of the *Orion* and the Paladin emerged from its interior.

The Paladin captain stepped onto the dockside platform, followed by three of her sisters. They stood in the half-light of the foil sails, dark and sinister.

'Where is the boy?' the captain shouted. 'Where is Jack Morrow?'

Eloise turned, raising up her sword. Davey looked back and saw their way blocked by two more Paladin.

'You will tell me now!' the Paladin captain bellowed.

'This ain't gonna end well,' Davey said to himself.

Hardacre put his hand firmly on Davey's shoulder. 'They outnumber us, but we are not dead yet! If we can just get on board the *Orion*...'

Francesco nodded her agreement. 'We need to draw them off.'

Eloise said, 'They will anticipate our plan.'

Davey's face broke into a devilish smile. 'So we'll create a little diversion.'

'What sort of diversion?' Francesco asked, drawing her gun from its hiding place.

'Not sure yet, I'll have to make something up,' Davey said, pointing ahead. Two Paladin had begun to advance cautiously towards them.

Eloise sighed regretfully as she prepared for battle. 'It will have to do.'

Francesco fired her gun twice, flooring the approaching Paladin. Almost immediately they were on their feet again and running towards them. Instinctively the group broke apart. Eloise retreated into the warren of platforms, drawing the Paladin with her. Francesco and Hardacre ran in the opposite direction, hiding amongst the cargo. Davey watched as the Paladin took up the chase, then he too scurried away, alone amongst the junk and rubbish.

Davey felt exulted, unburdened and liberated. This had been the only life he had known for so long – living on his wits. Being surrounded by people, by friends, felt uncomfortable, like a great weight pressing down on him. Now it was just him, free to live or die. He spotted an open hatch and sank below the uneven decks, finding a way through a tangle of pipes and pistons. Above him, through the gaps in the planks he saw three Paladin. They slowed, then stopped, as if listening for his breathing. Davey held his breath, and for a moment the Paladin hesitated.

'There!' one of them shouted, pointing down towards him. Davey crawled away, along the pipes, jumping down to a lower level, rolling onto his side, falling over a ledge, clawing at some cables, swinging himself into a new hiding place. All the time he heard the Paladin behind him. Below him was another platform, too far away to jump to safety. He rummaged in his pocket until he felt the familiar shape of his penknife. He flicked the old blade open and began to cut at one of the thick pipes that snaked past him. Oil started to gush out of the slit, pouring down his arm. He cursed to himself, not having anticipated the pumping fluid. He worked furiously, jabbing the knife through the thick pipe until it was cut loose, then he grabbed the end and swung clumsily out of his hiding place.

'Seize him, sisters!' A voice followed him as he swung. Almost as soon as he was clear of the pipes his hands began to slip and slide, his grip on the severed cable loosening. He saw the platform below him approaching rapidly as the cable slipped through his oily hands. He fell onto the lower platform, landing heavily on his knee then rolling onto his side, his shoulder ramming into the wooden slats. His head bounced off the beams and blood mixed with oil, stinging his eyes. His vision blurred, but he fought to stay conscious.

Two mighty thuds reverberated through the wooden floor. Davey looked up and saw two Paladin in front of him. He limped to his feet as needles of white-hot pain shot through his leg. He took several clumsy steps back, away from the growing pool of oil in between him and the Paladin.

One of the Paladin mocked, 'Nowhere left to run, boy.'

Davey watched them approach, his fingers searching in his pockets. 'Don't kill me! I'll tell you where you can find Jack.' He smiled wearily and raised his hands. As the Paladin stepped forward, Davey struck the cigarette lighter he had concealed in his hand and dropped it into the pool of oil in front of him. The fumes ignited immediately and a wall of fire erupted between Davey and the Paladin. He felt a sharp pain along his fingers: his arm was on fire! He yanked off his burning jacket and wrapped it round the flames, smothering them. He looked at his hand: the skin was sore but unburnt, unlike his coat. For a brief moment he considered discarding it, but it was a bloody good coat, burnt or not. He brushed it down and threw it back on as he retreated away from the heat, watching with satisfaction as the fire took hold of his pursuers.

The flames began to lick at the swinging cable above him and fire crawled upwards. A sickening dread grew in the pit of Davey's stomach.

'No, no, no!' he muttered as he stared at the climbing fire. For a moment it seemed to die away, and Davey felt relief wash over him. Then there was a mighty crack, and something exploded high above him. A sequence of deafening bangs erupted, each louder than the last, and the fire spread. He watched as one of the docked realm ships wheezed and groaned. As its hull crackled with fire he pulled himself away, running with all the speed his injured body would provide. Behind him the realm ship disappeared into a fireball. Fragments of its body rained down on the platform, cracking its wooden planks. Davey's legs vibrated with the shocks.

Then the realm ship began to fall.

19

BONE, STONE AND SORROW

The council chambers were modest compared to some of the sights Jack had seen on his way through Ealdwyc. The room had the same attention to detail, the same over-abundance of sculpture and decadence, but its scale was reserved, almost comfortable. Only the long curve of glass betrayed its First World provenance. The windows took up the entire length of the room, from floor to ceiling. Some of the panels were made of vibrant stained-glass pictures; others gave uncluttered views out to the great expanse of Newton Harbour beyond.

Jack and Hilda sat at a vast mahogany table, eating from the many platters of food that had been brought to them. There was an assortment of cold meats, as well as bread, cheese and fruit. They had been left alone for almost half an hour since their arrival in the chambers. Ealdorman Sinclair had been called away on urgent business, and Jack was beginning to wonder if waiting for him was such a wise idea.

'Relax,' Hilda said as she noisily ate a chicken leg.

Jack frowned. 'Are you reading my mind again?'

'I don't need to. You've hardly eaten anything, and you have that dreamy faraway look on your face. You should stop that, it makes you look simple.'

Jack smiled in spite of himself. It felt almost alien, like a forgotten expression. He stood up and stared out of the window. The view of Newton Harbour was spectacular. This port was like no other Jack had witnessed before, lacking as it did a shoreline. Great vessels – realm ships, Hilda had called them – were moored along the dockside. Superficially they reminded Jack of the Spitfires and Lancaster bombers he'd seen over war-time London, as if they shared the same manufacturers, but that is where any similarities to a Second World vessel ended. Each ship was different, varying in size and shape, but they all had a bulbous front section, which tapered away to the rear. These were ships of metal, made from riveted panels with porthole windows sitting above and below their profile. The largest of the realm ships was perhaps ten floors high, and twice as long. Towards the rear each ship had a configuration of three concentric rings, which turned lazily, even on the docked vessels. The ships hung in their docks, kept in place by dozens of guide ropes stretched tightly between ship and port, giving the mighty craft the appearance of harpooned whales. Cantilevered walkways joined the ships to the dock platforms, like castle drawbridges the size of motorways.

Jack watched as a realm ship appeared from above, drifting down slowly towards an empty dock. As it approached a hatch opened on its side and the first of the mooring ropes fired outwards towards a device on the dockside. The end of the rope connected and the rope was pulled tight as a set of cogs turned. The realm ship was drawn closer to the dock as its rotating rings – Jack presumed this to be an engine of some sort – slowed to the speed of the other resting ships. There was a flurry of activity as a dozen more mooring ropes fired outwards towards the dock, until the craft came to rest, like a giant metal spider at the heart of a delicate web.

'Remarkable, isn't it?'

Jack turned to see Ealdorman Sinclair had returned to the chamber. He stood next to Jack, admiring the view.

'Newton Harbour is, to my eye, the most impressive part of Ealdwyc,' the old man sighed wistfully. 'I would come here as a small boy and sit with my brother, down on the dockside, there.' He pointed to a bustling platform far below. 'I would stare up at those magnificent ships, coming and going, and wish that I was on board, heading to some undiscovered realm.'

'Did you go?' Jack asked.

'No.'

'Why not?'

A half-smile broke over Jodrell's scarred face, before it disappeared behind his stern visage. 'Family. Duty. Tradition. You could not be expected to understand.'

'Fear?' Jack said without thinking.

Jodrell turned his back on the windows. 'Fear is a great motivator. Fear of change the greatest of all. Change has fallen on the First World, has it not? And you, Jack, are its catalyst.'

'I told you before,' Jack said resolutely, 'I'm not going to be your leader.'

'Yes, yes, I know. But there is more at play here than you are aware of.' Jodrell fell into a chair with a heavy sigh. 'The Paladin are back in Ealdwyc...'

Jack shuddered. He looked out the vast windows and wondered what had happened to Davey and Eloise.

'They will not tolerate the loss of Rouland. Even now they seek to restore him. They are searching for Durendal.'

Jack tried to hide his recognition, but Jodrell smiled coolly.

'Yes,' said Jodrell. 'I know what they – and you – seek. Is it such a surprise to you?'

Hilda put down her food and faced Jodrell, her features like steel. 'Are you holding us prisoner again? Because it won't do. Jack's not going to help you, and neither will I.'

The old man chuckled to himself wearily. 'For two intelligent, gifted children you can be extremely dim. I was never your enemy. I have been protecting you.'

'Protecting us?' Jack replied. 'You might have helped us on the bridge but—'

'We knew where you were within minutes of your escape from us.' Jodrell's manner was that of a teacher losing his patience. 'Your little trick didn't slow us down for long, young lady.' He smiled at Hilda, who blushed and looked away.

'Trick?' Jack said, bemused.

'You didn't tell him?' Jodrell asked Hilda. He turned to Jack. 'My young man, she took you an hour into the past.'

Jack thought about this for a moment, hardly able to understand what Jodrell meant.

'She's a Yard Boy, Jack,' Jodrell said impatiently. 'I am right.' He raised a bushy eyebrow at Hilda. She stood frozen like a desperate trapped animal. Jack thought she might flee the room, but she remained still, puffing out her narrow chest until her cheeks flushed red.

'How dare you—'

'Do not bother to deny it!' Jodrell interrupted angrily, his gloved fist thumping down onto the table. 'I know you are. That is how you evaded us, using the memori-mortuus to travel the Sorrowlines. How far did you go? An hour into the past? Two?'

Hilda's eyes burned with rage.

Jack stared at Sinclair. 'What do you mean?'

Jodrell breathed deeply, letting his bony fists unfurl before he spoke. 'You recall the skulls in the wall outside of my chambers? They are our most recent dead – the memori-mortuus. Their skulls are placed there for one year after their death, so that we might remember them and mark their passing. After that time they are moved deeper into the catacombs.' Jodrell's leathery brow lowered, forcing his surviving eye into a pencil-line grimace as he leaned closer to Jack. 'A Sorrowline needs three things to exist: bone, stone and sorrow. Each of those skulls has its own Sorrowline, just like a headstone does in the Second World. When you wanted to escape Hilda simply opened up a Sorrowline and took you both into it. She didn't need to go far, just an hour or so into the past was enough for you to evade my Protectors.'

Jack suddenly understood. He remembered the strange sensation when they had run from Jodrell's chambers, how the Protectors had suddenly disappeared, how he had felt dizzy and disorientated. Now all the confused events clicked into place.

'But a Yard Boy . . .' Jack spluttered, his thoughts racing to catch up. 'A Yard Boy can't take someone else into a Sorrowline . . .'

'Or leap out of it after only an hour,' Jodrell said, completing Jack's thought. 'Those things are impossible, even for the most skilled of Yard Boys. A Sorrowline is a fixed passage from the present to the date of a person's death. You know that, Jack.'

Jack stared in wonder at Hilda. Her eyes darted

between Jodrell and Jack as she slowly backed away from them.

Jodrell stood wearily, following Hilda's hesitant retreat. 'She is far more than a mere Yard Boy. There is only one thing she can be: a Timesmith.'

'What?' Jack stepped closer to Hilda, amazed. 'Is this true?'

Hilda opened her mouth, but it was as if the words were stuck in her throat.

'Timesmiths are rare indeed, full of legend and portents,' Jodrell snarled. 'How far have you travelled upstream, girl? How far in our past do you really belong?'

Hilda's back thumped into the wall. Nowhere left to run.

'And why would you come all the way here, to 1940? It is no coincidence that you stumbled upon Jack, is it? It is not mere chance that has brought you two together. No, there is nothing random at work here. And that enticing thought brings with it a new question, a question around which your future now turns: who sent you?'

Hilda glanced quickly at Jack. There was the briefest hint of regret, of apology, on her face, then a wall of anger hid all other emotions. She leaped towards Jodrell like a wild creature, clawing at his already painfully torn face. He fell back onto the table, sending plates of food clattering to the ground. Hilda pushed away from him and scrambled towards the door.

Jack seemed dumbstruck, frozen where he stood. His senses reeled from it all. His leg twitched, as if urging him to run with his friend, but something held him back. The smallest germ of mistrust had been planted, and already its insidious roots were breaking apart the bond between him and Hilda. He wanted to run, to be free, but he stood still and watched her pull at the door.

Jodrell's Protectors appeared and were upon her immediately, pushing her to the ground, restraining her as she kicked and screamed. Her teeth gnashed, spitting and biting as she tried to wriggle free.

'Please!' Hilda cried out over the cacophony of noise. 'He'll kill them! Let me go!'

Jodrell pulled himself upright, pushing slices of meat off his expensive jacket. 'Who? Who do you speak of?'

'Rouland,' Jack said pathetically, overcome with an uncanny clarity. 'Rouland has her family. He's going to kill them.'

Suddenly the room shook with a terrible vibration. Jack looked to the line of windows. Far below, in Newton Harbour, one of the realm ships had exploded. A fireball erupted, raining fragments of metal onto the dockside. Flames leaped along the platforms as fuel spilled from the stricken vessel and ignited. The craft listed to one side, the rotating rings slowed, then stopped as gravity took hold and pulled the ship free of its moorings.

The burning wreck fell down onto another realm ship, tearing through its outer skin, breaking its hull in two. Then there was a new explosion as the second craft surrendered to the flames.

20

THE HIGH ROAD

Eloise closed her dark eyes, allowing herself a brief instant to clear her mind. The Paladin had cornered her in amongst the crates and barrels on the dockside – just as she wanted it.

She raised her head up and found the two Paladin – Véronique and Geneviève – raging towards her down the alley of cargo. They rushed into battle without thinking, Eloise observed with disappointment. They had forgotten everything she had taught them so long ago. She waited until they were almost upon her before she drew her sword.

They could not attack together in the confined space and Geneviève was forced to hold back and watch as Véronique charged ahead. The conflict was brief. Eloise's sword found Véronique's side, cutting through the armour and puncturing the skin beneath. As she pulled her sword free she leaped up onto a tiny ledge, then another, until she was high above the Paladin. Geneviève rose up, her eyes on her prey. It was only at the last second that she spotted the sword, thrown expertly like a spear, falling out of the air directly at her. Geneviève rolled to the left and the sword hit her leg, shattering the bone within and pinning her to the ground.

Eloise landed in front of her and yanked the sword free. She heard a faint scratching from behind, and without looking she swung the sword round. Véronique gave out a short gasp as she clattered to the ground.

Eloise ran out of the alley before the Paladin could recover. Ahead of her she saw Captain Jonah Hardacre limping towards her.

'The way is clear, for now,' she informed him without slowing down. 'Where is Francesco?'

'A Paladin attacked us. She lured her away.'

A ripple of fear passed through Eloise. She did her best to hide it. 'You left her?'

'No, I didn't!' Hardacre said defensively as they turned a corner. 'She left me. Besides, that old girl seems to manage well enough on her own. What's our next move?'

Eloise hesitated, uncertain. 'I do not know,' she replied. 'I wonder if Davey has created his diversion yet?'

The floor rumbled under them as a giant fireball erupted nearby. Debris was thrown in arcs of fire, landing close by on the platform.

Eloise sighed. 'Davey must learn subtlety.'

'He's got balls, I'll give him that much,' Hardacre laughed, 'but if he gets so much as a scratch on the *Orion* I'll personally lynch him!'

The burning dockside, the smoke and the cries of terrified workers prompted Eloise into a run. Behind her Hardacre struggled to keep up as they weaved through the people running blindly towards them. Her senses were alert – she knew the Paladin would not crumble so easily. Somewhere ahead, Captain de Vienne would be waiting.

'You're going the wrong way!' Hardacre coughed from behind her.

Eloise stopped and waited until he had caught up with her. 'You would rather walk up the *Orion*'s gantry and have the Paladin slit your throat?'

Hardacre harrumphed. 'What do you have in mind?'

'We approach from above.'

The *Orion*'s metallic surface seemed to glow in the reflected light of the flames. Two floors above it Eloise and Hardacre inched closer, trying to gain the best vantage point.

'Anything?' Hardacre asked impatiently.

Eloise shook her head. 'I see no one nearby.'

'So we move!'

'Not yet. Something is not right here.' She scrutinised the ship again. The entrance ramp was still open, a bluish light flickering from somewhere within. She let her eyes drift upwards, over the burnished skin of the vessel, to a window about halfway up. At first she could see nothing, then there was a flash of movement. She forced her eyes to focus beyond the glass, and whispered, 'There!'

Hardacre pushed himself forward, eager to see what Eloise was pointing at. 'I can't see anything.'

'There are people on board.' Even as she spoke, staring into the window, she was rising, her hand finding her sword. Briefly someone came up to the window, clattering against it, then rushed into the darkness again. The face had been there for less than a second, but it was enough for Eloise to recognise.

'Francesco!' she gasped.

The muffled noise of gunfire echoed out of the entrance ramp below.

Hardacre cursed under his breath. Eloise was already on her feet and leaping towards one of the anchor ropes that held the ship fast. She scrambled along its length, climbing onto the hull, grabbing at the grooves between the plates, clawing up to the top of the ship. She glanced back at Hardacre; he was descending towards the entrance ramp.

Eloise looked along the curved mass of the ship. In front of her was a window – a hemisphere of glass that broke the smooth profile of the vessel. As she reached it Eloise attacked the latch with her sword, popping it open. She somersaulted inside, rolling into the shadows, her senses twitching, listening, trying to pinpoint the battle. There were noises, somewhere below.

Eloise rushed towards a ladder and slid down it to the next floor. The signs of battle were everywhere. The walls were covered in long scars from a Paladin sword. Here and there were bullet holes, perfect circles that cut through the metal walls. *Why?* she wondered. *Why didn't you wait, Francesco?*

She forced herself to pause, slowing her breathing, sensing. There, lower still, was life. The broad clashes of battle had been replaced by heavier vibrations, as if something – someone – was being dragged through the ship.

Eloise rushed down the ladder, to the lowest level, to the entrance ramp. As she turned the corner she saw Hardacre first, outside with his hands raised up in a gesture of surrender. Then she saw a Paladin – Captain de Vienne – on the ramp, her mechanical sword rotating slowly as blood fell from it. Finally she saw Francesco Carhoop.

Captain de Vienne released the lifeless body from her hand and smiled as it fell to the ground.

21

INSTANT OF RAGE

The room vibrated from the aftershock of the explosions, causing the plates to rattle on the tabletop. A terrifying crack appeared in one of the vast panes of glass, dividing it into almost equal halves. Jack instinctively ducked.

'What's happening?' Jodrell demanded as his aides and Protectors crowded around the frail Ealdorman. One of them, a pencil-thin man, replied forcefully, 'Sir, we must get you to safety. The Paladin are in Newton Harbour.'

'I know that!' Jodrell boomed impatiently. 'And there's a battle raging down there.' He gestured towards the spreading flames and a thick wall of smoke that obscured the dockside from his vantage point.

Jack tore his eyes away from the windows and found Hilda, small and alone. He rushed to her side and grabbed her hand. Together they discreetly slipped out of the room while Jodrell and his aides stared at the flames.

As they retreated down the sloping corridor Jack heard the shouts of Jodrell emanating from the chamber. He stole a glance over his shoulder as they turned a corner: three Protectors appeared from the room and gave chase.

Jack ran faster, dragging Hilda behind him. She seemed stunned, lost inside her head. Suddenly she yanked her hand from his and stopped running.

'What are you doing?' Jack demanded,

'It's pointless, Jack,' Hilda replied. 'It's all pointless.'

Behind her the Protectors appeared, almost falling over her. One of them seized her in his heavy arms, lifting her off the ground.

'Come on, sunshine,' the Protector said to Jack, trying to sound friendly. 'We've got the girl. You'll come back quietly now.'

Hilda whimpered softly, no fight left in her. Seeing her tiny frame held aloft in the Protector's arms fed a rage deep within Jack. Without thinking he called to the Rose and it responded.

He felt his tension swell and dissipate. A wave of serene confidence grew from deep within him. His back straightened, his fists opened, he even smiled. The Protectors saw the change and exchanged uncertain glances with each other.

Jack began to speak, his tone charged with a hitherto unknown gravitas. 'No,' he said slowly, 'you'll put her down and leave us.'

The Protector turned to his hesitant comrades and laughed. 'Come on, he's just a boy.' He reached for his gun holster, but his fingers twitched above the weapon, spasming and shaking.

Jack was inside his mind.

And Jack's confidence swelled, growing into a controlled rage. He smiled to himself, wallowing in his superiority: these men did not deserve to live.

The Protector released Hilda, his fists clawing at his helmet. The other Protectors took a step backwards as Hilda limped to Jack's side. He barely noticed her. His focus was on the Protector, pushing deeper into his brain. The man fell to his knees as he ripped the helmet free. Blood filled his nostrils, spilling down into his mouth.

Jack pushed further, finding his way deeper, deeper. There. He had found what he was looking for. He sliced into his mind. The man screamed, but Jack knew it would soon be over. All he had to do was give one last, tiny push.

An ice-cool sensation entered his mind, rocking him sideways. Hilda's hand was in his.

'Don't, Jack,' she said. 'Don't be a monster.' There was no pleading, no anger in her voice, just love, calming and soothing.

Jack retreated from the Protector's mind. The man stumbled, crying out in pain as his hand finally found his gun and fired off a round. The confined space rattled with a deafening crack and a flash of light. When the smoke cleared, Jack saw the Protector had dropped the weapon and was edging back round the corner, shaking with fear.

Jack gasped for breath. He felt dizzy and nauseous.

Hilda let go of his hand and picked up the abandoned gun, pointing it at the retreating Protectors.

'Quickly,' she said to Jack as she returned to his side. 'They'll come to their senses again soon. We should go while we can.'

Jack found himself running with her, retreating from the stunned Protectors. Several shots rang out, whizzing over Jack and Hilda's heads. Jack looked back. The Protectors were not giving chase; instead, they tended to their downed comrade. A new wave of sickness gripped him as he thought how easily he could have given in to his darker thoughts. 'I . . . I could have killed him.'

'But you didn't,' Hilda said angrily.

Jack's hand reached for his mother's pendant. He missed her more and more, yearning to learn how she had coped with the burden of the Rose.

The walls of the corridors and stairways bled one into the other until Jack was completely lost. His only anchor was Hilda's hand, gripped firmly in his. Everything else faded into a blur of greys and black. Eventually, exhausted and disorientated, he pulled at Hilda to stop.

'Please,' he gasped, 'I need to breathe.'

Hilda released her grip and Jack fell to the ground, his chest rattling like an old man's. After a moment his gasping lessened and his eyes focused on his world. Hilda stood away from him, leaning against one of the many ornate statues that overlooked the southernmost part of the docks. She watched him cautiously, her arms hugging her body.

'Jack,' Hilda said firmly, 'you need to decide who you are, before the Rose does it for you. It's powerful. All those little angry thoughts, we all have them, but with the Rose you can carry them out.'

Hilda was right. The flashes of fury, the instants of rage that swam deep inside him, had a way out now. 'I should have died,' he said softly.

'What?'

'My mum, she gave me the Rose to save my life,' Jack replied bitterly. 'She gave me this, and now I'm turning into some sort of monster, and everyone wants a piece of me. She should have let me die.'

Hilda unfolded her arms, her frame full of rage. 'Don't ever, ever wish that. Don't you ever be that wretched, that self-pitying!'

Jack felt ashamed. 'I . . . I'm sorry, Hilda.'

'So you should be!' She turned her back on him angrily.

Jack stood up and walked towards the wall. Fire still raged in the docks below them. Burning embers and fragments of wood rained down onto lower decks, spreading the destruction ever further. The distant rumble of the conflagration unsettled him.

'Hilda,' he said cautiously. 'What happened to your family?'

She didn't look at him. Her tear-streaked face glowed red in the unnatural light. 'My family are all dead. They die every second of my life, over and over again.'

'So it's true, what the Ealdorman said about you?'

Hilda nodded hesitantly. 'Jack, I'm from the past, from 1813. I can travel through Sorrowlines, like you. I've been sent here by Rouland to find you and bring you to him.'

Jack stared at her, hardly able to take in what she had just said. 'You came for me? We didn't just meet by accident?'

Hilda shook her head, avoiding his stare. 'I was waiting for you. I followed you from 1813, back here to 1940. I followed you and your friend from the graveyard to Whitechapel, but I lost you. I thought you might eventually come back to the First World. I've spent weeks going back and forth through Sorrowlines, waiting at junction chambers to the First World, waiting and hoping that you might show up. I knew, if you were still alive, I'd get lucky eventually. And I did.'

'All this time, you tricked me?'

'Haven't you been listening, Jack? My family! He has my family! If I don't find you and that damned book, if I fail, then my family will die.' The words broke apart as her lip quivered uncontrollably. 'Rouland has them hostage, in my house. I have an hour to bring you and the book you stole back to him. That hour might as well be an eternity.'

Jack stood nervously, letting the magnitude of Hilda's statement sink in, uncertain what to say. He took the book out of his pocket and turned it over in his hands. It was a small volume, battered and well worn. On its front cover was its title, embossed into the leather and picked out in faded gold: *On the Nature of the Concealed Realms* by Magnus Hafgan.

'What is it about that book?' Hilda asked. 'Why is it so important?'

Jack shrugged. 'I was sent back to 1813 to find it for a man. He knew things about my mother, about the Rose. I went back to 1813 to find it in exchange for what he knew. My friend, Davey – my grandfather – he came with me.'

'So he's a Yard Boy as well?'

Jack shook his head pensively.

'Then,' Hilda continued, 'you're a Timesmith, like me.'

'Yeah, I think so,' Jack replied. He was still uncertain what he really was capable of. 'We went back to 1813 and found this book.'

'Found?' Hilda scoffed.

'We stole it, from one of Rouland's people, a woman called—'

'Jane McBride,' Hilda interrupted. 'Yes, I know. And you killed her husband to get it!'

'No!' Jack protested. 'We didn't kill him! He chased us and was knocked over. It was an accident!'

Hilda shook her head bitterly. 'How many people have died for that book? How many more will die?'

Guilt-ridden, Jack opened the book, staring at the intricately coded pages – all indecipherable to his eyes, except for the last page. It was a grid of letters and numbers. He'd already found clues to the future hidden in the text, a secret code inexplicably written in his own handwriting. It was as if this small, insignificant book was like a great stone thrown into the lake of time, sending out ripples that disturbed the paths of those it crossed. Now Hilda's family had been drawn into those ripples, and their very lives were at stake.

'I have this amazing power, Jack,' Hilda said. 'I can do such fantastic things, but no matter what I do I end up back at this point, with no other way out.'

'We could go back,' Jack said, thinking quickly. 'We could go back, together, to before your family were taken hostage. We could get them to safety, we could . . .'

His words faded away as he saw the look of disgust on Hilda's face.

'Don't you think I've tried already?' she said feebly. 'I've been back a dozen times, and each time things turn out the same. I have to watch my family go through the same torment.'

Jack shuddered as he thought of his own efforts to save his mother. He had tried, and failed, to change events. Instead, he had become entwined in them, part of events, herded towards the same terrible outcome. The image of the Grimnire came to mind. They had been there, over-seeing his path. He had thought one of them had helped him to defeat Rouland. Now he was less sure. Perhaps he had only served to fulfil the Grimnire's unknown plans.

He realised Hilda was staring at him.

'The Grimnire are not your allies, Jack,' she said icily.

Jack suppressed his frustration. After all, Hilda was right: he had to learn how to control his thoughts, to hide them from prying minds.

'There must be something we can do!' he said at last.

Hilda looked away, her large eyes alive with tears. 'There is only one thing I can do. I'm sorry, but there's no other way.' As she spoke she seemed to reassure herself, growing in determination. 'I can see how hopeless it all is, but I have to try. I've been putting it off, you see?'

'No, I don't,' Jack replied, confused.

'I'm not a bad person,' Hilda said, 'but sometimes good people have to do bad things. There's no other way. I am so very sorry, Jack.' Hilda whirled around and flung her arms around him, gripping him tightly. She pulled him backwards, towards the statue, its discreet alcove full of skulls, coming into focus at the last moment. Only then did he understand.

'Hilda, please!' Jack's words stretched and evaporated as he felt an all-too familiar sensation. Whiteness engulfed them both as they fell into the Sorrowline, back through time, downstream.

Jack felt the Sorrowline deform and they were moving in a new direction, shifting, riding the paths of sorrow. He sensed Hilda's dexterity with the Sorrowlines, navigating them, surfing their potential, and he understood the depth of her ability. He had so much to learn.

The tides of loss and regret from a dozen deaths blended together, breaking him into submission, one tear at a time. He cried out in despair, and then, finally, he felt the journey coming to an abrupt end.

Jack knew where Hilda was dragging him: they were going to the year 1813, long before his first encounter with Rouland, long before Jack put a sword in his heart and buried him in the earth. Everything seemed so uncertain now, and the possibility of Jack dying in the past seemed very, very real.

The walls of the Sorrowline fell away. They had arrived in 1813.

22

THE MAN AT THE FIREPLACE

'What's all the noise?' Anton said groggily. 'Why aren't you in bed?'

'Quiet!' Hilda insisted. She stood by the bedroom door, her ear squeezed into the small opening.

Anton crept out of bed and across the chilly floor to his sister's side. He tugged on the hem of her nightgown and looked up at her with his oversized eyes.

Hilda frowned, frustrated by his interruption. 'There's someone downstairs,' she said in a rushed whisper.

Anton, unimpressed, wandered over to the window. His head disappeared under the curtain as he studied the night sky. 'It's late,' he concluded.

'It's after two,' Hilda replied. 'Go back to bed.'

'Who's downstairs?'

Hilda hesitated. 'I'm not sure.'

'They're not happy,' Anton observed casually, yawning as he burrowed down under his still-warm blankets.

Hilda broke away from the door and stared at her brother. 'You're sensing stuff again?'

'Bits.'

'What?'

Anton didn't reply, his head tucked down deep into his curled body.

'Anton!' Hilda hissed, pushing her brother awake.

'Just bits, I told you. A man and woman. They're angry. I don't like them. The man, he's scary. His mind is black.' Suddenly Anton became agitated, consumed by fear. 'They're here for you! Oh, Hilda, you should hide!'

The silence filled with a groaning creak: feet on the stairs. Hilda jumped into her bed and pulled her blankets down until she was deep within its protective shell. She curled up into a ball, lying to herself that she was safe.

The bedroom door opened with a pensive rasp. Hilda held her breath, listening. She felt a hand on her blanket and she flinched, curling up tighter and tighter. Then the sheets were pulled away and her face was bathed in the accusing light of her father's lantern.

'Hilda,' he said grimly, 'come with me.' He turned to Anton's nest of blankets. 'You too, little one.'

As the door to the sitting room was pushed open Hilda saw two strangers, a man and a woman just as Anton had perceived. The man warmed his hands on the fire, his chiselled features bathed in the orange glow. His dark eyes looked up and he smiled at Hilda, welcoming and soothing. She felt her father's hand on her back, pushing her hesitant frame into the room. In the flickering shadows was the woman, her pale skin contrasting with her red hair, like the sun and the moon colliding.

'You must be Hilda,' the man said. His voice was friendly, reassuring. Hilda felt her defences dropping, then she saw her mother sat in an armchair, her face hidden in her hands.

'I will talk to her,' her father's voice retorted with a quiet anger, and the man at the fireplace lost his smile. 'Sit down, Hilda.'

Hilda and Anton sat on the couch, huddling together for protection. Anton sniffled to himself, hardly holding back his fearful tears. Hilda straightened her back and put her arm round her younger brother. 'It's all right, Anton,' she said doggedly. 'I'm here.' She felt better focusing on her brother, protecting him. It took her mind off the man at the fireplace. She hardly dared look at him.

Her father, an indomitable man at the best of times, stood in front of her, shrunken, a broken echo of his usual character. He brushed his thick moustache nervously, his deep-set eyes flitting between the two strangers. 'Now, listen here, Hilda,' he said awkwardly. 'These people, well, they want you to do something for them.'

'They'll kill me!' Anton cried out pathetically. 'And Mother! And Father!'

179

'That's enough!' Hilda's father shouted, but Anton wailed defiantly.

Suddenly the flames in the fireplace grew violently, turning a deep golden green. The tendrils of flame licked at the edges of the fireplace, singeing the wallpaper before retreating back into the hearth. The man stared at the fire, seemingly unaffected by the great burst of heat and light that had silenced the room.

'It is very late,' the man said at last in a calm resonance. 'I am sure these young minds are tired, so I will make this as brief as I possibly can. My name is Rouland Delamare and this is Mrs Jane McBride. Hilda, we need your help.' He turned from the fire and faced her again, his magnetic gaze unavoidable.

'You are a Yard Boy,' Rouland continued.

Hilda suppressed a gasp. How could this stranger know her secret?

'Yes,' the man smiled coldly, 'your family has tried to hide this from me, but I have known of you for some time.'

Hilda looked up at her father and she suddenly knew she was alone at the centre of a great and terrible storm.

'Something was stolen from me tonight,' Rouland said bitterly. 'A book was taken from my companion' – his eyes flashed momentarily to the flame-haired woman – 'a book that is very important to me. Two boys from upstream came into Mrs McBride's home, stole the book and murdered her poor husband. The book is called *On the*

Nature of the Concealed Realms by Magnus Hafgan. It was taken out of time, from this year of 1813. It was taken upstream. To the future. Do you understand?'

Hilda nodded cautiously.

'Good. I would like you to find this book for me, Hilda.'

Hilda pushed herself into the soft back of the couch. She felt hemmed in, trapped. 'I can't...' she said feebly.

The man at the fireplace smiled patiently, his eyes burning like the coal in front of him. 'You can. You will find it and return it to me here or...' Rouland stared at Anton, his smile growing.

'Or he'll kill us,' Anton sniffed. 'All of us.'

Rouland chuckled. 'Thank you, Anton, you are a clever young fellow.'

Hilda's brain erupted with a thousand questions. Her normally ordered thoughts crumbled, eroded by the flood of emotions that suddenly consumed her. She looked to her father. His deep, stern eyes were glassy with tears.

Her mother began to sob uncontrollably. 'She's a slip of a girl. She can't help you. Please, leave us in peace.' The words fell into the rhythm of her tears until her pleading became unintelligible.

Rouland looked to his companion. 'Take her out. Get her a drink.'

The woman nodded and lifted Hilda's mother out of her chair, in defiance of her cries and protests. The terrible sound faded into the depths of the house until the room drowned in silence.

At last Rouland spoke again, his voice low and potent. 'You know what you must do.'

'No,' Hilda shivered.

'You must go to the future and find my book, or I will kill your family.'

'But that's not possible. I can't—'

Rouland's eyes flashed with a fury that choked Hilda's words. 'I do not care for what you think is possible! Do you believe it possible for me to kill your family? Do you? Perhaps if I killed the boy now you would believe me. Or your father. Better still, your whining mother.'

'No!' Hilda sobbed. 'I believe you. I believe you.'

Rouland smiled, 'Of course you do. And you are wise to do so. You may doubt your own talents, but I know better. You are a Timesmith, Hilda Jude, and you are the only one who can retrieve my precious book now. I will give you' – he opened his fob watch and checked the time – 'an hour to return here with it.'

'But—' Hilda spluttered.

Rouland raised a silencing finger. 'You have as much time as the Sorrowlines allow. You can return to me as an old woman, if the task takes you that long. I really don't care, as long as you are back here in an hour with my book.' He opened his jacket and retrieved a small brown envelope and threw it at Hilda. 'This contains everything you need to know about the book and descriptions of the boys who took it from me. It is not much, but it is all I have.'

Hilda caught the envelope, her hands trembling. 'But...' she began, faltering.

'You are about to ask me how you can possibly find them, yes?' Rouland said impatiently. 'Come now, girl. A Timesmith understands the patterns of ebb and flow within the Sorrowlines. The grave the boys used is detailed in the paperwork I have given you: if you are quick you will sense the route they took. You will be able to follow them.'

Hilda stared at her father, his broad face streaked with tears.

'Go,' he said quietly. 'Live your life. Forget us and this monster—'

'But she won't,' Rouland interrupted. 'How can a girl ever forget her father? Her mother? Her brother? Knowing she is the key to saving their lives? Such a burden can crush a soul. Hilda will not give up on you.'

Hilda looked at Anton. His frightened pale face pleaded with her to take him away, to make it all better.

'Father...' Hilda blurted out. 'Why don't you fight for me?'

'Child,' her father grimaced. 'I cannot.' His fists tensed by his sides, as if held in place by an unseen force.

'Oh, he is a good man,' Rouland soothed. 'He would fight for you until the very last drop of his blood, if he could. But I will not allow it. Brute force is not my weapon. My powers are more . . . persuasive.' His finger touched the side of his forehead. 'The mind is far more powerful than muscle and flesh.' Rouland nodded and her father fell into a chair.

'Go, child,' her father insisted breathlessly, 'while you still can.'

Hilda turned away. She couldn't bear to look at any of them any more.

In the hallway was the family crypt, a sacred alcove found in the larger First World households. In it were memorials to her ancestors, a fine lineage for a noble family. Her eyes rested on the skull of her grandmother. She had died last autumn and since then she had rested here on the stone plinth.

Bone, stone and sorrow.

Hilda touched the skull lightly with her trembling fingertips and she vanished into the Sorrowlines beyond.

23

SUBMISSION

Jack's lungs filled with air, dusty and dry. He coughed violently, knocking himself off balance.

'Shush!' Hilda scolded from somewhere nearby.

Jack's hand found a wall and he steadied his fragile frame. All around him was shrouded in darkness. As his stinging eyes adjusted to the gloom, the frail glow of a dying fire revealed a large living room. Above the fire was a circular crest, like a coat of arms. The design caught his eye; it was vaguely familiar. Where had he seen it before? he wondered.

'Where are we? When?' Jack asked warily, already guessing at the answers.

Hilda replied meekly, 'This is my home, in 1813.'

The date rang like a bell inside Jack's mind. He'd been to this time before, with Davey, to retrieve the book by Magnus Hafgan. It had been an arduous adventure, but they had stolen it from a woman, a servant of Rouland's, called Jane McBride. Now he was back and every nerve in his body screamed for him to get out. He was about to search out the Sorrowline that had brought him here, desperate to escape, when movement caught his eye. His stomach sank.

'I had a wager,' a woman's penetrating voice echoed from the darkness. 'I swore you would not return, young girl, but Rouland thought otherwise.'

A form grew out of the blackness and became recognisable. The woman, tall and elegant, with a pale face crowned by distinctive red hair, stepped into the light. Jack gasped.

'I see you found the boy,' Jane McBride said to Hilda. 'He has the book?'

Hilda turned away from Jack and nodded regretfully.

Jane McBride smiled. She walked up to Jack, her face bubbling with rage. 'You stole that book from me, and killed my husband. I was grateful for the latter, but I will have my book back now.'

'It was an accident,' Jack replied, stalling to think.

'Yes, I know. He was trampled by a horse and cart. But he was chasing you, wasn't he?' Jane laughed to herself. 'You carry the guilt well for one so young. It ages you. Now: the book.' She held out her hand.

'No.'

'Then the girl's family dies. Surely she has already told you this. You are dealing with powers greater than a mere Yard Boy, even a Timesmith, can understand. Give it to me now and you might yet live.'

'I said no.' Jack felt the tendrils of the Rose clamouring to the surface from somewhere deep within him. He fought to calm his mind, to quell his tempestuous impulses, but this time he refused to turn to Hilda for help. He shut her out. Jack allowed the Rose to grow out from his mind, to touch the woman in front of him . . . a gentle push, just enough.

'How?' Jane said in amazement. She took a step back. 'Give me the book!'

'Jack!' Hilda pleaded. 'They'll kill my family. It's just a book.'

Jack listened, the Rose fine-tuning his senses: the house was still, empty and quiet – Hilda's family were not here. He turned back to Jane and bore into her mind.

'Please!' Hilda begged, pulling at his arm. 'Give her the book!' Her fingers clawed at his clothes, searching.

He ignored her and pushed further into Jane McBride's dark mind. One question burrowed into her synapses: *Where is the family?*

Suddenly, like an electric charge, the reply came back to him, loud and painful. His concentration faltered and he fell out of her mind.

Hilda was hitting him in the face, clawing and screaming for her mother, her father, her brother. Jack grabbed her hands and held her close to him, forcing her to stop.

'Your family,' he began, but emotion took over his voice. Tears rivered over his cheeks as he tried to tell her what he had discovered. 'Hilda, your family, I'm sorry but they're already dead. Rouland killed them, moments after you left.'

The images stolen from Jane McBride's mind bled out involuntarily. Hilda couldn't avoid it. She saw first-hand the execution of them all. She closed her eyes but the images would not stop, bursting into her mind like a blast of radio signal with the dial turned up to full, Jack's mind the uncontrolled transmitter. He tried to stop it, to shut her out, but it was too late. The horrifying images were embedded in both their minds like grotesque paintings.

Rouland had choked her father with his bare hands, smiling as he watched the old man's eyes roll back into his skull and his face turn red, then blue. The memories were so real Jack's throat closed up and he clawed to push away phantom hands.

Hilda's mother: Rouland had snapped her neck. The deadly deed was rapid, but death came only after long minutes of unbearable pain. The crack set Jack's teeth on edge. His face cooled as he felt the blood in her veins stop pumping. He could feel it all, and he knew Hilda could too.

And Anton, poor tiny Anton, he watched it all, his eyes as wide as saucers, watching his parents die. Then Rouland turned on him, filling his terrified mind with lies about his family, about Hilda. She had abandoned him, he said. She hated her snotty-nosed sibling, with his constant whining and moaning. She was glad he would soon be dead. And in the end Anton had believed it all. Rouland had then pushed inside his brain and burst a blood vessel, watching with morbid fascination as the boy died in his arms. And then he drank tea as his servants removed the bodies and cleaned the room. When his drink was finished Rouland had left. Only Jane McBride remained.

Hilda fell to the floor, screaming with grief as her world collapsed in on itself.

A slow, devious cackle erupted from Jane McBride. 'You have power, yes. But you lack experience. You dare to enter my mind, and you do not protect your own. You gave away many things, boy.'

'You can't hurt me now,' Jack said angrily.

'I can! I will! I know of Durendal, I know of your search. Do you think I will not warn my master?'

The rage of the Rose filled Jack's veins. 'How can you warn him...' He hesitated, his doubts fighting with the temptations surging within him, and then he continued, 'If you're already dead?'

Jane's voice trembled with hatred, 'You think you can kill me? Stop me before I tell what I know? You are not the warrior you think you are. Besides,' Jane mocked, 'my master is here.'

There was a dull click as the front door opened. A chill breeze passed through the room and the glowing embers danced in the fireplace.

Hilda rose up quickly in a blur of rage and rushed for the door. Jack pulled her back as she kicked and clawed to be free.

'You can't kill him, Hilda. He's too strong for you,' Jack said quickly.

She turned to him, her glassy eyes pleading. 'No, but you can. The Rose can.'

She took his hand in hers and was immediately inside his mind. But this time she wasn't soothing him, she wasn't calming him. Her rage flooded into him, stirring up the Rose, encouraging him to let it loose.

The echo of footsteps grew closer.

'We have company?' Rouland's smooth voice called out playfully.

'Please, don't! You have to help me control it!' Jack cried softly to Hilda. 'You have to make me stronger!'

'No!' Hilda replied dispassionately. 'Let it out, Jack. Let the Rose free. Do it!'

He felt the Rose respond, surging up, and he couldn't fight it any longer. He stretched out his arm in front of his face and a glowing ball of white energy grew in his palm.

The door opened and Rouland entered. At first his face was full of smug contempt, then his world went white.

Jack felt the Rose's energy unleash itself on Rouland, burning into him like arrows of fire. The room was awash with the primal fires of Otherworld. At its centre were the dark silhouettes of Jack and Hilda.

Rouland recoiled, unprepared for this attack, unable to see beyond the wall of white.

Jack pushed home his advantage. With each passing moment he felt his control of the Rose strengthen, his understanding increase. He saw the skin evaporate from Rouland's skull and his jaw sagging open as fire spewed out from his mouth. The walls around Rouland caught fire and he began to scream.

A wave of calm circled into Jack, and he felt the Rose recede again deep into him. Satisfaction filled his body, a weary blissfulness that made him feel whole again. But then his mother's face came into his mind and the satisfaction was doused by guilt.

Rouland slumped to the ground, his cindered hand clawing at his long coat.

'Enough,' Jack said weakly, feeling suddenly vulnerable.

Hilda looked up at him in a daze. 'Finish him!'

Jack lowered his voice to a whisper: 'We have to go, now.'

Rouland didn't move. Flames licked at his clothes. What remained of his skin was stretched tight over his bones, his skeletal face contorted in a frozen sculpture of agony.

Jack turned to find Jane McBride cowering in the corner, still stunned and dazed from his assault. She stared at Rouland's broken body, disbelief written across her sinister features, hardly noticing Jack and Hilda.

He had to get out of here. Jack dragged Hilda's sobbing frame past the hideously burned body, shielding them from the burning doorway, to the shrine in the hall. He put his hand on the skull and searched for a Sorrowline. He didn't care where it took them. Anywhere but here.

Nothing. He could find nothing. He felt sick.

'Hilda,' Jack pleaded.

She took her shaking hand and placed it on top of his. He felt his senses combine with hers, searching, sensing, pleading. The faintest of Sorrowlines suddenly opened up and Jack and Hilda disappeared from 1813.

The burning heat in Rouland's body began to subside, but it was too late for his eyes – they didn't work any more and he was trapped in darkness. What had happened to him? He could hardly comprehend it: he had almost been killed. *Him!* That was impossible.

He had not seen his attacker, hidden behind the lightning, but he could guess: Hilda Jude. But although the girl may be a Timesmith, she did not possess the sort of power that he had suffered. And the smell had stayed with him, the fragrant odour of Otherworld. He was sure his attacker was connected to that elusive realm some- how. Could it be, he wondered, that this attack was the work of the Rose of Annwn? Long ago he had taken the

Rose from Otherworld and briefly wallowed in its power before it was lost to him. Had it really been in front of him? Within his grasp? It was a puzzle that occupied his mind between the pulses of unbearable pain. His broken fingers touched the sword hidden under his coat and his burnt heart surged with relief.

Durendal.

Almost at once he felt its healing energy trickle into his limbs.

Not enough. Not nearly enough.

After a moment he could move his arms. Another moment and he tested his jaw. It opened and closed, but he could not speak. His throat gurgled.

'Master?'

The voice was far away, muffled.

'You live?'

This time it was louder, clearer, and he felt a hand on his. Jane. He smelled her perfume. His relief was tempered with pity as he realised what he must do. If only he could speak, he could explain it to her. She would understand, he was certain.

His fingers cracked loudly as they found the hilt of his sword and tightened around it. He summoned up all his strength, all his rage and thrust the sword forwards, hoping it would find its target.

Jane made a small noise, a half-cry carried on a gasp of surprise.

Durendal had not failed him. Already it began to feed, and Rouland felt its energies surging through him.

Vision returned as a blur of colour, slowly fixing itself into focus. There was Jane in front of him, the sword in her chest. An expression of confusion settled on her beautiful face, and Rouland felt a pang of guilt. He shrugged it away. It was a weakness after all.

She would understand.

'When...' His mouth still hurt, and the words came slowly at first, slurred and delicate. 'When I am well... when I am restored, I will resurrect you. I promise you that much, Jane. You will be my servant again, the last and greatest of my Paladin. I will make you more than you ever were...more than you ever could possibly be. I will remake you into something infinitely better.'

He leaned forward, his restored features illuminated in the green glow of the sword, and kissed her tenderly on her cold face, watching as the life left her eyes.

24

FAMILY TREE

Davey stared in disbelief at the expanding fireball as it rushed towards him. A rasp of hot air preceded it, shaking him from his daze. Instincts took over and he began to sprint away. He stole a brief glance over his shoulder and saw the twisted metal hull of the burning realm ship falling towards him, spitting molten droplets ahead of it. He ran faster, turning down a smaller gantry, desperate to evade the descending vessel.

He heard a fierce impact, and another explosion lifted him off his feet. The air about him rippled with heat and Davey was thrown onto the gantry. He scrambled for cover as a wall of soot and fire and smoke consumed him. For an instant he felt he was back in the firestorm that had destroyed the Hanging Tavern.

As his world went dark his fingers found a metal grate in the floor. He pulled at it as his back became uncomfortably hot. The grate came away and Davey threw himself into the waste pipe below. He fell into it, propelled by a rush of burning wind behind him. Faster and faster he slid down the pipe, away from the scalding orange fire until he fell into a pool of stinking water. He scrambled to the side as hot fragments of metal showered down from above, igniting the fumes from the liquid. Davey climbed the outer fence that lined the pool and ran aimlessly from the spreading fire.

He rested a safe distance from the flames, coughing his lungs clean. He watched the fire for a time, in awe of its hypnotic beauty, then he remembered his mission and he began to ascend again, moving quickly back towards the *Orion*'s berth. As he came to the next level he felt the hairs on his neck bristle. Something was wrong. Davey stopped and turned towards a stone statue in the middle on an opening. He recognised it immediately – these memori-mortuus were dotted all over Ealdwyc. The larger houses had their own family memorials inside their homes but the rest of the First World population made do with these public spaces.

'What is it, Davey?' he wondered aloud, staring at the recesses full of bones. 'What's up?' He reached out and touched one of the skulls, uncertain what he expected to sense. His fingertips tingled. The sensation rose up his hand, then his arm. He was suddenly afraid, and retreated back from the statue. A brief wind picked up around him, swirling for a moment then dying again. Suddenly Davey realised he was no longer alone. There were two people, a boy and a girl, standing next to the statue exactly where he had just been. His heart raced faster as excitement grew. The boy was the right build, he had the same unkempt wavy brown hair, the same clothes. He was certain now: it was Jack!

Davey began to run towards him and the girl, his mission momentarily abandoned as he was overcome with joy at the sight of his friend.

'Jack!' Davey laughed. Then he saw his friend's face, grim, haggard, covered in grime. Jack managed a feeble smile back as he leaned against him. He felt slight, like he might blow away. 'What happened to you?'

'Later,' Jack said heavily.

Davey faced the girl. She looked even worse than Jack, her face streaked with tears. Her wild hair fell about her lowered head, but Davey caught a flash of her green eyes before she looked away. He registered the girl's grief, the hopelessness that pushed her shoulders down, and he felt an instinctive urge to care for her.

He realised he was staring and looked away. 'Who's she?' he asked Jack.

'Hilda,' Jack said regretfully. 'She's a Timesmith, from 1813' – he leaned in closer – 'and Rouland's just killed her family.'

'Why didn't you kill him?' The two boys turned to see Hilda. Her voice was small but filled with rage. 'You had the chance to kill Rouland, but you didn't! You could have killed him for good!'

'He looked pretty dead to me!' Jack replied anxiously.

'Rouland was still alive,' she continued. 'We both knew it. I felt you hold back. You stopped when you could have finished it. He survived. He killed my family and you let him live.'

Jack stood in silence, staring at Hilda. 'I'm sorry. I . . . I couldn't do it.'

Davey edged up to them anxiously. 'Jack, we have to go.'

Jack suddenly grabbed Davey by his collar, scrutinising his neck. 'What's that?' he said eventually, his words tinged with hostility.

'What?'

'On your neck.' Jack gestured to the green tattoo that curled up from his shoulder, snaking behind his ear.

'It's from Gremmen sap,' Davey said proudly. 'It saved my life.'

'*He* had that mark,' Jack said, his eyes unreadable.

'Who?'

'Old David.'

The words fell on Davey like a death sentence. Jack was talking about Davey's future self. They had met him in 2008 at the climax of the battle with Rouland – the battle that had led to Jack's mother's death. Old David had been in league with Rouland, full of hate and bitterness. Davey stroked the mark on his neck. 'It don't mean nothing!' he said defensively. 'I'm still me!'

Jack did not reply. His eyes were cold, untrusting.

'Really, Jack! I was dying. Hardacre – he's a realm ship captain – he saved my life with his blood. The mark is just the Gremmen sap! That's how I got it. I've not changed. It's just a mark, is all.'

Jack remained silent, his face full of uncertainty, then he let go of Davey's shirt.

In the distance something popped, reminding Davey of the fire. 'Never mind that anyway!' he said. 'The Paladin are here, and I've made a little diversion' – Davey glanced over his shoulder at the flames – 'which might have gotten a bit out of hand. We can talk about all this later! We need to get to the *Orion*, now!'

'The *Orion*?' Jack asked.

'A realm ship. You want to stop Rouland coming back, don't you?'

Suddenly Hilda focused on Davey for the first time. 'Yes!' she said.

'Well, we're gonna find Durendal before the Paladin. We can stop him for good!'

'Lead on,' Hilda said, pushing past Jack.

Davey looked at Jack. He had a terrible feeling, deep in his gut, that things had changed between them, and that it might never be the same again. Remorsefully he turned his back on his grandson-to-be and led the way towards the *Orion*.

25

INSIDE THE CLOUD

Rage consumed Eloise, pure, red and primal. Francesco's motionless body lay in a pool of blood close to the feet of her Paladin attacker. Captain de Vienne laughed as she waited for the inevitable attack.

Eloise lunged forward, attacking Captain de Vienne with an animal fury. The Paladin captain reacted quickly, blocking the wild onslaught. Eloise cried out above the clatter of their swords, a guttural, wordless scream. They moved as one, each parrying the other's move. Their arms became a blur as they fought on, moving along the dockside.

'You will tell me where the Morrow boy is hidden!' Captain de Vienne shouted.

'I'll kill you!' Eloise screamed.

The Paladin captain lunged forwards, forcing Eloise to retreat. She felt the cold metal hull of the *Orion* slam into her back and the Paladin's sword arm whirred towards her head. She rolled to the side, narrowly missing the deadly blade. Instead, it tore into the ship, ripping at the pipes embedded just below the hull. Steam erupted out of the gash, clouding the platform. Suddenly Eloise and Captain de Vienne were alone in the cloud, their surroundings hidden behind the wall of white.

Eloise rushed at the Paladin captain, her need for vengeance overwhelming everything else. Almost at once she knew it was a mistake. Her opponent parried, rolled aside and was behind her. She felt the blade cut into her back as she spun away.

Stupid, she scolded herself. She should not have let her anger cloud her thoughts. She retreated into the haze as she tried to calm her mind.

'Eloise!' The voice seemed far away, dampened by the gas. It belonged to Hardacre. She ignored it. She had to block out the pain in her back and focus on the Paladin. She had to end this quickly.

'You have lost!' Captain de Vienne was upon her, raising her sword above Eloise.

The pain in her back was growing, climbing up in between her shoulders. Her vision flickered in and out of focus and Captain de Vienne's face drifted like a ghost. Her sword had gone, lost in the mist, and Eloise felt her very life-force ebbing away.

She heard the spinning sword coming at her and she moved without thinking, surprising even herself with her latent agility. Where was the Paladin now? She had lost sight of her. Eloise rolled to the left, a gamble, hoping it would take her away from her attacker. She felt something cold under her leg and reached for it, grabbing the hilt of her sword. At that same moment Captain de Vienne lunged at her, piercing Eloise's arm.

The Paladin captain laughed, her teeth flashing like a wolf's. Then a puzzled expression crossed her brow, and she looked down: Eloise's sword was in her chest.

'Better,' Captain de Vienne said with a smile, but Eloise heard the suppressed pain in her voice. She took her chance and pulled her sword out, readying it for the next strike. Captain de Vienne saw it coming and retreated, yanking her own sword from Eloise's arm.

The pain raged through Eloise's body and for a moment she could barely stand. She opened her eyes, focusing, and saw the Paladin. The instant seemed to freeze in front of her, as her attacker's sword swung for her throat. Eloise danced free, barely clearing the blade. She felt it tear into the side of her neck. But the Paladin captain had overreached herself and began to fall towards Eloise.

At that moment Cayden's youthful face came to her mind. 'You killed my husband!' Eloise cried out.

Captain de Vienne scoffed, adjusting her stance as she readied herself for the next assault. 'We are Paladin! We serve only Rouland. We love only Rouland! There can be nothing more!' She swung her blade again, its angry mechanism spinning noisily.

Eloise retaliated, and her sword found its mark: the only certain way she knew to despatch a Paladin. Captain de Vienne's headless body flopped onto the floor and a stillness descended around Eloise. She felt an uneasy remorse for her former sister, finally at peace after so many decades of hatred.

'You were wrong, Alda,' she said. 'You were always wrong. There is so much more.'

'That's her: the *Orion*!' Davey said excitedly as he led Jack and Hilda towards one of the odd-looking realm ships. He held up a cautionary hand as he slowed his approach. 'There's someone there.'

'Where?' Jack couldn't see anyone, a cloud of drifting steam hiding part of the platform from view. Then he heard the faint noises of battle, sword hitting sword. 'Is it the Paladin?'

Davey grimaced, then ducked behind a stack of cargo crates, weaving in between them to get closer to the ship. Jack kept at Davey's heels. He turned to check on Hilda. She seemed far away, unfocused, following Jack blindly. He pitied her.

'It looks like Hardacre,' Davey said quietly. For a brief instant Jack saw the shape of a man in the cloud, then he disappeared into it.

'Who's Hardacre?' Jack asked.

'Captain Jonah Hardacre. The *Orion*'s his ship.' Davey smiled enthusiastically and Jack realised how much he had missed that stupid grin.

Davey rushed forward, and Jack and Hilda followed him into the cloud. Within seconds they were surrounded by the fog. Even the massive bulk of the ship disappeared from view. They edged forward, not knowing what was ahead of them.

'There!' Jack whispered to Davey, pointing to an indefinite shape ahead of them. 'Someone's there.'

Eloise appeared out of the dissipating cloud and limped towards them. In her arms she carried the body of an old woman. Behind her another figure appeared, a lean man whose face was surrounded by a wild mane of hair.

Jack ran forward, relieved to see Eloise again. At that moment he felt his feet buckle under him and he looked down to see the entire dockside had listed to one side. The framework groaned and whined. In between the planks he saw flames licking at the pier, eating away at its structure.

The howl of fire erupted into the air as the platform began to fall apart.

'This way!' Captain Hardacre called, waving Jack and the others towards the *Orion*'s entrance ramp. The floor about them was collapsing, falling into the great void below. Fire took its place, clawing up to eat at the remaining dockside. Jack ran towards the stranger, Davey and Eloise in front of him. He took Hilda's hand and dragged her with him, up the ramp of the realm ship.

Jack felt sick as he watched the *Orion*'s entrance ramp closing. The hellish vision of fire consuming the dockside disappeared from view.

'Davey!' Hardacre cried as he ran deeper into the ship. 'I need you on the flight deck, now!'

Davey ran after him. Eloise laid the body she was carrying on the floor, touching her face tenderly. Jack edged closer, wanting to help his friend, but not knowing how.

'Her name was Francesco Carhoop,' Eloise said quietly. 'I have known her for a century. She was a dear friend, perhaps my only friend.'

Jack put his hand on Eloise's shoulder. 'You still have friends,' he managed. Eloise put her cold hand on his, her face hidden from him. He was sure she was sobbing.

'I would like to be alone now,' Eloise said, her back straightening.

Jack nodded, retreating towards Hilda. 'Come on.' He took her hand again and pulled her out of the cargo hold.

He followed his senses, listening for the faint shouting voices, until they ascended to the top of the ship. By the time they had arrived at the flight deck the ship was already moving, its engines rumbling as the *Orion* tilted away from its berth. Like the rest of the ship the flight deck looked functional, with open wall panels that exposed a multitude of pipes, but here some effort had been made to insulate the room. The curved walls were covered in places with what appeared to be a faded patterned carpet, tacked tightly into place against the metal beams. Jack surmised this was where the captain spent most of his time, and he had afforded it some small amount of comfort. There were four seats in a horseshoe layout, facing out onto a bubble of glass that gave a wide view of the harbour outside. Hardacre and Davey sat at a console of switches and dials.

Hardacre was saying to Davey, 'Anything we can do about that fire out there? *Orion*'s been sitting here for weeks. Water tanks need emptying anyway.'

Davey flicked a switch and there was a deep vibration. Jack looked out of one of the tiny windows. The fire had done its worst, but still raged on, eating up anything in its path. As he watched, the ship dipped back towards the platform, then rose upwards. A spray of water erupted from somewhere beneath him, and doused the flames. A wall of grey-white smoke rolled up to the window, caking it with wet ash that obliterated Jack's view.

Eloise appeared behind Jack and Hilda, her grubby face fixed in a grim expression.

Captain Hardacre turned to see her step onto the flight deck. 'The death of Francesco was a pity, and I'm sorry. But a deal is a deal. I have the *Orion* and we are underway.

I have fulfilled my part of the bargain. It is your turn now. If we stand a hope of finding Niflheim, I'll need to see Hafgan's book.'

Eloise wiped her face and said, 'I have led you here under a false pretence. I do not have the book.' She looked up and acknowledged Jack for the first time, her dark eyes adrift in a sea of hopeless tears. 'Do you have it, Jack?'

Jack stepped forwards, nodding. 'Yes. Why does he want it?'

'To find a way to Niflheim, where Durendal's supposed to be,' Davey butted in before either Eloise or Hardacre could reply.

Jack hesitated. He'd looked after this book since he and Davey had brought it back from 1813. The thought of giving it over to a stranger filled him with apprehension. But when he looked at Eloise he felt reassured and he offered up the book to the captain.

Hardacre held it with both hands, as if it was made of glass. His face changed as he stared at it, his wiry eyebrows raised, and his grim demeanour consumed by awe. 'Is this genuine? Is this Hafgan's book?'

'I believe it is,' Eloise replied. 'But you tell me.'

Hardacre switched an overhead lamp on and stooped to look closer at the book cover. He remained there for several long minutes, turning the book over in his hand, studying the embossed letters. Eventually he said, 'The leather is of the correct age, and the lettering seems to be of the period. But all of that can easily be forged, of course. Tell me, how did you come upon this?'

'I stole it,' Davey said proudly. 'I went through a Sorrowline to 1813.'

Hardacre looked doubtfully at Davey. 'Nonsense.'

'It is true,' confirmed Eloise.

'Course it's true. I don't lie!' said Davey. 'I took it from Jane McBride and brought it back to 1940.'

'And Jack brought *you* back,' Eloise said reproachfully.

'True enough,' Davey conceded, smiling at Jack.

Hardacre whistled. 'Jane McBride. Hafgan's book. You dabble in legends.' He let out a chuckle of amazement, oblivious to his companions, and opened the cover, inspecting each new page with growing respect.

'When you came to me in my prison I thought you were lying,' he said at last. 'I was content to be free, to return to my *Orion*. I never thought you really had this book. I see now I was wrong. Amazing!' The captain stared intently at the pages. 'It's written in Luidian, one of the old languages of Otherworld.'

'Reckon you can read it?' Davey sniffed, putting his feet up on the console.

Hardacre scowled until Davey sat up properly. 'It shares some common traits with Old Norse and Gaelic writing. It is all but a dead language.'

Davey peered at the confusing text. 'Is that a no?'

Hardacre smirked. 'I can read it well enough! But it will take some time to understand it.'

'Time? How long?'

Hardacre closed the book. 'If you continue to interrupt my thoughts it will be an eternity, I am certain!'

Davey feigned offence as he climbed out of the seat.

'And get off my flight deck!' Hardacre growled. 'All of you!'

'I can fly this thing better than you!' Davey protested.

'Get out, boy!'

'It's boring anyway,' Davey grumbled as he herded Jack, Eloise and Hilda away. 'Let's go see if the galley has anything in it worth eating.'

As they walked away from the flight deck Jack heard Captain Hardacre shout, 'I'm taking us out of Newton Harbour, to the Interim. We'll wait there till I can plot our course.'

Davey grinned at Jack and grabbed hold of an exposed hull beam. 'Oh, you won't like this, not one bit!'

'Like what?' Jack asked. 'And what's the Interim?'

Davey didn't reply. The ship's engines shifted up in pitch and the hull vibrated noisily. Jack felt the deck beneath his feet lurch up, tilting steeply, and they all fell to the side. An uneasy sensation ripped at his legs, like they were being pulled away from him. His face went cold, and he was gripped by vertigo. By the expressions on Davey and Hilda's faces, Jack knew they felt it too.

His vision became blurred, his throat dry. He felt as if his skull was too small for his brain. He managed to raise his head and look out of the flight-deck windows. They appeared to be far away, at the end of a vast metal tunnel, and the harbour outside was being torn apart.

26

IN THE INTERIM

Almost as soon as it began the discomfort passed. As Jack's watery eyes refocused, Davey's grinning face loomed into view. 'It's good, innit?' his grandfather-to-be laughed.

'No, not really.'

Hilda was patting herself down, rearranging her dress. 'The first time is always the worst,' she offered.

Jack staggered back along the corridor that led to the flight deck and peered through the windows: the harbour was gone. In its place was a sea of red, thick with patterns, swirling and shifting like currents in a lake.

'It's the Interim,' Hardacre said, looking over his shoulder at Jack. 'Beautiful.'

There was a hypnotic quality to the red motion, but it made Jack feel uneasy, afraid, like it was alive and gazing back at him. His head began to spin.

'Don't stare too much, Jack,' Davey said, pulling at his arm. 'Not till you get used to it.'

Jack held his stomach, sucked in the cool air and

waited for the sickly sensation to pass. Hilda stared at him, her expression fixed. Then, to his surprise, she offered him her hand. Jack took it, steadying himself.

'Better?' she asked eventually.

Jack nodded, noticing the faint green tattoo markings on Captain Hardacre's skin, the same as those on Davey's neck. They reminded him so much of Old David. He knew it was irrational, but he couldn't shake those dark memories of betrayal. One day, he thought, Davey would follow that destructive path. He looked at his young grandfather; he seemed as jovial as ever, the same as when he had first met him. But Jack knew that Davey's mental powers were stirring – he'd seen the first evidence of it in their battle in St Paul's, the first tentative steps on the road to becoming an Operator.

'What're you staring at?' Davey asked.

Jack forced a smile and looked away, still feeling light-headed.

'Come on!' Davey said. 'This view isn't doing you any good.' He led the way out of the flight deck to the ship's galley, barely hiding his impatience at Jack's slow progress. The room was cramped and functional, dominated by a rectangular table with benches fitted to the floor. A narrow kitchen lay beyond the old table. Hilda guided Jack to a seat, while Davey peered out of one of the small windows.

'It's not very nice, is it?' Hilda said quietly.

'Outside?'

She nodded. 'The Interim. It's the place between realms. No one likes it, not really. They say you get used to it, but I don't think that's true. I never have.' Hilda shuddered.

Jack glanced at Davey, staring out of the window. 'Will we be here long?'

'Nah,' Davey replied without looking. 'Hardacre won't want to hang around.'

'Why not?'

Davey strode over to Jack, smiling devilishly. 'Reckon there's things out there' – he gestured to the window – 'weird things!'

'Rubbish!' Hilda grumbled loudly. 'You talk such nonsense!'

'It's true!' Davey protested. 'Ask Hardacre, he'll tell you! Anyway, you don't know nothing about me!'

Hilda rolled her eyes. 'I know who you are, Davey. You're Jack's grandfather.'

'That's true,' Davey said, winking at Jack. 'I've been around. I know a thing or two about stuff. And I've been on a few of these realm ships 'n'all, not just as a passenger, I've helped fly these things! I know what I'm talking about.'

'As have I.' Hilda smiled.

Davey hesitated, then dismissed Hilda's claim with a shrug. 'You don't know what's out there!'

'*I* know,' said Eloise, entering the room, 'and there is little to fear.'

Jack was pleased to see her. He'd barely spoken to her since his return to 1940, as things had happened so quickly. He hoped now they might have time to rest, to recover, to talk. As he looked about the room he was struck by how much they had all endured.

Eloise had lost an old friend and Jack wondered what Francesco had meant to her, how much they had been through together.

Outwardly Hilda seemed the most damaged; having witnessed her family's execution, it was little wonder. It would take years to come to terms with those images.

And then Jack thought of himself and was shocked to realise it was only a handful of days since he had seen his mother die. It was strange to think of it in those terms. After all, he'd lived with his mother's death since he was seven. When he had discovered he was a Yard Boy and learned about Sorrowlines he had returned to that time to try to change her fate. But he had changed nothing. As he stared at his companions he felt cold and small.

'Empty!' Davey exclaimed. 'Not a thing to eat!' He slammed the cupboard shut and joined Jack and Hilda at the table. 'Some realm ship!'

'What does a realm ship do, exactly?' Jack enquired.

Davey stared at Jack, smiling. 'I forgot how thick you

214

were! Realm ships connect our realm to all the other ones. We can come and go on these realm ships. But it ain't easy. And hardly anyone has been to Niflheim before.'

'Because it's a Concealed Realm?'

'See!' Davey laughed. 'You're learning. How about I give you a tour of the ship? Show you where everything is?'

Jack nodded, then remembered Eloise at his side. 'Eloise? How are—'

'Go,' she said flatly.

Jack understood her desire to be alone.

'Hilda?' Jack called out. She looked up slowly, her mind elsewhere. 'Come with us.'

She pulled herself up and sheepishly followed Jack and Davey without a word.

Davey wallowed in his role as host and tour guide, showing them around the three decks of the *Orion*, pointing out the weapons locker, the hammocks, the grappling hooks, the storage hold and the oddly fascinating engine room with its multitude of rotating parts that generated some sort of magnetic field.

Jack turned to Hilda, wanting to share the strangeness of this place with her, but she didn't seem to notice. She viewed the world with the same detachment she'd displayed since they'd returned from 1813. At first he felt frustration, then he recalled the terrible images of her tortured family and he felt nothing but guilt and shame.

'You've been on realm ships often?' Jack asked, hoping to engage her.

Hilda nodded solemnly.

It was with her father, Jack presumed, feeling foolish, so he let the subject drop.

It was some hours later that Hardacre finally appeared in the galley. The captain had changed out of his grey prison clothes. He wore dark trousers tucked into polished leather boots and a long red coat that gave him the appearance of a great general. Only his wild grey hair and piercing eyes defied the air of respectability. In his hand was a four-barrelled pistol that he caressed and polished with admiration. Jack had dozed off, stretched out on the floor. He awoke to the sound of excited voices around him.

'It's blindingly simple!' Hardacre said to Eloise, laughing.

Jack raised himself up onto his elbow, rubbing the sleep from his eyes.

'What is?' Eloise replied.

'Hafgan's solution! Are you not listening?'

'To be fair, you ain't making much sense yet!' Davey put in.

Jack realised Hilda was sat next to him, her arms crossed over her knees. She smiled as he looked up at her. There was kindness in those eyes, just like he remembered in his mother's.

'They were right!' Hardacre said, waving the ancient book in the air. 'Hafgan is a genius. The text is a journal of his experiments, and his travels into the Concealed Realms, including Niflheim. No one else has ever been there—'

'Except Rouland,' Eloise injected.

'Except Rouland.' Hardacre nodded. 'And now I know why.'

'Negative frequency,' Hilda said. She was still smiling.

Hardacre stopped, as if he had been hit in the stomach, a comical expression of amazement on his face. 'Yes... negative frequency. How? How did you know?'

'What on earth is negative frequency?' Davey asked as he found a cigarette in his pocket and put it to his mouth.

'No smoking on my ship!' Hardacre shouted. Davey's face danced with anger, then annoyance, and finally resignation. He put the cigarette back into his pocket.

'Each realm has its own frequency, a resonance point,' Hilda said. 'If you know the frequency you can travel to that realm. The realms we travel to mostly sit in a narrow band of frequencies. Some realms have a higher frequency and are more difficult to get to. Most of the

Concealed Realms sit in this higher frequency range. But some are in the negative frequencies.'

'How come you know so much?' Davey grumbled.

'My father.'

Hardacre smoothed his peppery beard with his hand as he stared dumbfounded at Hilda. 'He was a realm ship captain?'

Hilda shook her head. 'He was a scientist and engineer, like Hafgan.'

Eloise frowned. 'Like Rouland.'

'No!' Hilda replied angrily. 'Not like Rouland. Not at all. He was a good man. He designed realm ship engines.'

'And he understood how to travel to the Concealed Realms?' Hardacre said, impressed.

'It was a theory. He would often tell me about his work, but he never got the chance to find out if he was right.'

'I think he was. Hafgan used negative frequencies to travel to Niflheim, and so can we.'

'Then do it quickly!' Eloise said. 'If the Paladin get there first, if they find the sword, then we are lost.'

'I have more study to do,' Hardacre replied, holding up the book. 'There is much to learn here.'

'Once we have the sword then you can study. If you know how to get to Niflheim then we must get underway immediately. I insist.'

Davey suppressed a chuckle, catching Jack's eye.

'Well,' Hardacre said eventually, 'if you insist . . .'

'I do.'

'Then I can hardly refuse you, can I?'

'It would be unwise.' The smallest of smiles escaped from Eloise's face.

Hardacre saw it and laughed. 'You are a formidable woman.' He bowed slightly. 'I will make preparations. We will be underway soon.' He spun round and was about to leave the galley when he spoke to Hilda, 'Perhaps you might like to join me? I think you might be able to help.'

'Her?' Davey said, aghast.

Captain Hardacre laughed heartily. Davey frowned, scowling at him.

To Jack's surprise Hilda followed the captain towards the flight deck. Jack laughed as she left. He saw that Hilda was smiling too and his heart lifted.

Davey sat down on the table, his feet on a chair, and brought out his cigarette again, forcing a casual pose. 'What's her story then?'

'Hilda?'

'No, the Queen of Sheba!' Davey said sarcastically.

Jack thought for a moment, wondering where to start. 'You already know most of it. She's a Timesmith from 1813. Rouland sent her to find us, to find that book.'

'She works for Rouland?' Eloise said tensely.

'No, no,' Jack replied. 'Rouland made her, threatened to kill her family if she didn't do it. We went back together, to 1813, but her family were dead.'

Eloise shifted uncomfortably. 'You saw Rouland?'

Jack shrugged. 'He didn't see me.' The blinding image of Rouland screaming came back into his mind.

'You're not safe left alone, Jack!' Davey laughed. 'Stick with me in future.'

Jack avoided his smiling eyes. Davey's future filled him with dread. He turned to Eloise, hoping to change the subject. 'Do you have a plan? For when we get to Niflheim, I mean.'

'Francesco told me Niflheim is a frozen wasteland of ice and darkness. There are three frozen rivers that meet at a waterfall. The sword is embedded in the ice at the top of the waterfall.'

Jack sighed. 'Why can't it be easy, just for once?'

'If it were easy,' Eloise replied, 'it would have been found and retrieved before now.'

Davey lit his cigarette and said, 'But how we gonna find this waterfall?'

'The sword is like my own,' Eloise said, tapping her weapon. 'I will be able to sense it.'

'And so will the Paladin,' Davey said.

Eloise nodded. 'We must hope we are there first.'

The metal walls rattled at the engines' changed pitch. The ship groaned, as if in protest.

Hardacre's scratchy voice came out of a speaker hanging on the wall. 'Hold onto something. We're about to give this a go.'

The engines began to vibrate again, and the rest of the ship joined in. Outside, the world of red blipped for an instant, turning white, then Jack's senses screamed.

The ship's interior flashed with a painful blue glow as it disappeared from the Interim.

27

ADRIFT WITH THE WIDOW

Dominica tensed as she entered the cabin. She had become accustomed to the appearance, the disgusting vision hidden behind lace veils, but the smell took her by surprise every time.

She cursed her Paladin captain for giving this mission to her. She understood its importance but she knew the real reason why de Vienne had chosen her. It wasn't because she was the most suited, the most able to complete it – although Dominica doubted any of her sisters would have managed to get this far. No – Captain de Vienne wanted her out of the way.

'One day I will have you, de Vienne,' Dominica cursed under her breath.

'Is that you, my master?' The voice was frail and drawn. It came from within the chamber, somewhere near the bed. Dominica straightened and remembered where she was. She stepped into the room, closing the door behind her.

'No, my Lady. It is your servant, Dominica.' She stepped forward and bowed to the rancid creature sitting in a chair next to the empty bed. 'Forgive me, I did not know you were awake.'

'I am still capable of dressing myself, girl.' The rattly voice still had strength behind it, in spite of the years. A gnarled hand came up from under the gown and pulled back the veil covering her face.

Dominica suppressed a gasp. She was wrong; she would never get used to it. The tight white translucent flesh covered a once-beautiful face with dark veins, making it appear embalmed. The eye sockets were wide, no more than skin-covered bone with receded lids that left the dry bloodshot orbs almost completely exposed. The pupils were nothing more than tiny red sightless dots. Her flame-red hair was all but gone and barely a few patches of it endured, dry and bleached, like broken twigs in winter. Her lipless, empty mouth was cracked and sore, its edges red like a scabbed-over wound.

The terrible red dots appeared to focus on Dominica as a twisted hand rose up and beckoned her to come closer. 'Why are you here?' asked the Widow.

'My Lady,' Dominica began hesitantly. 'We are lost in the Interim, adrift. Our pilot is—'

'Where am I? Tell me now?' the Widow interrupted.

Dominica cursed her mistake. It did no good to overload the Widow with too much information. She had tried to explain their situation to her before, many times. She had told her of their journey from Ealdwyc on board

Rouland's realm ship, she had explained how they had travelled far, that they had tried and failed to find Niflheim. Dominica realised it was a mistake to burden her with their failures, with the damaged engines, with the fading power supplies. She must keep it simple. 'My Lady, we are on board the *Veillantif*. We—'

'The *Veillantif*?'

'It is Master Rouland's realm ship,' Dominica said. She cursed inwardly. It was the same conversation every time she entered the Widow's chamber, the same circular discussion which led nowhere.

'Rouland!' the Widow exclaimed, her eyes drifting about the room. 'Where is my beautiful Rouland?'

'He is lost, my Lady. That is why—'

'Lost?' The Widow became agitated. 'How can he be lost? I must see his beautiful face again!'

'My Lady, we are on our way to find his sword, Durendal, so that we can revive him. He—'

'Durendal...' the Widow said wistfully. 'Yes, Durendal. It's coming back to me now. Yes, yes, I recall. The sword.'

'Yes,' Dominica replied patiently, 'the sword.'

'Rouland hated it, you know? He hated that sword. It is a living thing. We must place it out of sight, on Niflheim.'

'Yes, exactly!' Dominica said, seizing this lucid moment. 'You know the way to Niflheim, don't you?'

The Widow ceased her wild unfocused staring. Her eyes seemed to flicker with life again. 'Yes, of course I do.

Rouland entrusted me with many secrets. I was his last Paladin, you know? His greatest. He could not bear to live without me. I cheated death to be at his side, for all time.'

'I know,' Dominica said impatiently.

'He needs me, you see? I know many things. Things about the future, things even Rouland does not know.'

It was true enough, Dominica conceded to herself, that the Widow did possess insights into what awaited upstream. But her revelations were confused and incomplete, sometimes no better than a fairground fortune teller's. But she had warned Rouland about the boy from upstream, about his arrival in 1940. She had prophesised his coming. Yet that warning had been of little help. Master Rouland had been defeated.

The Widow raised up her bony hand, as if trying to reach for something in front of her. 'I met a boy, long ago. He tried to kill me, but I stopped him. I saw deep into his mind, saw the future, many things, many mysteries. It was a great gift. I learned so much in that moment. It was all so clear at the time, so clear. Now' – she let her hand drop – 'my memories elude me.'

'Yes, I know, my Lady. But your sisters have faith in you. We need the knowledge hidden in your mind. Tell me of Durendal.'

'Durendal?' the Widow said, her voice tiny now. 'You wish to know?'

'Yes!'

'I have told only one other of Durendal. Are you her?'

'Tell me, my Lady. Tell me of Durendal.'

'Are you Francesco?'

The Widow had said this name before. It was not one Dominica knew.

'You are not her. Francesco was my friend. We spoke often. Such a lovely girl.' The Widow's voice became a cracked whisper, barely audible. 'I told her of Durendal.' She brought her hand up to her dry mouth, as if she had said too much.

'I am your friend now,' Dominica said, forcing a smile. 'You can tell me.'

The Widow scowled. 'I do not know you. You are not my friend. Send me the maid, the girl Francesco. She can attend to me, not you! Where is she? It seems like years since I have seen her.' The Widow became agitated, her voice rising to its full feeble strength. 'Who are you? What have you done with her? Send me my maid at once!'

Dominica sighed. The Widow had been lucid in their travels in the Interim, loose with her secrets, and Dominica had learned her true name, something known only to Rouland. She swallowed hard, uncertain if she dared to speak it out loud. But she was losing her again. There was no time for caution.

'Jane McBride!' she demanded. 'Master Rouland commands that you assist me.'

'Jane...Mc...Bride...' The words fell from her cracked mouth one syllable at a time as the Widow drifted into a sea of recollection. 'Jane McBride. Yes, I was that woman once, long, long ago. Before I died. Before Rouland promised to resurrect me, to make me greater than any of you Paladin. But his sword had the best of me, so not even Rouland's will could make me whole again.' She clawed at her breast with stiff hands, wallowing in self-pity.

'You *will* help me!' Dominica shouted angrily.

The Widow stared up at her, confused like a child. 'Who are you? What do you want?'

'My name is Dominica. Rouland demands you travel to Niflheim. You must give me the correct frequency for our journey there, or he will be lost for ever. Rouland will be truly dead.'

Finally the Widow seemed to understand the urgency. 'Yes...yes. Quickly, fetch me paper, before I am adrift again.'

Dominica collected a notebook and pencil from the dresser. She closed the Widow's hand around the pencil and held the pad up to its tip.

'Niflheim,' the Widow whispered under her foul breath and she scrawled notes onto the paper. After several moments she dropped the pencil, exhausted. 'Give that to your pilot. He will know the way.' Her head fell back onto the chair and her eyes gazed up at the ceiling.

'Thank you, my Lady,' Dominica said reverently, reading the string of numbers and equations, barely visible on the paper. 'It is a great service that you do for our master. He will be most grateful.'

'Yes . . . yes,' the Widow replied wearily. 'Rouland . . . my beautiful Rouland. Tell me, girl, where is he? Where is my beautiful Rouland? Will he call upon me this night?'

Dominica stared at the pathetic creature in front of her. Every fibre of her yearned to wipe this abomination from the world, to eradicate her offensive face for ever. Order was beauty, after all. But she could not. In spite of everything, Rouland still cared for her. Was it guilt? she wondered.

'Rest, my Lady. Master Rouland will be with you shortly.'

The Widow's gaunt face shifted, the old muscles replaying the memory of a smile.

Dominica took the paper and left the Widow to fester in the prison of her mind.

28

NIFLHEIM

The world outside the windows was a sculpture of ice and frost. Windblown shapes, bulbous and gargantuan, stretched out of the mist to scratch at the low sky. The *Orion* weaved its way through them, beneath them, gliding nimbly past the unearthly formations. As it did so a flurry of snow rose, partially obscuring Jack's view.

'Welcome to Niflheim. Lovely, ain't it?' Davey said sarcastically.

Jack replied, 'I think it's beautiful, in a weird sort of way.'

Davey pushed in closer, steaming up the window with his hot breath. 'You ain't getting me out there! Have you seen it? Nothing could live here! We'll freeze to death.'

'We must find the sword,' Eloise reminded them from the table.

'Yeah, yeah,' Davey replied flatly.

Hardacre's voice burst over the radio from the flight deck. 'Harpoons!'

Jack was suddenly alert, expecting some sort of attack. Davey saw his fear and laughed. 'It's OK, Jack. It's the mooring harpoons. The captain needs us to help him land this thing.'

Jack nodded, not really understanding.

'Come on,' Davey put his arm round him. 'I'll show you.'

As they left the galley Eloise stood. 'This size of realm ship has at least six mooring harpoons. I will find Hilda, we will take the starboard side.'

'OK,' Davey shouted back as he led Jack down a narrow corridor that ran along the length of the realm ship. He stopped at a tiny window with a telescopic apparatus over the glass.

'See this?' Davey explained. 'Look through the eyepiece and get the target in sight. Then, when Hardacre gives the order, you press these two buttons together.' He pointed to a pair of concealed switches under the eyepiece.

'Then what?' Jack asked.

Davey smiled. 'You'll see.'

Jack frowned. Sometimes Davey annoyed him intensely. Before he could complain Davey was rushing down the corridor towards the next window. After a moment he gave a thumbs-up gesture. 'Be ready!'

Jack pushed his face into the viewfinder. The world outside was magnified through the glass. The centre was marked by a cross-hair target, but he could see nothing to aim at. Glass-like ice blurred past him, dancing in and out of snow clouds. Then the ground came into view: rugged, ice-covered rock blanketed in patchy mist. The familiar tinny noise of the communication radio crackled with Hardacre's voice. 'Now!'

Jack heard Davey firing his harpoon, then rushing to the end of the corridor to fire another one. The ship began to tilt as it became tethered. Then he felt the vibrations of the harpoons on the other side of the ship, and the deck listed back. His view was now full of grey mist again.

'Come on, Jack!' Davey was stood behind him, leaning over his shoulder.

'I can't see anything!' he replied. Then, as the ship moved closer to the ground, the mist blew up and a patch of rock loomed into view. Jack pressed the buttons and the harpoon flew free. He saw the rope spool out beneath the window and disappear into the swirling mist. The line became taut as mechanical winches reeled in the slack, drawing the ship's belly closer and closer to the rock. The engines slowed, whining and roaring until the ship's motion ceased.

'Have we landed?' Jack asked.

'Not exactly.' Davey raced along the corridor again and Jack followed, weaving his way through the ship, jumping through the tiny bulkhead doors, then down a ladder into the darkness of the floor below. Davey's voice guided him, shouting half-intelligible directions for him to follow.

Eventually Jack found him on the lowest level, back in the hold where they had entered the ship.

Davey's head was pushed up against one of the little windows that dotted either side of the room. 'Here, look!' he shouted.

Jack saw a cool mist come out of Davey's mouth, and he felt the drop in temperature, even here. He dreaded to think what it would be like outside. He peered out of the frosted glass: the ship appeared to be drifting just above the surface, gently pulling and swaying on its tethered lines.

'We're floating?' Jack asked, his breath steaming up the window.

Hilda and Eloise appeared next to them, breathless and full of anticipation.

'The engines don't stop,' Hilda explained before Davey could open his mouth. 'They just slow down enough so that we come close to the ground. The ropes stop us from drifting away.'

Davey stared at Hilda, smiling with surprised admiration. 'Yeah ... yeah, exactly.'

Hilda and Jack exchanged a smile. Davey saw it and reddened.

Captain Hardacre appeared nearby, rubbing his hands with an oily cloth. 'If you're going outside you'll need something warm on.' He cocked his head towards a wall of storage cupboards. 'I'll stay here on the flight deck, in case we need to get out of here quickly. Besides' – he tapped his pocket – 'I have some reading to do.'

Davey rushed at the storage cupboards, opening each one in turn. Inside was equipment and clothing for all weathers, including fur-lined hooded coats. Jack stepped closer and touched the soft material. They were made of animal skins, held together with thick stitches. They looked crude and well-worn, but perfect for the inhospitable weather outside.

'They might be a bit big,' Hardacre mused, 'but they'll do the job.'

Within minutes they were clad in layers of warm skins. Jack felt the sweat trickle down his neck and wondered if he'd overdone it.

Eloise smiled at the odd sight of Jack, Davey and Hilda dressed in furs.

'You can laugh!' Davey shouted through his fur hood. 'I don't care what I look like as long as I'm warm out there. You'll look just as bad.'

Eloise shook her head, a hint of superiority about her. 'I do not need them: one advantage of being OnceDead. I do not feel the cold.'

Captain Hardacre scrutinised Davey as he upholstered his gun. 'You've shot before?'

Davey nodded grimly.

Hardacre spun the weapon round and offered it to Davey. 'You might need this out there.'

Reluctantly Davey took it, feeling its weight.

'But I want her back!' Hardacre said, pointing to the gun. 'You look after her! Understand?'

Davey grinned. 'Don't panic! I'll bring her back.'

As Captain Hardacre instructed Davey on the proper use of the gun, Jack turned to find Eloise. 'So: what's our plan?'

'You will follow me,' Eloise said quietly. 'I will lead you to the sword.'

'And then what?'

'We must destroy it.'

'Sounds easy enough.'

Eloise looked away pensively. 'Rouland would not choose Niflheim without good cause. We must expect danger.'

'What do you know of this place?' Hilda said.

'Vague recollections...nothing certain.' Eloise hesitated, then said, 'There are creatures in this realm, creatures of the mist.'

Hilda frowned. 'Is that all you know?'

Eloise's lips tensed. 'We must be on our guard.'

'Good luck to you,' Hardacre shouted as he pulled at a lever hidden in the wall and the entrance ramp opened with a judder of pistons. A blast of icy air hit Jack's face and he was instantly glad of the heavy coat. The wind rattled around them, cold and powerful, and it sounded to Jack like it was crying out, howling like a lost beast.

The hold began to fill with the grey mist and a flurry of snow turned the floor from rust-red to pink.

Eloise waved them down the ramp. With every step Jack took he became cooler, the persistent wind finding the smallest gaps in his clothes and burrowing in. In front of him was Eloise, then Davey, each of them becoming blue-grey cut-out shapes in the thickening mist. Behind him was Hilda.

As he stepped away from the *Orion* the world around him became vague, made of grey silhouettes hidden behind snow and mist. Under the wind he heard the noise of ice pushing against itself, gasping and groaning against its confinements.

'Stay close!' Eloise barked from ahead.

Instinctively Jack held out his hand to Hilda. When she didn't take it he turned round. The great dark mass of the ship was still visible, but Hilda was nowhere to be seen.

Jack whipped around frantically, his eyes straining to see. The swirling mists seemed to close in on him, and Davey and the others vanished from view. Even the ship was lost to him now. He staggered forward a few steps, shouting out to the others. His cries were dampened by the darkening mist, and he felt cut off, completely alone.

The wind seemed to whisper half-formed words in his ears and his heart pounded in his chest – it was as if the wind really was talking to him.

'Who's there?' Jack shouted. He saw nothing but snow and mist and ice. The wind dropped suddenly, and the blur of noise in his ears lessened. He stepped forward and—

'Jack.'

He tensed. Was that the wind, or had someone just called his name? He felt a tingle of terror ride up his spine.

'Jack, help me!'

It *was* a voice! He was certain this time. He turned, trying to find the source of the call. He heard his name again and he sprinted towards it, his feet slipping and sliding. In front of him was a shape in the mist, indistinct at first, coming towards him. The shape seemed to take on form, becoming clearer as it approached him until it was unmistakable.

There in the snow, only a few metres in front of him, was his mother.

29

FRACTURES

'Mum?' Jack spluttered. He had forgotten the cold, forgotten all about Hilda and Davey and the others, forgotten all about their mission. Instead, his brain reeled from the vision of his mother standing before him. He knew it was impossible, and yet...

'What are you doing here?' he managed eventually.

His mother smiled. 'Jack, give your old mum a hug!'

In spite of his doubts Jack stepped forward and buried himself in his mother's embrace. His mind filled with confusion and nostalgia.

'But how did you—'

'Shh. Just hold me,' his mother soothed, pulling him in tightly. Her arms held him strongly, wrapping him up with her comfort. She was exactly as he remembered: the same clothes, the same jewellery – she even had the pendant necklace that he now wore. But there was no warmth, and she didn't smell right. Where was her unique mix of cigarettes and perfume?

Jack felt a wave of fear rise up through him. He tried to

pull away from his mother, but her grip held firm. 'Mum, let me go!'

'It's all right, Jack.' Her voice was so calming, so reassuring that for a moment his muscles relaxed. He didn't need to fight any more; his mother was here, back from the dead.

My mother is dead, he thought.

'Let me go!' He pushed again to be free but his mother's grip only tightened. The brief relief he'd felt at seeing her evaporated, coalescing into an instinctual fear. This was *not* his mother.

His skin began to tingle, then burn as the heat was drawn out of it. This thing was sucking the warmth from his body, killing him slowly. His desperate mind called out to the Rose. In seconds it responded and filled his senses. He looked up and the image of his mother churned and became a tower of blue mist. He felt its malevolence, its sickly intent. This mist was alive, deceiving him with images of his dead mother, drawing him in to feed on his warmth.

He felt his strength fortified by the Rose and he pulled away from the mist. The gaseous form responded and smothered him. His lungs were freezing up, he couldn't breathe. He reached out with the Rose, finding the dark mind within the mist and he struck out, burning it with hot needles of fire. The mist reacted, retreating. Cold clean air filled Jack's stinging lungs. He watched, panting, shivering, as the mist drifted away and faded from view.

Jack sensed he was not alone. He peered into the snow and perceived more of the mist creatures. With a start he realised they were attacking his companions. He rushed to the closest one, skidding on the icy rock. Within the blue column of churning smoke he saw Hilda.

'Father, please, you're hurting me!' she cried.

Jack reached out and found the creature's mind. There was little intelligence there, just the raw instinct for survival, a desire for heat. The Rose surged up, willing him on. He could kill this mist, he realised. But he didn't need to. Shaking, he fought the urge, suppressing the Rose just enough. He struck deep inside the mist's mind, stinging it into retreat. He composed himself as he helped Hilda to her feet.

'Jack . . . my father . . . he was—'

Jack shook his head. 'That wasn't your father, Hilda. It was a trap. I need to free the others, but I need your help.'

She took his hand in hers – her touch was ice-cold. Almost immediately he felt her now-familiar calming influence. He briefly wondered if Hilda might not be a better custodian for the Rose than he was. She seemed so much more in control.

'Concentrate!' Hilda urged.

Jack squinted and saw more of the mist creatures. He counted two: one each for Eloise and Davey. He reached out to the two bodiless minds, rooted deep within and administered a forceful sting to both of them. He felt them recoil and retreat. Their minds were easily startled but he saw their hunger. They would not give up on such a rich prize lightly.

Davey walked towards them, confused and dazed. 'What just happened?'

'A trick,' Jack said, still shaking. 'There are creatures here, mists that trick us. I saw my mother.'

'And I my father,' Hilda said, sobbing.

'What did you see?' Jack asked.

Davey became awkward and uncomfortable. 'My old man. Though ... he was kinder, friendly. But he's been dead for years.'

'We have been lucky.' The shaken voice belonged to Eloise. She appeared out of the fog, her hand on her sword.

Jack smiled with relief as she joined him, Hilda and Davey in a small circle. 'Those things could be back soon,' he said.

'The sword is nearby,' Eloise said. 'We are standing on the frozen river that will lead us to it.' She turned without hesitation and began to trudge along the ice.

'Wait!' Davey shouted. 'What did you see?'

Eloise stopped, her head down, then she returned to Davey. Her stoic expression could not hide her obvious confusion.

'I saw ...' Eloise began, shook her head, then started again. 'I saw my husband.'

'Your husband?!' Davey exclaimed. 'But...but I thought you were only, what? Seventeen maybe?'

'I was sixteen on the day I died,' Eloise said bitterly. 'It has been many years since that day.'

Jack reeled, struck by how little he knew about Eloise and her past. He had so many questions he wanted to ask her, but he saw her eyes glass over and he suppressed them all.

Davey, however, did not. 'You got married *after* you died? How is that even possible?'

Eloise said nothing, her face as cool as the ice under Jack's feet.

Davey laughed. 'I can't believe you're married!'

Rage burst onto Eloise's face and she struck Davey with her hand, sending him falling onto his back. 'I am *not* married! I am a widow.' She turned away and marched into the fog.

Jack and Hilda helped Davey onto his feet.

'I think you probably deserved that!' Hilda said angrily.

'Yeah,' Davey replied, rubbing his cheek. 'Yeah, I think I probably did.'

They trudged on for almost an hour, following Eloise's path through the treacherous ice floe. Along the way they endured two further mist attacks, each one more unsettling than the last. Only Jack's connection to the

Rose helped them avoid succumbing to these creatures, but each time he became more exhausted. He wished this trek would come to an end.

Jack was recovering from his third fall on the unforgiving ice, nursing a bruised thigh, when he caught a glimpse of something moving in the snow. 'What was that?' he said.

'What?' Davey asked.

'I don't know. Something moved over there.' Jack pointed into the swirling dense fog ahead of them.

'Another mist?'

'No, I think it was a person.'

Eloise unsheathed her sword. 'We may not be the first to arrive here.'

Davey drew Captain Hardacre's gun. Slowly everyone retreated into a circle, their backs almost touching.

'Rouland's sword is nearby,' Eloise whispered. 'The Paladin may also be here.'

Jack stared into the hypnotic fog. He saw only ice and rock. If anything was there it had stopped moving. 'Can't you sense them?'

'I feel nothing here, in this realm, except that terrible sword,' Eloise said tersely. 'Be on your guard, all of you.'

The circle began to break up as each one fell in line behind Eloise again, but there was a new sense of tension now as they scrutinised the swirling atmosphere.

They had not travelled much further when Eloise stopped again.

Davey halted next to her and whispered, 'See something?'

'We are here.'

'Where?' Davey said, blowing warm air through holes in his gloves.

'The sword,' Eloise said bitterly.

Jack looked around him. The terrain was as foggy and featureless it had been on the rest of the trek. Just then the wind kicked up and the fog parted to reveal a wall of ice climbing into the snow-filled sky.

'A frozen waterfall!' Hilda exclaimed.

The sight was equally disturbing and beautiful. The water had been shaped into cascading sculptures of ice, caught forever as they fell over the rock. Mirror-like stalactites and stalagmites had formed up and down the waterfall, like giant sets of shiny teeth, ready to ensnare a misguided climber. The waterfall stretched out in a horseshoe shape, wrapping them in on three sides. Jack felt uncomfortably confined under that tower of ice.

'Look!' Hilda pointed to the top of the waterfall, half-hidden in the perpetual grey fog. The shape of a sword could be seen, embedded into the ice.

'Durendal,' Eloise gasped.

'Well, I ain't climbing up there!' Davey said pointedly.

'It is too late,' Eloise replied, her voice full of despair.

Jack stared up at the sword. The cloud above broke, and a shaft of sunlight caught the blade, sending a kaleidoscope of colour bouncing off the monochromatic ice. Then a dark shape moved above the sword.

Eloise hissed, 'We are defeated.'

As the brooding clouds snuffed out the fleeting sun the shape above the sword revealed itself: a Paladin stood triumphantly over Durendal.

As Jack watched, the warrior grasped the ancient sword and pulled at its hilt. A noise like the scream of a thousand defeated souls echoed down the walls towards Jack. With a roar of triumph the Paladin drew the sword from the ice and raised it into the air. A mighty crack opened up where the sword had been and zigzagged its way down through the waterfall.

Great chunks of ice began to break apart, launching themselves into the air high above Jack and the others. The noise grew until it was a deafening roar.

30

ESCAPE

'Run!' Davey cried, pulling at Jack. He had Hilda by the hand as well, dragging them both with him. The fragments of ice hit the ground around them. At first it sounded like a heavy rain shower, but the noise grew and grew as larger chunks struck the frozen river. The roar of ice and rock smashing together pounded Jack's ears. The ground beneath his feet trembled and shifted with the onslaught, and minute debris filled the air with a haze of icy vapour that stung his face. He could barely see, he was running on instinct, no time to think.

An island of ice landed a few paces in front of him, burying itself into the ground. Jack skidded to a halt, falling on his back as he crashed into the impromptu wall. Hilda and Davey fell next to him, gasping for air. What had happened to Eloise? Jack couldn't see her anywhere.

Before they could pull themselves up, the ice beneath them juddered violently. With a terrible cracking noise the river ruptured. Cold liquid water burst up through the break, spraying over the trio. As Jack stood up he felt the ice tilt under him. He rushed forward, desperate to stay ahead of the breaking ice. He glanced over his shoulder; Hilda and Davey were scrambling to join him, leaping over growing chasms full of spitting water and cascades of slush.

Jack put his hand out as Hilda leaped towards him. He grabbed her arm and helped her stay upright. Davey was right behind, grabbing at Jack. Together they skidded away from the gaping, collapsing fracture.

Jack's hands found an outcrop of exposed rock and he pulled himself up above the river's broken surface. As Davey and Hilda joined him, panting breathlessly, Jack took in the chaos around him.

The smooth glass-like surface of the frozen river had been broken into a million fragments. In amongst them sat new structures: giant pieces of ice resting at dangerous angles. High above the waterfall flowed again, but already the liquid was freezing, forming a new coat of ice. The air was thick with disturbed snow falling back to earth through the swirling mist. Eloise was still nowhere to be seen.

Davey stared at the carnage. 'Do you think she got out?'

'I – I hope so,' Jack managed, hardly convincing himself. His stomach ached with fear.

'There!' Hilda cried out, pointing at a shape moving in the freezing waters.

Jack saw it was Eloise, clawing her way towards them. As she reached the rock Jack and Davey pulled her out of the river. She limped to her feet, her head tilting skyward. Jack followed her gaze: the dark shape of a realm ship had appeared above the waterfall. It drifted slowly over the sky, its engines churning, building up speed. Its metallic cobalt surface shone like an oily mirror, reflecting the ice structures it navigated past. It was bigger than the *Orion*, a grander and newer vessel. Its shape reminded Jack of a shark.

'The Paladin,' Hilda said remorsefully.

Davey nodded. 'That's Rouland's ship: the *Veillantif*.' He slumped down onto the rock, his head in his hands, exhausted. 'What do we do now? If they've got Durendal—'

'Do not use that name.' Eloise's voice was weak, full of defeat. Frost formed over her wet body, painting her with the ghostly flotsam of the ice fall. Above them the *Veillantif* arced up into the dark clouds as its engines grew louder.

Davey suddenly reached for Hardacre's gun and aimed at the ship. Jack's ears cracked with round after round, but the *Veillantif* carried on climbing into the clouds. On the last shot Jack saw a puff of smoke eject from one of the rotating arms of the ship's engines. The whining shifted tone, pitching down, and the vessel stalled. Its upward journey halted and it began to drop back down towards the ground – towards Jack and the others.

The dark shape grew in size and the injured roaring became louder and louder.

'Good shot!' Hilda observed dryly.

Jack began to retreat away, as did the others. Their hesitant steps became a sprint over the rock as the shadow of the *Veillantif* covered them. Beneath Jack's feet the rock began to tremble. He looked up and saw the dark mirrored surface coming closer and closer – he could even see their reflection in it now. Running away seemed hopeless. Then the other two curved engine arms picked up pace, spinning faster and faster, compensating for the damaged arm.

The air around the engines crackled with electricity, then the sky ripped apart and the realm ship fell into the rupture – disappearing into the red squall of the Interim. The opening snapped shut with a peal of thunder that echoed off the waterfall. The shock wave threw them all to the ground, dragging them over the rock and ice. When Jack finally came to rest he couldn't see the others. He stood up and ran back to the top of the outcrop. He saw Davey first, brushing himself down.

'That was close!' Davey laughed as Hilda and Eloise appeared out of the fog. 'You OK?'

'I'm alive,' Hilda observed. 'No thanks to you and your shooting!'

Davey shrugged nonchalantly. 'Was worth a try, wasn't it?'

'I suppose it was,' Hilda conceded. Her clothes were ragged and dirty, her face bruised and scratched. Jack wondered what he must look like now. He ran his cold fingers through his unkempt hair, hardly able to push them through the icy knots.

'Y'know, I thought we'd won there, just for a minute,' Davey said bitterly.

'It will take them time to divine Rouland's hiding place, even with his sword,' Eloise said as she straightened her back.

'Then there is still a chance?' Jack asked, hardly believing it.

Eloise nodded slowly. 'You know where he is hidden?'

'Yes,' Jack replied, recalling the fateful events that had led to Rouland's defeat. Jack had dragged him back through a Sorrowline to 1805 and thrust a Paladin sword into his heart. He was all but dead.

'He's buried in London: in a grave in St Bartholomew's Church.'

'Quickly!' Eloise ordered, already marching off. 'We must return to the *Orion*.'

They huddled together, hanging onto each other on the slippery surface, desperate to return to the realm ship as soon as possible. Jack remained alert for further mist encounters but he sensed none. He wondered if the destruction of the ice floe had startled them into retreat.

Finally a great shape appeared out of the shifting fog, massive and solid. There was the *Orion*, but something was wrong: its ever-turning engine arms were still, and the body of the ship rested on the ice, tilted to one side. Without thinking they rushed towards the open ramp and into its sheltering interior.

'This hatch should not be open,' Eloise observed quietly.

'And the engines . . .' Davey whispered. 'This is bad.'

Jack stared about him: frost coloured every surface with its white fur. He followed Eloise up to the flight deck. Even on the upper levels the heat had lost its battle with the cold, and a sickening feeling of dread began to grow in the pit of Jack's stomach.

'Captain?' Davey cried ahead. No one replied.

They turned the corridor and stepped onto the chilly flight deck. There was Captain Jonah Hardacre, sat in his usual chair with Jack's stolen book clutched in his hand. Eloise stepped cautiously forward and touched the captain's body. The lifeless husk that had once been Hardacre slumped forwards, shattering into icy fragments as it hit the control panel. The book fell to the floor by Davey's feet. Remorsefully he picked it up and put it in his pocket.

Jack's heart pounded as he realised the horrible truth. The *Orion*'s internal heat source must have shone out for miles, drawing the creatures to it. 'The mists have been here. Inside.'

He saw Eloise was crying, her shoulders slumped in defeat. 'All is lost,' she said.

Only then did Jack fully understand how serious their situation was. Without Hardacre they couldn't navigate the *Orion* back to their own realm.

The Paladin would eventually find Rouland and restore him.

And Jack, Hilda, Davey and Eloise would soon be dead, frozen in Niflheim.

31

RETRIEVAL

Rouland hated winter, when the pinpricks of frost would eat into his bones and splinter them into dust.

He had suffered the decline of autumn, felt the heat leave the earth around him, sensed the tide of life ebbing away again. The roots of the trees had finally rested from their summer growth. Each year the hair-like vanguard would touch and pry, reaching out further and further. Then the thicker roots would follow, penetrating without mercy, bullying their way past him – through him – until he was wrapped in their fragile claws.

The burrowing animals were quieter now as well, hidden in preparation for the grip of winter. It would be a hard chill this year, he could tell. He had learned to read the turn of the world above, even though he could not see it. He could feel the sun's mighty influence even here, six feet under. The springtime scratching and digging, the nocturnal home-making of his tiny neighbours was a distant memory now as the blanket of leaves was slowly dragged earthwards by the persistent worms, wriggling,

wriggling. In the stillness their minute movements became deafening, like overlapping earthquakes tapping on his fragmented skull. He hated winter, with its stillness, its freezing touch, its damp embrace.

He had prepared himself well this year, steeling his mind against the monotony, preparing for the long nothing, when he felt something.

Something new.

In his moment of angry reflection he had almost missed it: a distant vibration penetrating the earth. He stilled his thoughts and the vibration hit him like a freight train. There followed an instant of silence, then another shock wave. There it was again, and again – a sharp thrust into the earth above, then a dull scraping. He focused past the vastness of the invasion and heard more: the obvious *thud, thud, thud* of feet upon the ground.

There were people upon his grave. After all this time without a single visitor to disturb his prison he was no longer alone. Something approximating hope curdled at the edges of his mind. He felt a terrifying anticipation race through his rotten form. He had imagined this moment for decades, wondering if he might be found one day. Now it seemed that day was here, and he felt a strange mix of emotions.

Rage had sustained him over the years, rage for the boy who had buried him here. He had made little time for less subtle feelings. But in the last few decades, as the final scraps of his muscles had been eaten away, he had found some sort of calm, alone with his thoughts. His great mind still worked, and he had no interruptions, beyond the worms and the moles and the mice, to distract him. He had made plans more magnificent than any man before him. In his damp cold prison he had laid out the foundations of a mighty future where he would rule for ever. And nothing could stop him. Nothing except this prison in the soil.

The digging grew closer and closer. He could hear the muffled vibrations of voices. He counted at least three, their words unintelligible.

The metallic thrust of digging became more frantic. Then one of the spades struck the sword in his chest. Even now the pain was unbearable.

The digging stopped.

As his senses refocused he perceived scratching, clawing: hands in the soil, removing it from around the sword. He wished he still had eyes to see what was happening.

Was that a breeze? He was certain he felt air about him again.

Before he could process this new sensation his world erupted in white fire.

The pain lasted an eternity. Then, as it receded, he grasped its origin: the sword in his heart was gone. It was almost too much to bear.

The voices were clearer now, but his ears transmitted only the feeblest of tones. The words were indecipherable. The touching and scratching continued, moving up from his open chest, searching out his skull, his shoulders, his arms, then down to his hands.

He lay there, hope rising like a tide that threatened to drown him, until, finally, something cold touched the bones of his right hand. He knew it at once.

Durendal.

32

FLIGHT

Jack's ears stung with the tense silence that filled the flight deck. Davey, Eloise and Hilda sat with him, each exhausted and dejected.

He reflected on the dream-like events that had occurred since their grim discovery of Captain Hardacre's body. It had been a struggle to close the entrance ramp; its pistons were seized up with ice. Eventually they had succeeded, checking first that none of the insidious mists were still on board. He and Davey had removed Hardacre's remains, placing them in a box in the hold. It had been a difficult and undignified task, the body breaking into smaller and smaller icy fragments with every touch. All this had happened in an urgent matter-of-fact way that disturbed Jack deeply. The captain had died, his passing marked not with reflection and ceremony, but with tasks to be finished without delay. Now those grim duties were completed. Davey had managed to restart the engines, raising the ship up from the ice. They were warm again, and safe from the mists. Only now could the true

256

terror of their predicament take hold.

'I can't bloody fly this!' Davey seethed, his fists punching the console in front of him.

'If you can't we're all gonna die here!' Jack heard himself saying.

Davey's eyes punched through him. 'You want to have a go? Fancy a play?'

'You've been on this thing before!' Jack replied angrily. 'You know something about how it works!'

'Something, yeah!' Davey sighed. 'But not enough.'

Hilda stepped past Jack and sat in the seat beside Davey. 'I've never flown one either,' she said matter-of-factly. 'But we have nothing to lose.' She smiled at Davey.

'I've got plenty to lose!'

'How long will the engines idle like this before they run out of power?' she asked. 'Two days? Three? Then we fall back to the ice and the mists will find a way in.'

'And the Paladin will find Rouland,' Eloise added quietly from the back of the flight deck.

'This isn't my bloody fault!' Davey shouted. 'You think I want to stay here?'

Hilda's patient smile remained. She took Davey's hand, forcing him to focus on her alone. 'My father taught me about realm ships, but I'm sure you know a lot more than me.'

Jack smiled with relief, watching Davey soften.

'Well, I know a few things, yeah,' Davey said.

'Then perhaps between us we might know enough?'

Davey looked to the console with its myriad switches and dials, then back to Hilda. Hesitantly he nodded.

'Good,' Hilda said brightly. 'Let's start with the mooring harpoons.'

Jack inched closer, fascinated. He watched as Davey's hand hovered over the switches.

'That one, there,' Hilda offered patiently, pointing to a red lever.

'Yeah, right,' Davey replied, pulling the lever.

There was a rhythmic clatter from deep below in the ship, followed by the low rumble of machinery. The ship began to rise up, drifting to the left, tilting softly as the winds outside pushed on the loosed vessel.

'Where's the drift stabilisers?' Davey said urgently.

'Check the ballast first,' Hilda said, tapping at a dial in front of her. 'Sixteen point two. It's low.'

'Cos of all the water Hardacre used in Newton Harbour. She'll be hard to keep steady.'

'Yes,' Hilda replied. 'But you can manage.'

Davey flashed a confident smile at her, but Jack saw the wide-eyed fear.

'Stabilisers set at sixteen point two,' Davey said, hitting a series of buttons.

'Splendid. Can you take the flight controls?' Hilda said, pointing to the stick-like apparatus in front of Davey. He hesitated, staring at the device, then grasped it and released a lever on its side. The *Orion* immediately shifted, jolting up. Jack and Eloise grabbed hold of the bulkhead, steadying themselves. Davey tilted the control stick, guiding the ship upwards. As the moments passed his navigation became more subtle, more controlled, and the unsteady gyrations of the ship lessened.

'You're a natural, Davey,' Hilda said.

'I dunno,' Davey replied meekly. Jack had rarely seen him like this before. It was as if Hilda had tamed his bravado. Davey's guard had lowered, melted away by her kindness.

The ship levelled off inside the clouds. Ice formed on the windows outside, fracturing the misty view.

'Good,' Hilda said. 'I think it's safe to try for the Interim, don't you, Davey?'

Davey shrugged. 'I ain't about to get any better at this. Now's as good a time as any.'

Hilda nodded as she read off a series of dials in front of her. 'Power is at seven. Can you take it up to nine?'

Davey pushed down on the control lever and the ship's engines responded. At the same time Hilda turned a set of dials. 'Frequency set for the Interim,' she said.

'Engines up to speed,' Davey noted.

Hilda smiled her encouragement as she hit a switch. 'Take us in.'

Davey rotated the control lever and pulled at a handle on the panel in front of him. The *Orion* rattled violently as the icy clouds of Niflheim disappeared from view, replaced by the red milk of the Interim.

As the vibrations lessened everyone laughed with relief.

'That went better than I thought!' Davey confessed.

'Well done,' Eloise said. 'Now comes the hard part.'

Hilda leaned over to a rack to her left and found a large notebook. 'The captain's ledger: the frequency for Newton Harbour should be in here somewhere.'

'We are not going to Newton Harbour,' Eloise said icily. 'There is no time.'

'What?' Davey said, exasperated.

Eloise paced impatiently. 'We must go directly to London – to Rouland's burial place at St Bartholomew's Church.'

'I can't take the *Orion* over London!' Davey barked his tense reply as the engines shifted in pitch.

'You must!'

'This is a realm ship!' Hilda said, her voice clipped. 'You know what that means! You know what would happen if we flew it over London!'

'There are greater things at stake than the First World's secrets! Rouland cannot return.' There was desperation in Eloise's voice. 'We cannot allow more to die. You *must* fly us in!'

Davey stared at Hilda, his face full of doubts. 'Can't you use the Sorrowlines?'

'How?' Jack asked.

Davey shrugged. 'I dunno! What if you went back in time and took Rouland's body and moved it somewhere else?'

'He is already hidden,' Eloise said sternly. 'The Paladin can find him with Durendal. Moving him would achieve nothing. There is too much that could go wrong with such a plan. Our only hope is to stop this happening *now*!'

For a moment the only noise cutting the tension was the whine of the engines, then Davey turned to look at Eloise. 'OK, I'll fly us in!'

'But what about the war?' Jack said urgently. 'London's on high alert for bombing raids from Germany. If we fly over the city in this thing we'll be shot down!'

'Jack's right!' Davey replied.

Eloise shook her head. 'If we are to stop Rouland we must take that chance. We are running out of time.'

Hilda looked up from the ledger open in front of her. 'I think I can work out the frequency to bring us in over London. From there it'll be up to you, Davey.'

'I'll keep us low, under the anti-aircraft guns. But I ain't promising you an easy trip.'

'Just get us there, Davey.' Eloise's tone softened as she patted him on the shoulder.

'You remember the church?' Jack asked, recalling his previous adventure there with Davey.

'Course I do!' Davey barked. 'That's the easy bit! Flying this ship – that's gonna be hard!'

'Can I do anything?' Jack asked.

Hilda spoke up. 'You must be ready on the mooring harpoons.'

Jack wanted to stay, to see what would happen. He felt safer there rather than in the dark bowels of the ship where he couldn't see what was coming. Reluctantly he left the flight deck, following Eloise down to the mooring harpoons. When they were alone he stopped her. 'Are . . . are you OK?' he said, feeling uncomfortable.

Doubt coloured Eloise's pale face.

'I mean . . .' Jack struggled, wishing he'd never started. 'Well, what you said earlier. About being a widow. I'm sorry if Davey upset—'

Eloise raised her hand, and the words dried up in Jack's mouth. Her stern face softened with kindness. 'It's all right, Jack.' She paused, thinking. 'I fell in love.' A rare smile tugged at Eloise's mouth as she looked into the distance of her memories. 'Rouland could not bear it, so I ran away and we married in secret. The Paladin found me. Captain de Vienne . . . she killed my husband.' Her smile evaporated. 'Now the score is settled.'

Jack felt like an intruder, treading through personal memories. 'I'm sorry.'

'At least I loved.' Tears pooled at the edges of her eyes. 'Even with this terrible pain I am glad of that.'

She smiled again as she turned towards the starboard mooring harpoons, leaving Jack alone. After a moment he moved towards the port stations, inching along the tight corridor, and took up his position at the first harpoon, waiting, watching the dark red world outside as it flowed past his tiny window.

He must have fallen asleep, he supposed, the hypnotic patterns working on his tired mind as he waited for the engines to kick in. A rumble shook the ship, robbing Jack of his rest. His eyes scanned the exterior; the red light outside suddenly buckled and fractured into a thousand shades of ochre. For a second he wondered how long he'd been asleep, then Davey's voice crackled over the speaker, sounding older. 'Here we go!'

The hull trembled and Jack instinctively closed his eyes. He heard a series of cracks and pops. The ship was tossed about and he fell to the floor. As the shaking subsided he clawed his way to the window. Outside the world was black, devoid of features. Then, slowly, fragile dots of light appeared. They dipped and shifted in front of him as the *Orion* turned, and an orb of mottled blue and white filled his view.

'The moon!' Jack laughed. 'It's the moon!'

Clouds whipped by, radiating in the vibrant moonlight. The dots of light were stars, Jack realised. He shifted his view downwards, pushing his forehead up against the cold glass. Below him was land, shrouded in darkness. A winding river stood out, catching the reflection of the moon above. Was it the Thames? he wondered.

The sky erupted in fire, and the *Orion* swung sharply away from it. The ship dipped forwards and began to plummet towards the ground. It weaved left and right as more explosions cracked at the hull. Dotted lines cut up the sky, bright points of light following each other into the clouds.

'Anti-aircraft fire,' Hilda shouted over the speaker.

The hull close to Jack's feet was punctured by six tiny holes as some of the gunfire found its target. He ducked as the bullets embedded themselves into the ceiling. He wondered if Eloise was OK on the other side of the ship.

The *Orion* tilted again and the river loomed into view outside.

'We're nearly on top of the water!' Jack exclaimed with fear, uncertain if he could be heard on the flight deck. He saw the shapes of buildings rush past outside, a blur of dark rectangles. The unmistakable tower of Big Ben passed by, its darkened clock face gleaming in the moonlight. The river disappeared from view and midnight-coloured streets took its place. The ship accelerated quickly, tipping Jack off balance, then almost immediately it began to decelerate, weaving left and right. The *Orion* arced back on itself, losing speed, and an ancient church tower came into view.

'Now!' Davey's voice boomed.

Jack peered into the eyepiece and saw line after line of

gravestones hidden in the darkness. He fired the trigger and watched as the harpoon rope thudded into the earth. The ship jerked to a halt as the rope tightened, dragging it towards the graveyard. He ran to the next harpoon and fired it into the ground. As he reached the third gun he felt the vibrations from the other side of the ship as it inched closer to the surface.

'This is the place?' Eloise asked, joining Jack as he fired his last harpoon.

'This is it,' Jack said, feeling apprehensive. The thought of returning to Rouland's grave filled him with dread.

Within seconds Jack was at the entrance, waiting with nervous anticipation as Davey, Hilda and Eloise crowded around him. With a hiss of steam the ramp touched the soil of the graveyard, pushing into the damp surface.

Silence fell like a great smothering blanket.

Eloise edged cautiously down the ramp, her sword at hand. Behind her followed Davey wielding Hardacre's gun, then Jack and Hilda.

The night air was crisp and the graveyard seemed eerily still, a tiny island of calm in a city at war.

'Are we alone?' Hilda asked.

'I think so,' Eloise replied, 'but landing the *Orion* here has robbed us of any surprise. We must be swift.'

Jack ran with the others towards the church. The greying clouds began to rain, softly at first then more forcefully until the headstones glittered in the moonlight.

'Which way?' Eloise asked, looking at Jack.

He took a deep breath and stepped out from the shelter of the church wall. He could see the twisted dead tree from here. Below it he had buried Rouland in 1805. The glow of a distant fire illuminated the clouds behind the tree, casting a dancing glow over the earth.

Jack led Eloise, Davey and Hilda towards the tree. As he got closer he saw something that terrified him: the soil had been disturbed.

'Eloise . . .' Jack said nervously. He was close enough now to see the dark hole where he had buried the body. All around were the signs he had dreaded: piles of unearthed soil with footprints embedded in them, abandoned spades thrown haphazardly to the ground. His legs began to shake under him. 'Someone's been here.'

Davey looked into the dark pit. 'They've dug him up, ain't they?'

'Then we are already too late,' Eloise gasped.

33

THE HALF-MAN

Rouland felt exhausted – even bracing against the tilting motion of the *Veillantif* seemed like a gargantuan effort. He stood alone in his bedroom with Durendal in his calcified hand. It was difficult to move after so long in the ground. Standing seemed like the best option.

He struggled towards a full-length mirror, and then wished he hadn't.

He saw the hideous skeleton of a half-man, a rotting zombie bathed in the red glow of the sword. Rouland stared at his face, once beautiful, now disgusting. Even as he watched he could see it change, as the stolen energies of Durendal replenished his body. A misshapen eye stared out of the deep sockets as the broken mouth flexed over gumless teeth. He turned away, feeling uneasy.

There was a polite knock at the door and one of his Paladin entered. It took him a moment to remember her name, it had been so long.

'Come in, Dominica.' Speaking, he discovered, was hard. His voice was slow and deliberate, gravelly like an old man's. He hardly recognised it.

Dominica bowed respectfully and crossed the room to stand before him. 'We are returning to Newton Harbour, Master. We are receiving reports of a disturbance there.'

Rouland waved his hand for her to continue. It was less effort than trying to talk.

'There has been a fire, and Captain de Vienne is no more.'

With a great effort Rouland lowered himself into a chair. 'A fire would not kill her.'

Dominica shook her head. 'No, Master, it did not. There was a battle, and a realm ship was taken. We believe it was the *Orion*, on its way to Niflheim. The Exile fought with Captain de Vienne. The captain was decapitated.'

Rouland listened, considering. 'Then she truly is no more. That is . . . disappointing.' He suppressed his anger, his remorse. He had known de Vienne for an age, and he felt her loss greatly. But it would be wrong to display such weak emotions here, in front of Dominica. Instead, he shifted the focus onto her. 'You must be greatly saddened.'

Dominica did not betray any emotion. 'The Exile must be destroyed.'

Rouland nodded patiently. 'What other news do you bring?'

'Ealdwyc is in disarray, Master. Since your departure the Houses have fallen into civil war. They are leaderless, but there are rumours that Jodrell Sinclair is still alive.'

'Impossible!' Rouland seethed, recalling his actions in the Parliament Chamber. He had killed them all, every last one of them. 'Sinclair is dead.'

Dominica nodded.

'And the boy?'

'Surely he perished on Niflheim. The mists—'

'Do not presume!' Rouland scolded, finding some of his old strength.

'He will be found,' Dominica replied diplomatically. 'I have left two sisters at the site of your burial, to watch in case he returns there.'

'Good,' Rouland said quietly, his mind already drifting into a million possibilities.

Dominica cleared her throat deliberately. 'There is one more thing, Master. The Widow is on board. She is keen to see you.'

Even after all these years Rouland felt a pang of guilt at the mention of the Widow. He would not usually entertain such pathetic nostalgia, but she held a unique place in his heart. His experiment had failed. *He* had failed. He had promised her a superior existence, a grand reward for her noble sacrifice. Instead, she had suffered greatly at his hand, each new surgery taking her further away from him. 'I will go to her when I am restored – it would only distress her to see me like this. First, there are many things that must be done,' he said.

'As you wish, Master.' Dominica bowed. 'Is that all?'

Rouland took in a deep breath, thinking. He wished de Vienne were here.

'I am grateful for your journey to Niflheim, Dominica,' he said. 'I know it was not an easy mission. You risked much to restore me.'

Dominica straightened.

'We grieve for your lost captain but order must be maintained.' Rouland smiled. It was almost without pain now. 'That is all, Captain Dominica Huon. Please inform the others of your promotion.'

Dominica blinked quickly, her surprise obvious. She opened her mouth, about to say something.

'Do not be foolish enough to question my decision, Captain,' Rouland said.

'I would not,' Dominica replied. 'I am most grateful, Master.'

Rouland's smile fell away quickly; the effort was tiring him. 'One more thing, Captain.'

'Yes, Master.'

'The sword is not enough. Bring me three – no, four – subjects. They must be young and healthy.'

Captain Huon nodded her understanding.

Rouland waved her away. He watched as his new captain turned brusquely towards the door.

34

COMMUNION IN MEMORIES

'He can't be too far away,' Davey said hopefully. 'Maybe we can still get him before—'

'It is already too late!' Eloise interrupted bitterly. 'Rouland is resurrected. He has his sword. Every passing second restores him to his former self.'

Jack stared into the dark hole. The rain pounded onto the graveyard, forming tiny waterfalls that cascaded down the rough walls of earth. Had it all been for nothing? 'We have to find him!'

'Where?' Davey said breathlessly.

'He will return to the First World, to Newton Harbour. It is the only dock big enough for the *Veillantif*,' Eloise noted. 'We must go there at once.'

As Jack turned away from the grave he saw two Paladin waiting in the shadows, their drawn swords glinting in a burst of lightning. There was a deafening pop that drowned out the thunder. Another followed, then another.

Jack's eyes chased the trail of smoke and saw Davey, his outstretched gun in front of him, the barrel steaming as the rain splashed onto the hot metal.

Jack turned back to the Paladin. The one closest to Davey smiled as she inspected the bullet wounds to her body. 'You think your gun can kill me?' the Paladin mocked.

'No, but I bet it hurts like hell!' Davey taunted them as he cautiously retreated, reloading the gun.

Eloise raised her sword up and attacked the bullet-ridden Paladin. The second assailant leaped through the opening, straight towards Jack and Davey. Jack felt Hilda's hand in his, her calming voice in his mind. He understood, and called out to the Rose, allowing it to rise up.

He held up his hand to the Paladin. Almost at once the warrior fell to the ground, writhing in agony. Jack pushed further into his opponent, letting the Rose seek out the fibres within her brain and—

'Steady,' Hilda said calmly. Jack understood, reining in the fierce power of the Rose. Just enough, that was all he needed.

The Paladin staggered to her knees, reaching for her displaced sword. She looked up, confusion on her pale face. 'You . . . hurt me?'

'Keep back!' Jack warned. At the same moment he was aware of Eloise striking down the other Paladin close by. It was as if his senses were heightened, reaching out into the rain-soaked graveyard. Eloise's racing heart pounded in his ears like a drum beat as she struck the final fatal blow against her attacker. He could almost feel the tension in her arm muscles. In that instant he knew every movement around him. Every tiny noise, even the complex swirl of the wind through the rain became clear. And yet Hilda was more distant, like she was falling away from him, her calming influence becoming smaller and smaller.

Jack refocused on the Paladin in front of him. He saw the tiny twitch of a vein in her forearm, the signal for her hand to raise her weapon. Jack saw it all before it happened. As the Paladin swung the sword and lunged towards him, Jack raised his hand. The Paladin fell back again.

She looked up at him, her face full of an animal rage. 'You will yield!' The Paladin cried out, launching herself into the air towards him.

Time appeared frozen, the Paladin only centimetres from him, her sword falling towards his neck. He sensed her rage, her unstoppable intent. She served Rouland. She could not be reasoned with. Inside his mind he felt the Rose, willing him on: kill or be killed. Jack let go, throwing his might at the Paladin.

There was a fury of noise and light, then silence. The Paladin fell at his feet. Jack turned away; he did not want to see. Instead, he saw Davey's stunned face, staring back, terrified. As Jack stepped towards him Davey flinched, retreating away.

'Hey, it's OK, Davey.'

Davey stopped, his frame trembling. 'You . . . you did that.' He pointed at the charred remains of the Paladin.

Jack had never tried to kill before, except for Rouland. And that had been an impulsive move driven by desperation. This time he'd calculated, he'd chosen to kill. He felt a change deep within him. Part of him liked it. 'I know,' he said eventually, strangely proud. He almost smiled, then he saw Hilda's face. 'It was self-defence!' he added tersely.

Hilda nodded. 'But you enjoyed it,' she whispered.

Jack pulled his hand from hers. He didn't need her telling him what he felt.

'You can do that,' Davey gasped, 'and you worry about me? About what I might become?'

The drum of the rain filled Jack's ears, each drop like an accusation. He wanted to walk away, wanted never to look back, but Davey was his friend – his grandfather! He couldn't ignore his words. And Hilda – he relished her support, yet now he stood alone. Even Eloise seemed to be judging him with her stern expression.

Slowly, deliberately, he turned from the horrified faces of Hilda and Davey to the remains of the Paladin. At first he saw nothing, only smoke. Then the breeze ripped the smoke aside, and the horror of the Rose revealed itself to him.

Jack shook his head, stepping back from the nightmare that had been a living thing until a moment ago. *The Paladin are already dead*, he told himself. *She would have killed me*, his mind offered up in his defence.

He could live with being a killer – after all, he'd tried to kill Rouland, but Hilda was right: he had *enjoyed* it. He had felt powerful. Part of him felt no remorse; he'd wanted to do it. Wanted to kill. Wanted revenge for his mother. Wanted to make someone, anyone, pay for what had happened to her, to Francesco, to Hardacre, to Hilda's family.

He looked at his hands. He couldn't drop this weapon, like a smoking gun, and vow never to use it again. It was too late: he was transformed. He was no longer Jack Morrow, the boy with the Rose.

He had become a monster who enjoyed killing.

Like Rouland.

He fell to his knees and sobbed. He couldn't blame the Rose, not any more. He felt as if he was at a precipice where he might soar or fall depending on his next choice. And he didn't know what to do, not any more.

The rain howled around him.

His head felt light. He closed his eyes.

Jack was somewhere else, a world of honey-toned light. Everything was out of focus, soft shapes that seemed to shift gently into new formations. The shapes coalesced into recognisable forms: he was on a hillside of rock and heathers. Far below was a lake of perfect glass. Above him was the great mass of a mountain capped with snow, and at its very peak was a circular structure made of polished stone. It reminded Jack of a castle from a fairy tale. The air was cool but comfortable, blowing gently towards him from the lake. The isolation was glorious and he felt instantly safe here.

'Beautiful, isn't it?'

Jack knew who had spoken, even before he looked to see. That voice was instantly recognisable. He felt no fear, no trepidation, just warmth.

'Hello, Mum.' He smiled, turning to see his mother next to him on the hillside, knowing immediately how different this felt to the illusion created by the mists. He looked at the stunning location and furrowed his brow. 'Am I dead?'

His mother smiled, looking out to a boat crossing the wide lake. 'No. You're not dead, Jack.'

'Where are we?'

'Inside a memory,' she replied.

Jack took in the valley anew. 'I don't know this place. Is this one of your memories, Mum?'

She shook her head. She was more beautiful than he remembered. 'This is a memory of the Rose.'

Jack leaned back on his elbows, thinking. He felt no urgency here, no desperate life-threatening problem to solve. He could stay here for ever. 'Is this Otherworld?'

'It is how the Rose remembers it.'

Jack felt a wave of sadness. 'So, you're not real?'

'I carried the Rose. My memories are enshrined here.

I'm always here, Jack.' She tapped the side of his head playfully, smiling her broad smile.

He took her hand in his and laughed. He didn't want this moment to end.

'I'm sorry. You know you have to go back, don't you, Jack?'

He shook his head. 'I can stay here, with you.'

'This is a memory, nothing more. It will be over soon.'

Jack pulled his hand away. 'Then why am I here?'

His mother stood and began to walk down the slope. '*You* came here, Jack. Why?'

Jack caught up with his mother. He saw a mountain range at the far side of the lake. Above it a wall of dark storm clouds brooded.

'I've done something terrible, Mum. I've killed.' The words seemed to fill his throat uncomfortably. He couldn't look at her. 'And I liked it.'

His mother hooked her hair behind her ear, gazing at him sympathetically. 'I'm sorry that I never had time to teach you about the Rose, to explain its purpose to you. You are so young to be its host. But remember, you are in command. The Rose must submit to its host.' Her voice was laden with regret and pity. 'You still have control, Jack.'

'I don't! I'm not strong enough!'

His mother took his shoulders, forcing him to look at her kind face. 'You are stronger than you know. You are the last of a great and noble family.' She lifted the pendant from inside his shirt, letting it dazzle in the clear light. 'You must remember who you are. The Rose will do your bidding. You have to choose what sort of person you want to be. It's *your* choice.'

The storm clouds had reached the lake, turning its silver surface a dark purple.

'I have a choice?' Jack said, thinking.

His mother smiled, nodding softly as she let go of the pendant. 'You have a choice.'

At that the rain reached them, warm and clean. He rejoiced in the torrent, closing his eyes as the smells of the heathers erupted from the hillside.

'This land was a paradise until Rouland took the Rose from it. Much has changed since then. Otherworld suffers. It is dying. And the fate of Otherworld has an effect on all realms, even your own.'

Jack's thoughts cleared. He seemed to understand intuitively here. 'The Rose must be returned to Otherworld?'

His mother nodded. 'The Rose *belongs* here. It is the soul of Otherworld.'

Jack felt light-headed again, and the rain became cool. A chilly breeze stole the floral smells from his nostrils. He began to cry again, knowing that when he opened his eyes he would be back in the graveyard, far from the memory of his mother.

He held onto the moment for as long as he could, until he felt a hand upon his shoulder.

'Jack,' Davey said nervously. 'You OK? We need to go.'

Wearily, Jack opened his eyes. There was the Paladin – a view forever burned onto his retina. He pulled himself up on Davey, standing unsteadily. He took in a series of deep breaths and wiped the tears from his cheeks. Davey watched him with concern, as did Eloise. Finally he saw Hilda, her eyes reflecting his own emotions. She, most of all, understood his turmoil, the tribulations that had tugged at his heart.

'We must leave now,' Eloise said urgently as she headed for the *Orion*'s ramp. Davey hesitated, staring at Jack before he shrugged to himself and turned towards the ship.

Hilda hung back, watching Jack as he moved slowly towards her. 'Have you given up?' she asked firmly.

Jack stopped, as if her question had hit him in the face. He paused for a moment, trying to arrange his conflicting thoughts. Already the *Orion*'s engines were powering up, spinning faster and faster above his head.

He held out his hand to Hilda. 'We should leave, if we're going to stop Rouland.'

Hilda nodded and walked up the entrance ramp. As it closed Jack glanced back to the patch of earth where the Paladin fell, his mother's words still ringing in his ears.

You have a choice.

35

HOMECOMINGS

'There!' Eloise exclaimed, pointing to the realm ship berthed below them. 'The *Veillantif*: Rouland's ship.'

The flight deck was cramped and tense. Davey and Hilda sat at the controls, both grimly silent as the *Orion* swung in a tight circle, manoeuvring unsteadily closer to the other ship. Behind them were Jack and Eloise, peering through the dirty glass at the impressive expanse of Newton Harbour.

Jack saw the final wisps of smoke rising from the burnt-out docks. Rouland's ship, the *Veillantif*, had berthed on the far side of Newton Harbour. Spotlights illuminated the dark marble ship, winched into place by its moorings. Suddenly a spotlight swung upwards, blinding the *Orion*'s flight deck.

The radio burst with static, followed by a clipped voice: 'Newton harbourmaster to unmarked realm ship: identify yourself immediately.'

Davey smiled ruefully. 'This could be interesting.'

'What's happening?' Hilda asked.

Davey picked up the radio intercom, his voice unnaturally formal. 'Harbourmaster, this is Captain Vale of the realm ship' – he looked at Hilda and smiled – 'the realm ship, *Hilda's Hope*, requesting an emergency berth.'

'Captain?' Hilda whispered to Davey.

'Why not? I'd make a good captain!'

The radio crackled. '*Hilda's Hope*, you have no transponder code. Our CBI signal is being blocked. What's your emergency?'

'Gyro stabilisers are misfiring, unable to hold position. Request emergency berth immediately!'

Davey tilted the control stick left then right, causing the ship to rock aggressively. 'Think they'll fall for that?' Davey asked, raising an eyebrow.

'No,' Hilda replied.

'Take us over the *Veillantif*,' Eloise barked.

Davey scowled. 'And do what? Shake my fist at them?'

Eloise was already stepping out of the flight-deck doorway. 'Get me close enough and I will jump.'

'Jump?' Jack gasped. 'Jump to where?'

Eloise turned back to the flight deck. 'To Rouland's ship. Every second we waste is madness. Do it, Davey!' She didn't wait for a reply, disappearing into the ship.

Davey growled, 'She'll get us all killed.' But he was already obeying, arcing the *Orion* towards the *Veillantif*.

'Newton Harbour control to *Hilda's Hope*,' the radio hissed, 'your gyros appear fine from here. Hold your position and prepare to be boarded by port authorities.'

'Told you!' Hilda said dryly.

'Squawk seven, seven, zero, zero,' Davey said to Hilda, pointing at a panel of switches. 'Emergency code,' he explained as he picked up the radio handset and shouted, 'We're going down, Harbour Control. Captain Vale out!'

'What does that mean?' Jack asked.

'It means hang on!' Davey swung the control column violently to the left. The *Orion* responded and the world outside the windows tipped dramatically.

'Davey, what on earth are you doing?' Hilda shouted, her fingers gripping the edge of the console.

'Taking her down, right on top!' A devilish grin erupted on Davey's face.

'On top of what? The *Veillantif*?'

Davey didn't answer, all his concentration on the dipping view. He jerked the controls down, nosing the ship into a dive. 'I'll need some help with the harpoons!'

'You're insane!' Jack screamed.

Hilda leaped out of her seat. 'I'll take the starboard side.'

Jack and Hilda rushed out of the flight deck, down to the harpoon bays. As they reached the harpoons the ship banked again, dipping and turning as if it was out of control. Jack peered through the little window and saw the shapes of moored realm ships just beneath him. There was a violent shudder as the *Orion* struck something.

The passageway vibrated with the impact, throwing clutter at him.

'Harpoons!' The shouted command from Davey filled Jack's ears.

Jack looked into the viewfinder again, saw the dockside in extreme close-up, and fired. The harpoon dug deep into the walkway, throwing up splinters of wood. The mechanism was already pulling in the slack, holding the ship in place on top of Rouland's vessel. As he fired off the second harpoon he felt crunching vibrations through his feet. It sounded like the belly of the ship was breaking apart. Jack ignored the sickly noise and fired the last harpoon. The ship jerked again and the engines howled for an instant, then settled into a passive hum.

Jack felt the rush of air as the entrance ramp was lowered. He followed Hilda towards it, just in time to see Eloise disappear out of the hatch. The sound of swords echoed into the ship, and Jack felt his heart sink.

He looked at Hilda and she seemed to understand, offering him her hand.

'Be noble. Be just,' she said.

Jack nodded grimly as the pair of them descended the ramp.

'Hey!' Davey shouted from behind them. 'Hang on!'

There was no time to wait, Jack concluded. He stepped off the ramp into a circle of Paladin. Eloise pushed at the circle, attacking and parrying, seeking out a weak spot.

283

The circle widened, and for the first time Jack saw where they had landed. He was stood on the dark reflective hull of the *Veillantif*, its surface marked and torn by the *Orion* resting upon it. The engines of the two ships sat above and below them, creating rhythmic wind with their sweeping arms.

Davey rushed out of the *Orion*, his weapon raised and cocked.

'Fight me!' Eloise screamed at the Paladin. 'Fight me, or are you cowards, like your captain?'

One of the Paladin stepped forward. '*I* am captain now.'

'Dominica?' Eloise said, half laughing.

'You will address me as Captain Huon.'

Eloise lowered her stance, her weapon tensing in her palm. 'Then you must make me. I have already killed one captain today . . .'

Captain Huon raised her sword up as she edged towards Eloise. Another Paladin circled behind her.

Jack held out his free hand, allowing energy to grow in his palm. The Paladin took a slow step back. Were they afraid of him? he wondered.

Suddenly Eloise was upon Captain Huon, like a ferocious animal. Captain Huon managed to smile as she pushed back, overpowering Eloise. She swung her sword down, missing her by mere centimetres, rooting it into the dark metal of the *Veillantif*. Eloise jumped up, pushing Huon off balance. The pair jostled to one side, sliding over

284

the smooth hull.

The rest of the Paladin watched, closing the circle again.

'What should we do?' Jack whispered. 'Why aren't they attacking?'

'They're waiting,' Hilda realised.

'What for?' Davey said, aiming his gun at the nearest Paladin.

'For Rouland,' Jack gasped, understanding what was happening.

Behind the circle of Paladin he saw a hatch. Out of it climbed a man clad in black armour. The face was less perfect, thinner, wrinkled around the eyes, but still instantly recognisable. The Paladin circle opened up, allowing the man to step forwards.

'Whose idea was it to land on top of my ship?' Rouland said with a deliberate smile. 'Did you think this would give you an advantage? The element of surprise, perhaps?'

'Sorry, that was me! I'm more of a doer than a planner,' Davey replied, pointing the shotgun at Rouland and pulling the trigger.

The air between them filled with smoke. As it cleared Jack saw Rouland, smiling still. At his feet was one of his Paladin who had leaped to his defence, clutching her chest.

'That was another bad idea,' Rouland seethed, raising his arm up.

Jack quickly stepped in between Davey and Rouland, his hand still clutching Hilda's. He let the energy build in his palm, hissing and fizzing in front of him.

'You!' Rouland said, shaking with rage. 'Jack Morrow. The boy who almost killed me!'

'I can finish the job,' Jack warned, glancing at Hilda.

'Ah, yes,' Rouland noted. 'You have the Rose. How strong are you? Can you control it? You have felt its wilfulness by now, yes?'

'I'm in control,' Jack replied calmly.

'Very good. But the human mind is easily distracted.'

There was a blur of movement and one of the Paladin attacked Hilda. She cried out as the blade struck her chest.

The calm in Jack's mind died as Hilda's hand fell from his. Fear congealed with anger and formed into a primal rage. The Rose fed on it immediately.

'No, Jack!' Hilda cried pathetically, her eyes rolling upwards.

Jack barely heard her. One thought drowned out everything else: *revenge.*

The nearest two Paladin did not stand a chance. Jack was inside their minds at once, crushing them from within. They fell to the ground in front of him. He picked up the sword from the hand of one of them and decapitated another Paladin, relishing the kill. He could move faster than them, he realised. He could react before they could.

He let the Rose move the sword and his muscles followed, felling one opponent after another until he stood in front of Rouland.

Why was he still smiling?

'Nicely done,' Rouland said. Slowly, almost casually, he raised his sword.

'This is Durendal,' he said, stroking the weapon. 'It yearns to feed on you. On the Rose.'

The noises of battle seemed to fade away behind him. Jack was vaguely aware of Eloise striking down a final Paladin nearby, of Davey reloading Hardacre's gun and firing, of Hilda slowly dying, but he ignored it all, letting his attention narrow until only he and Rouland remained. Nothing else mattered.

He seemed more terrifying than ever, Jack realised with a pulse of doubt. He cooled his mind and allowed the Rose to bloom, pushing it onwards with his spite. He tunnelled his way into Rouland's mind, like he had in 1805, and—

Jack fell back on the hard metal of the realm ship, stunned, disbelieving.

Rouland looked skywards and roared with laughter. 'You think to conquer me twice in the same way? You think I have idled since 1805? It never dawned on me that it was you, all those years ago, until I had the time to reflect during my long imprisonment. I have pondered, and learned, and planned. You beat me before, but I was unprepared. I have grown since then, tempered my skills. Now my mind is barricaded, fortified against your crude attack.' He stepped forwards, his sword pointing to Jack. 'I wonder . . . is *your* mind as well-guarded?'

A point of burning light impaled Jack's brain. The heat was terrible, like a fire inside his skull. He clawed backwards, retreating over the hull.

Rouland stepped closer, until he stood over him. 'You thought you were so good, didn't you, Jack? So clever!' he said bitterly. 'You kept the Rose from me! You defeated me! You! Just a boy who knows nothing! How did you succeed where so many greater men have failed?' He knelt in front of him, the tip of Durendal touching Jack's throat. 'Who *are* you? Who are you to defeat me?' Rouland looked down, puzzled. 'You, Jack, are an unanswered question.'

'I don't have any answers for you,' Jack gasped.

'Then,' Rouland said calmly, 'I will find my own answers.'

The point of light inside Jack's mind began to tear at his memories like they were pages being ripped from a book. He sensed his entire life replayed, every forgotten moment pulled apart and inspected. He was immobile, unable to resist. He called for the Rose to protect him but it seemed far away, cowering from sight. Then he felt it stir and his perception shifted.

Jack was no longer on the hull of the *Veillantif*. He was deep within his own memories. He was back in the tiny flat he'd grown up in, before his mother had died. He sat in the worn armchair by the window – the one his father preferred. Spring sunshine poured into the living room, pushing away the frosty morning air. Dust danced in the light, swirling in endless patterns. The room was peaceful, silent in a way it never was when he lived there. A clock on the shelf ticked away to itself, loud now in the absence of any other sound. Even the ever-present throb of rock music vibrating from Klara's flat above was gone.

But he was not alone: Rouland sat on the sofa, immaculate in a grey suit. There were no scars, no sunken wrinkles, just manicured, groomed perfection.

Rouland smiled, crossing his legs. 'This was your home, when you were young.'

Jack said nothing. Why were they here? he wondered.

'So mundane. You lived here with your mother,' Rouland noted. 'To have grown out of this squalor… you are hardly worthy to be the host of something as divine as the Rose of Annwn.' Rouland's face wrinkled with bitter anger. 'How? Tell me how you are more worthy than me?'

'I don't know if I am,' Jack replied honestly, 'but my mother was.'

'Your mother!' Rouland seethed. 'Your angelic mother! You hold her on such a high pedestal, don't you? You think her so perfect. She was not so different from me, you know?'

'Shut up!' Jack shouted. His hand touched his mother's pendant through his clothes. He knew at once it was a mistake. Rouland raised his hand and, with a tiny flick, the chain danced into the air, revealing the pendant.

'Of course,' Rouland whispered eventually. 'I am an old fool, you know? Even with all my wasted years of consideration I never guessed at your lineage.' He flicked his fingers dismissively and the pendant dropped back onto Jack's chest.

Jack felt suddenly afraid and tucked it back under his shirt, out of sight.

Rouland stood purposefully, walking around the room. He picked up a book and inspected its pages. 'The House of Jude lives still. Interesting. I had sought to wipe out that family years ago. It explains a great many things. You are from a great and noble House, and yet you live in this filth.' He looked at Jack, fixing him with a cold stare that lasted too long. 'You did not know, did you? Did your mother tell you nothing?'

'This is my family! This is my home!' Jack retorted.

'You wear the Seal of the House of Jude! You offend me with your piteous modesty.' Rouland stopped abruptly; something had caught his eye. Jack gasped as he saw it too. In the doorway was a dark hooded shape. He knew it at once: a Grimnire.

'Well,' Rouland smiled angrily, seeing the visitor.

'It seems we are observed even here, in the isolation of your past.'

The Grimnire bowed and retreated into the shadows, fading into the grubby wallpaper until it vanished completely.

An image of Hilda, bleeding, dying, came to Jack's mind and he felt a sickening rush of guilt. The walls of the flat began to crumble around them, falling away one brick after another, until nothing remained. The light changed. It was dawn and the orange circle of the sun clawed its way over a distant horizon.

They were not in London any more. The city had gone, replaced with a beach of pebbles and coarse sand. The water lapped towards them in rhythmic crescendos, marking time like the ticking of the clock had in the flat. Time was running out, he realised, for Hilda. Somewhere she was dying, her life fading with every passing moment. Jack knew he had to get back, but how? He had no idea where he was.

At first he thought this might be a lost memory of a trip with his family. Perhaps it was Brighton, where his aunty lived. No, he concluded, he had not been here before. This was not his memory, this was Rouland's.

'You brought us here? To this memory?' Rouland said, sounding hesitant. For the first time he looked pensive, almost helpless.

'Where are we?' Jack asked.

'You dare to bring me here!' Rouland seethed, his anger rising. 'I will tear your mind from . . .' His voice faded away as he spotted something along the shoreline. There were two people walking along the beach towards them: fishermen carrying lobster pots. They spoke amongst themselves, laughing and joking, oblivious to Rouland and Jack. They stopped as one of them pointed out to sea and dashed into the waves.

'No!' Rouland said. 'This is my memory! Get out!'

'*Benoît!*' the fishermen in the sea shouted to his friend. '*Aide-moi! Il y a un garçon ici!*'

Jack recognised the language; he had studied French at school. He struggled to translate. Had he said something about a boy?

'*Il est vivant?*' the other man said.

The first man replied, '*À peine. Il toujours respire.*'

Together they pulled at a body in the water, dragging it to the shallows. Jack squinted against the sun, the fishermen and their catch reduced to golden silhouettes against a burning yellow sky.

'*Comment tu t'appelles, gamin?*' the fisherman said to the coughing figure. *Comment tu t'appelles*, Jack recalled: *What's your name?*

'No more!' Rouland screamed, pulling Jack back.

The sand about Jack's feet began to sink away. The sea fell into it, turning into a mighty waterfall that stretched along the length of the beach. Jack turned away, wanting to run before he fell into the widening rift, and spied the distinctive shape of a Grimnire high on the clifftop.

Jack's vision blurred with painful colours. The memory collapsed to nothing and he saw that he was still sprawled on the pitted hull of the *Veillantif*. He sensed Hilda close by, barely conscious, her mind frail and silent.

Rouland stood over him, pensive, like he had forgotten Jack entirely.

The Rose stirred, festered deep within him. He summoned it again and struck while Rouland was pre-occupied, throwing his hatred for him into the attack.

Rouland staggered back, shaking his head. Finally his distraction disappeared and he bore down on Jack. The two minds met, like massive ocean liners unable to turn away from their course. Jack struck deeper, letting the tendrils of the Rose cut into Rouland's mind. But Rouland returned the attack, blistering into Jack's thoughts, fraying his concentration.

Too late he felt something strike him, cold and quick. He looked down and saw Rouland's sword in his leg. The pain was unbearable, and his concentration collapsed. The Rose recoiled, subsiding into him.

'Unpleasant, isn't it? The sword feeds. Soon you will be dead.' Rouland smiled as his mental onslaught on Jack's consciousness returned, stronger than ever.

Jack felt helpless, his thoughts disjointed, tumbling into a mire of chaos.

Where was the Rose?

Where was Hilda? Or Davey and Eloise?

His world became pain and despair and he cried out for his dead mother.

'Your mother can't save you now, boy!' Rouland said, twisting Durendal in Jack's leg. 'No one can save you now! I will have the Rose for myself and the House of Jude will finally be at an end!'

36

THE BEAUTIFUL BURDEN

Jack felt his grip on life loosening. Every second that passed took more of him away, draining his very essence into the sword.

He closed his eyes, praying that the pain might be brief. Then he heard a noise, a crack like a whip, followed by a gurgling cry. He looked up: Rouland's oil-like eyes were wide with disbelief – Davey had shot him.

Rouland staggered back, looking at the new wound in his chest. He laughed at it, regaining his composure. 'That actually hurt.'

'That was the idea!' Davey shouted, reloading his gun.

Rouland yanked Durendal from Jack's leg and circled it above his head, swinging it towards Davey's shocked face. At the last second another sword blocked Durendal's arc. Eloise stood in front of Davey, her weapon scratching against Rouland's.

'You still wish to oppose me?' Rouland said to Eloise.

'I always will.'

'That is a pity. I would have found a way to forgive you.

You were always my favourite; you know that, don't you? Why must you defy me?' Rouland raised Durendal up again, its gleaming surface shining in his eyes. 'And for what? For a mortal man.'

'For love!' Eloise shouted as she stormed forward.

'And yet you have nothing to show for it, do you?' Rouland mocked. 'No husband, no family, no ordinary life of toil and despair. We are greater than those things, Eloise.'

'I had something greater. Something you could never understand.' Eloise's sword rattled off Durendal as she rolled clear of its falling blade.

'Do not presume I know nothing of love! I am still human, child! But to love something so fleeting, so mortal – the investment is hardly worth the pain.'

'Then pain is all you will ever know.' Eloise turned quickly and her sword found Rouland's unprotected side.

Jack could hardly take it all in. He felt dizzy from the wound in his leg, and someone was pulling him up, dragging him away from the battle. He saw a body on the floor. Was that Hilda? Now he saw Davey frantically pulling at his arm. Jack shook his head, forcing his mind into focus.

His mother had shown him what to do; in the brief seconds before she had died, she had shown him humility and kindness. He had forgotten those things. Now Eloise echoed her example, putting love ahead of hate, no matter what the cost. Suddenly he understood the choice before him. He summoned the Rose again, but this time it filled him with a glorious surge of optimism. Its tendrils sought out his injured leg, soothing it, healing it from within. The pain became bearable.

He looked at Davey, moistening his dry lips. 'Thanks.' He gently pushed him away as he stood up straight. Jack knew what to do next: Hilda had been trying to show him all along, as had his mother and Eloise. He cleared his mind of hatred and anger, letting his mother's compassion take its place. He looked at Rouland and reached into his mind. At first the way was blocked, but then Jack felt new aspects to the Rose, like petals opening to the sun.

Rouland looked at him in shock, cowering in retreat.

Jack fought to keep his own fear contained, his anger in check, letting his sympathy guide him. Things seemed clearer now. He was circumventing Rouland's mental defences; he was unprepared for this sort of onslaught.

In his mind Jack saw Rouland's next move, and he blocked it, stepping closer and closer.

'Fight like a man!' Rouland screamed. He unleashed globes of lightning from his hand, but Jack managed to absorb their energy, his body glowing in a haze of gold, protecting his friends from Rouland's vengeful attacks. He glanced down at Hilda: she was consumed with pain and her face looked old, ragged and empty. She was dying, slowly, painfully. Hesitation took hold of him.

Rouland's laughter filled his mind as a new volley of energy struck him. 'Not so strong now, Jack?'

The calm inside his mind began to crumble and collapse. Fear, doubt, hatred clawed up, relentless and inevitable.

No. He held his hand up to Rouland, closed his eyes and pictured his mother giving him the Rose. There was no malice in her face, only contentment. Jack mirrored his mother.

He opened his eyes again and pushed once more at Rouland's mind, filling it with his pity, his compassion.

Rouland recoiled, pained. Jack allowed the warmth of the Rose to spread out from him in a growing shock wave. Rouland collapsed in tears, unable to deal with this new invasion as he crawled back towards the hatch.

Jack stepped forward. He had Rouland. He could end this now. He could use the Rose to destroy him for ever. Voices circled in his mind, like birds over a corpse: *Kill him! Rip his heart out! Revenge!* He rejoiced in the power, in the thoughts in his head. He allowed the Rose to swarm to his fingertips. He could unleash it any second, let it rip Rouland apart. It would all be at an end.

He turned to see Hilda, almost lifeless on the hull. She was beyond hope now. Only one thing could save her. Doubts pushed into his head. *Save her! Save your friend!*

He paused. This was the choice, he realised, the choice he always had to make, if he was really worthy to wield such a power as the Rose. In the end the choice was a simple one: life or death, create or destroy, love or hate, heal or kill.

But now that the choice was upon him he was racked with indecision. He could kill Rouland and his friend would die, or he could save Hilda, knowing that Rouland would prevail. He did not have the strength to do both.

The energy boiled in Jack's hands, red with hatred. Rouland retreated to the hatch, fear filling his eyes.

From nowhere Jack felt a wave of calm overcome him, like the refreshing breeze of Otherworld. The noises around him faded away until only one voice remained: his mother's.

I have nothing left to give you, except one thing. I'm giving it to you, Jack. You are the Rose now. Use it well, and it will sustain you. Abuse it, and you'll be consumed by it. Fight for me, Jack. Fight for me. I love you.

They were her last thoughts as she gave up everything for him. He remembered that moment and suddenly his choice was obvious.

Smiling, Jack lowered his hands and the balls of energy shifted from red to blue. Rouland, disbelieving, retreated into the ship, and the hatch closed behind him.

Quickly Jack turned to find Hilda, her blood tracing patterns over the hull. Davey was with her, holding her head, though there was nothing he could do to tend her wound now – nothing anyone could do.

Except Jack, and the Rose.

He remembered his mother's example. She had used the power of the Rose to heal him when he was sick, and again when he had fallen from St Paul's Cathedral. When even that could no longer save him she had given up the Rose, knowing it would kill her, so that he might live.

He placed his hands on Hilda's chest and brought the Rose to the front of his mind.

Heal my friend. Save Hilda.

His hands began to glow, golden energy flooding out of them and into Hilda. Jack felt the pain and grief as he lost some of the Rose's essence. It was the most horrible feeling, like he was falling out of himself. And yet he felt freed, like he was soaring higher than ever before, his beautiful burden finally at peace within him. And in that moment his thoughts cleared. He understood what the memory of his mother had been trying to tell him, realised why the family crest in Hilda's home had been so familiar: it was the same design on his mother's pendant.

There, around Hilda's neck, was a pendant on a chain, just like his mother's. It bore the same design, the same family crest. He knew his mother's pendant was a family heirloom, passed down to her from her parents. He was from a great and noble family – the Jude family.

Hilda's hand grabbed his arm and her eyes flickered open. She was alive!

It's OK, Jack said in his mind, soothing Hilda in the way his mother had soothed him. He felt the Rose seeking out her injuries, healing her wounds, bringing her back from the brink, back to life.

'Next time . . .' Hilda said feebly, 'do not leave it so long.'

Jack smiled as the Rose receded into him, resting, its work complete. He felt dizzy, unsteady on his feet. At first he thought it must be because of the Rose, then he saw Davey next to him, faltering, stumbling to his knees.

'What's happening?' Davey shouted.

Jack looked beyond the hull and saw the view listing to one side. 'We're moving!'

'The *Veillantif*, it is undocking,' Eloise gasped.

The engines were already turning more quickly, static building up in the wake of the rotating arms. The ship tilted backwards as it began to move away from its moorings. Above him Jack saw the first of the harpoons being released from the dockside and winding their way back into the ship.

'What have you done now?' Hilda asked, her strength returning.

The hull let out great groans and gasps as the two realm ships shifted against each other.

'Time to get aboard!' Davey shouted, lifting up Hilda and carrying her towards the *Orion*'s ramp. Jack turned to follow when the hull shifted, tipping him off balance.

Eloise plunged her sword into the hull, using it to steady herself. She reached out her hand to Jack. Their fingers briefly touched, then Jack slid past, down the tilting hull.

From the safety of the entrance ramp Davey cried out to him, watching as Jack rolled over the sleek surface towards the edge.

'Look after Hilda!' Jack shouted as he slid away, uncertain if his voice could be heard.

Ahead, the smooth hull flattened into the shape of a short wing, out of which one of the mooring ropes protruded. Jack grabbed the rope, his legs dangling over the receding platform. He quickly lowered himself down its length until he hung over the dockside. It looked so far away, getting further and further with each passing second. It was now or never, Jack realised, and he let go of the rope.

He braced himself, calling for the Rose to protect him as he fell through the air, smashing into the dockside, splintering the planks, almost breaking through them. The pain was unbearable. He lay there, unable to move, watching the conjoined realm ships above him.

The *Veillantif* began to turn, its dark mass glinting in the artificial light. On top of it was the *Orion*, still clinging to the back of Rouland's ship. He saw Eloise clawing over the hull towards the hatch when the *Veillantif* yawed to the side, sending her sliding down towards Jack. She fell helplessly to the dockside, smashing into it with a terrible fury. Jack picked himself up and ran to her side as she screamed out in pain.

'Eloise? Can you hear me?'

She opened her eyes, nodding tersely, then cried out again.

A noise above him caught his attention: the *Orion* was turning, unhooking itself from the mass of the *Veillantif*. Davey must be at the controls, Jack realised with a mixture of relief and fear. Sparks flew from between the two ships, followed by smoke, then fire. Machinery complained noisily under the metal skin, and the wing dipped violently as the ship began to lose height. Jack pulled at Eloise, dragging her out from under the shower of debris falling towards them.

The *Veillantif*'s engines increased their output and the ship began to climb again. He felt a rumble vibrate through his arms as an explosion tore through the rear of the *Veillantif*. The *Orion* skidded free, leaving the burning ship as it swung about defiantly, its engines roaring in spite of the smoke spewing from them.

Then, as if in slow motion, the two realm ships collided again. The *Veillantif* was the larger ship, and pushed the *Orion* aside, sending a shower of twisted metal into the air. The spinning engine section of the *Veillantif* caught on the *Orion*, ripping one of the rotating arms free. It swung through the air like a boomerang, then began to fall towards Jack and Eloise.

There was no time. Adrenalin pumped through Jack's body as he picked Eloise up in his arms. He carried her along the platform, looking over his shoulder at the falling debris. The smaller chunks hit first, ripping indiscriminately at the dockside. Great swathes of the platform broke apart and fell away, shaking the remnants like they were matchsticks. Jack managed to keep on his feet as he navigated through the devastation, ignoring the fragments bouncing off his battered body, struggling along with Eloise in his arms.

He came to a stone pillar, cowering in its shadow.

'We ... can't stop!' Eloise managed groggily. Above him Jack saw the two realm ships limping higher into the sky. The *Veillantif* seemed to be struggling, barely staying aloft. He looked behind him as a huge piece of the *Veillantif*'s engine struck the dockside, falling through it like it was dust. The platform juddered as it broke away.

Then the *Veillantif* began to fall out of the sky, crying out like a bird of prey. Its engines exploded, erupting into a giant fireball that lit up the entire cavern like it was a summer's day. Comets of fiery metal whirled along the dockside, spreading flames far and wide. As the explosion cleared, the burning wreck of the *Veillantif* came into view, falling directly towards Jack. A blast of hot air heralded its fall as drops of burning fuel splashed over the dockside.

Jack's heart pounded. It was too late to run to safety, he realised. Panic gripped him as he stared wide-eyed at the disintegrating platform.

'Jack,' Eloise said, 'it is a memori-mortuus.' She pointed weakly at the stone column they rested against. 'A communal grave to the dead . . . you understand?'

At the bottom of the column Jack saw several niches, filled with skulls, like the shrine in Jodrell Sinclair's house.

'*Bone, stone and sorrow,*' he gasped as he reached out to touch the column. 'There are Sorrowlines here?'

Eloise nodded.

Jack's fingers tingled. As that same moment the platform beneath his feet began to tilt and fall.

He felt the recognisable tug of memories as the memori-mortuus cracked apart. There *were* Sorrowlines here! Above him the noise of the falling realm ship was almost deafening. They had seconds left. Jack glanced up; the sky was afire. He caught a final glimpse of the *Orion*, high above, firing up its engines and disappearing into the Interim. Then as the air about him erupted with heat he felt the Sorrowline open up for him. The scream of death, the heat of fire, gave way to a cool light as the Sorrowline swallowed him and Eloise. Together they were falling back through time, without a notion of their destination.

Relief gave way to panic as the Sorrowline began to vibrate then shatter. His senses were burning. Where was Eloise? He gasped, realising he no longer held her. He felt hands about him, dragging him a great distance, hauling him onto a cold floor.

His senses settled, his eyes opened and focused on his surroundings – a world of formless white. He saw a great dark shape in front of him. At first he couldn't tell what it was, then its details came to his eye, one at a time: hands of bone adorned with ancient rings, a vast cloak of silvery black made from layers of crows' wings, a bejewelled scythe carved with runes, a ticking clock face on a heavy chain, a dark mysterious hood with grey smoke drifting from within.

Jack gasped as the Grimnire bowed to him.

37

THE PRICE

Rise, Timesmith.

Jack felt the demanding voice deep within him. He stood up, taking in his surroundings more carefully. He was back in the realm of the Grimnire, he realised with an awful dread. This time there was only one of the strange creatures. The space seemed even more vast than before, like an endless wasteland, a place without detail.

'Where's Eloise?' Jack demanded.

You have made your choice.

Jack was uncertain if this was a question or a statement. He said nothing in reply. The Grimnire swapped its scythe from one gnarled hand to another, turning away from him. It seemed to be thinking.

The Rose rests within you.

Jack could barely feel it now. The Rose was exhausted, dormant, somewhere far inside him. He smiled to himself, happy that he had finally come to understand its might. He knew he had yet to fathom its true potential, but he had chosen what sort of host he would be. Jack felt content.

The Grimnire turned round quickly, a cloud of smoke spewing from its hood.

The fire will never cease. Be on guard always. Many thought you too young for this responsibility. They may yet be right. Better minds wished you dead. There is a price to pay for your continued existence.

Jack shuddered. 'What's happened to my friends? Where is Eloise?'

The Grimnire turned away again. *They live.*

'But where are they? When?'

Enough! The Grimnire stamped its scythe onto the featureless floor. A shock wave rumbled through it, twisting its surface like it was water. As the ripples subsided the Grimnire turned to Jack, its hood lowering towards his face.

The price for your existence must now be paid.

'Price?' Jack asked nervously. 'What sort of price?'

The Grimnire straightened, its head looking upwards. *Exile.*

Before Jack could react he felt bony fingers on his shoulders as a dark cloth was pulled over his head. His hands and feet were held in place as he was lifted up. He struggled to be free, feeling more and more clicking fingers touching his body. The hands turned him upright again and his hood was pulled away.

As he opened his eyes he heard a hissing noise and the air filled with a red gas. He lifted his hands in front of him and touched glass. A burning white light above him blinded his eyes. Then the white crushed into a rich redness. Jack's lungs ached as he began to fall again. The red space became a wind of gas that roared about him, lifting him with it. He felt as if he was being torn apart, one molecule at a time, and cast adrift onto the wind.

The unearthly sensation lasted an eternity. He heard voices, echoes of conversations in the wind, like forgotten thoughts that made no conscious sense. The wind coalesced, and he did with it, his form returned to him at last.

He raised his hand up in front of him, wafting the red mist apart so he could see where he was, only to be confronted with a cold dark surface.

The hiss of pistons and machinery filled his ears as the red gas dissipated. A rectangle of featureless white light opened up in front of him. Then a pair of eyes appeared in the rectangle, looking in on his confined space.

Jack hammered on the wall in front of him. It rang like it was made of metal. The eyes studying him widened with surprise and he heard a distant muffled voice.

'Hello there,' the voice spoke tentatively.

'Let me out!' Jack replied. His own voice sounded strange, as if contained, and he realised he was inside some sort of chamber, no bigger than a coffin. The thought brought his claustrophobia back. The rectangle of light, he saw now, was a glass inspection window in the chamber. The eyes peering in blinked rapidly, then moved away, leaving the dazzling light in their place.

There was a low clunk and the sound of something heavy being pulled over metal. Then the chamber opened, allowing the crimson gases pooling around Jack's feet to escape.

A figure appeared out of the swirls of red mist, flapping its arms to help scatter the gas. At first Jack made out only a dark blur, then details emerged. A teenage boy – perhaps a few years older than Jack – appeared before him. His nervous face was crowned by neatly combed auburn hair brushed behind his protruding ears. His wide brown eyes stared in astonishment at Jack as he slowly stepped forwards.

'Are you real?' the boy asked.

Jack spluttered, coughing violently.

The boy suddenly poked Jack's sore flesh with his index finger.

'Ow!' Jack let out a weary gasp.

'Indeed you are,' the boy giggled. 'You're not another phantom after all.' He stood up straight, brushing down the neat waistcoat he wore over a crisp white shirt. 'Greetings, stranger,' he said formally. 'Welcome to my world. This is England.' He shook his head, as if disagreeing with himself. 'Well, that is to say, this is Earth. The planet Earth. England is an island, one of many on this great planet, but arguably the best of them all. Welcome, traveller. I bid you good tidings from our realm to yours. My name is Magnus Hafgan. Mag...nus... Haf...gan.'

He said it slowly, as if Jack was stupid. The name resonated like a bell inside Jack's head. Groggily he wondered where he'd heard it before.

'Do you have a name?'

Jack stumbled out of the chamber, his eyes puffy. 'Water!' he gasped.

'It is my honour to meet you, Water. I bid you peaceful greetings.'

Jack shook his head firmly. 'Water, to drink.'

Magnus stood momentarily as the new meaning sunk in. 'Ah, I see.' He jolted past the large desk, and produced a jug and glass, which he offered to Jack.

Jack ignored the glass, snatched at the jug and poured its contents directly over his stinging eyes and mouth. The water was a saviour, cooling his skin. He swallowed long gulps until the jug was empty, and handed it back to the stranger who stared back with a slack-jawed fascination.

'My name's Jack Morrow.'

'Hello, Jack Morrow,' Magnus said thoughtfully. 'I say, that's rather English-sounding.' He gasped suddenly as a new idea took him. 'And you speak English very well. I suppose English must be the language of God, and so is perhaps universal across the other realms. Is this the case, Jack Morrow?'

'I *am* English,' Jack replied testily. 'I'm from London.'

'Oh,' Magnus replied, deflated. 'So you're not from another realm?'

'No.'

'I see. So how did you get here?'

'I was hoping you could tell me.'

Magnus brushed down his perfectly neat hair, his eyes squinting at Jack. 'I'm sorry, I don't have the slightest idea what just happened. I was trying to contact another realm.'

As Magnus spoke he returned to his desk, picked up a thick leather-bound notebook and started to make unintelligible notes in it with a small well-chewed pencil.

'I've never had anything like this happen before. It is a fascinating occurrence, even if you are only human. I wonder what was different this time? This never happened in the library. Perhaps it's something to do with the acoustics down here.'

Jack walked unsteadily to the desk and gripped its edge. 'What year is this?' he asked.

Magnus stopped writing and glared at Jack. 'What is that supposed to mean? Do you know something of what I am doing here? Did my aunt send you? You can tell her I will not be stopped when I am so close to revealing the infinite cogs that turn the universe. Tell her!'

'I don't know your aunt. No one sent me. I was dragged here.'

'Dragged?' Magnus's eyebrows arched inquisitively.

'I think so,' Jack replied. 'Have you heard of a Sorrowline?'

Magnus mulled over the question, his lips silently toying with the word. 'Sorrowline? Sorrow...line? Sorrow, as in mourning, loss, that sort of common display of emotion?'

Jack sighed. 'What about a Grimnire?'

Magnus looked baffled.

'Magnus,' Jack said softly, 'the date is very important. Will you tell me, please?'

'February. The twenty-fifth, I think. Why is it so vital to you? Is it your birthday?'

'What year is it?'

Magnus laughed. Jack frowned and eventually Magnus stopped laughing. 'It is the fifth year of King Charles's Restoration: 1665.'

38

EXILE

Snow painted the graveyard in the palest of blues that promised spring would not be far away. Jack sat on his bench, wrapped up tightly against the cold. He liked to sit here, to think. It reminded him of when he would sit by his mother's grave, waiting for his father to show up. If he closed his eyes he could almost pretend the approaching figure was him, late as usual.

But the idea was folly. He was three hundred and forty-eight years away from his father, from his mother's grave. The rest of his family were almost as far. He had thought of them every day of his exile, wondering what had happened to them, where they might be, and if they still thought of him. Some days his mind fell on Rouland. Had he survived that terrible crash? Did he still live, desperate to take the Rose from him? The fear in those thoughts had lessened over the last few months. Everything that had happened to him seemed so long ago now, so far away.

'Why do you insist on coming here, even on such icy days!' Magnus smiled, his cheeks red from the cold.

He rubbed his gloved hands together for warmth. 'Come inside, I have something marvellous to show you! I think I am on the brink of mastering junction transportation.'

Jack smiled inwardly. He had witnessed so many amazing things this last year. It had not taken him long to recall the name of Magnus Hafgan, the purported father of the First World, the great inventor, statesman and explorer. Hafgan was merely sixteen, still in the care of his parents, but already his experiments marked him out as a genius. Jack had been there the night he had successfully contacted another realm and opened up a dialogue with the proud Boagymen. He had helped in his first experiments with mental abilities, his measurements of morphic fields, his construction of a working chronoscope. In the summer months they had spent weeks together, deep underground exploring the massive chasms that Jack knew would one day become the seat of the First World's capital.

He had especially enjoyed completing the cipher in the back of the book Magnus was writing: *On the Nature of the Concealed Realms*. He knew one day this secret code would help him in many ways.

But in spite of these wonders his heart was elsewhere, and every day since his arrival here he had come to this small graveyard and searched for a Sorrowline, a way back to his friends and family. But he had failed. Either he had lost his ability or there were no Sorrowlines to be found. He had travelled further afield, to other graves, but each time he had returned to Hafgan disappointed.

The Grimnire, it seemed, had banished him here, robbed him of a way home, confined him to this point in time. And the Rose? The Rose had been dormant since he had used it to heal Hilda. He had called to it but to no avail. It seemed diminished now, smaller somehow. Had part of it found a home in Hilda? he wondered. It was hard to tell.

Living here, he was just a boy again, without the weight of power. He was free of it all. And yet . . . he missed it. He missed the adventure, the bond of friendship with Hilda and Eloise. Davey, in spite of the knowledge of what he might one day become, he missed the most. And if he was no longer a Timesmith, he realised, he would never be able to travel upstream, to return to 1940 and find his friends.

His friendship with Magnus had been of some consolation. The boy and his family had shown him nothing but kindness, but Jack had suffered dark days of mourning for his lost life. Now that his exile had reached a full year he had become increasingly resigned to his fate, to this life of discovery in the seventeenth century. After all, it could have been much worse.

'You are in the future again, Timesmith!' Magnus teased.

Jack shook himself out of his reverie. 'You're right, Mag. Sorry.' He managed a tired smile.

'Oh, I don't blame you, old boy!' Magnus said jovially. 'How could I? You've seen everything I yearn to! The future, other realms. Your tales are like pages from my dreams. And I do so love to hear your stories. It's like having my research confirmed even before I've begun to consider what I wish to research. But I don't want to hear stories today. And besides, it's far too cold. Come inside and eat. Later, Father has some friends coming round. Old Sinclair and his son. I was hoping to tell him something of my plans for our First World project, and you would be the perfect piece of evidence to convince him. If he doesn't laugh us both into an asylum he might prove to be a good ally.'

Jack smiled. 'I think you're right.'

The sun was low in the sky, counting the minutes till it dipped below the horizon, taking its feeble heat with it.

Jack stood to leave. The future seemed so far away. But there was always tomorrow.

He walked with Magnus, half listening to his wild ideas, past the rows of gravestones. As they reached the exit Jack paused.

'What now?' Magnus said impatiently.

'Go on without me,' Jack said. 'I'll be just a while longer.'

Magnus hesitated, his eyes full of confusion. Then he smiled at his friend, patted him robustly on the back and strode off towards the big house hiding in the snow.

Jack waited until he was gone, until the graveyard was deathly silent, before he approached a small, broken headstone. Had he seen it before? he wondered. Had he tried this one? The surface was rough, like a barnacle, the chipped letters almost gone completely. But one word was still legible and had made Jack stop in his tracks.

Jude.

Was this an ancestor's grave? He removed his gloves, letting them drop into the snow. He hardly dared to bring his hands up – he'd been disappointed so many times before. The cold air nipped at his fingers. He rubbed them together, then touched the headstone, allowing his smoky breath to fall out of his mouth as his thoughts cleared. He closed his eyes and let the images of Eloise, Davey and Hilda appear in his mind.

Tears unexpectedly formed, rolling down his icy cheeks. There was something here! He felt it; he was sure this time. He could feel the Sorrowline.

For a moment he hesitated, looking back in the direction of Hafgan's house, before he succumbed to the lure of the future.

His exile was at an end. The stone softened, then melted away, and Jack Morrow fell into a world of possibilities.

ACKNOWLEDGEMENTS

I'll let you into a little secret: other people make an author look good. They catch our mistakes, politely point out our errors and guide us like grumpy, egotistical sheep towards the best possible version of our story.

For me this process starts with my wife, Diane, who is my first reader, my quality control and the person who always spots the obvious. Next it's my agent, Juliet Mushens of The Agency Group, who cheers at just the right moment, keeping me from doubting myself too much. Then it's over to Charlie Sheppard, Eloise Wilson, Ruth Knowles and Chloe Sackur at Andersen Press, a quartet of creative editors who fool the world into thinking I might know what I'm doing.

And it's not just English I need help with: I could tell you I speak French fluently but that would be a big fat lie. I wish I could but I can't. Instead I turned to Olivia Chapman for the French translations in Chapter 35. Latin proved equally baffling! Luckily I had some help and advice from my friend, Tony West. See, you thought I was clever, didn't you?

Finally my copy editor, Sue Cook, is the last line of defence that stops me looking like a silly sheep. She is like a literary Boss Level baddie – but in a good way! She spots those little things that most readers would never see but can make or break a story.

When you add in the extraordinary art direction of Kate Grove, the skills of designer James Fraser and the tenacity of publicist Eve Warlow you have a team that any egotistical grumpy sheep would be proud to have on his side. I know I am.

Niel Bushnell

2013

ABOUT THE AUTHOR

Niel Bushnell is an author, artist and animator who has worked on numerous films, TV shows and computer games, including *Space Jam*, *The Dumping Ground* and *Harry Potter and the Philosopher's Stone*.

Timesmith is his second novel. He'd like to take the credit for his creative output but he swears there's something living under his stairs that whispers secrets to him when no one else is around.

Niel lives in the north-east of England where he continues to write and draw. In his spare time he is building a teleport machine in his shed.

www.nielbushnell.com

GABRIEL'S CLOCK

HILTON PASHLEY

Jonathan is the only half-angel, half-demon in the universe, and now the forces of Hell want him for their own purpose.

Aided by a vicar with a broken heart, a big man with a cricket bat and a very rude cat, Jonathan races to find the mysterious Gabriel's Clock. If he doesn't find it then his family and friends will die, but, if he does, then he risks starting a war between Heaven and Hell that could engulf them all.

Gabriel's clock is ticking . . .
and time is running out.

9781849395786 £12.99 Hardback

THE ISLAND OF THIEVES

JOSH LACEY

Buried treasure. Ruthless gangsters. An ancient clue . . .

Our Captayne took the pinnace ashore and I went with hym and six men also, who were sworne by God to be secret in al they saw. Here we buried five chests filled with gold.

Tom Trelawney was looking for excitement. Now he's found it. With his eccentric Uncle Harvey, he's travelling to South America on a quest for hidden gold. But Uncle Harvey has some dangerous enemies and they want the treasure too. Who will be the first to uncover the secrets of the mysterious island?

Praise for other books by this author:

'A delight'
The Times

'Smart and pacy'
Sunday Times

9781849392457 £5.99